THE
POISONED
ROCK

THE
POISONED
ROCK

A SULLIVAN AND BRODERICK
MURDER MYSTERY

ROBERT DAWS

urbanepublications.com

First published in Great Britain in 2017
by Urbane Publications Ltd
Suite 3, Brown Europe House, 33/34 Gleaming Wood Drive,
Chatham, Kent ME5 8RZ
Copyright © Robert Daws, 2017

A CIP catalogue record for this book is available
from the British Library.

ISBN 978-1-911331-21-6

Design and Typeset by Michelle Morgan

Cover by Michelle Morgan and Debbie at The Cover Collection

Printed and bound by CPI Group (UK) Ltd, Croydon, CR0 4YY

urbanepublications.com

FSC
www.fsc.org
MIX
Paper from
responsible sources
FSC® C013604

For Janet and Clem

There is thy gold,
worse poison to men's souls,
Doing more murders
in this loathsome world,
Than these poor compounds
that thou mayst not sell.

William Shakespeare, Romeo and Juliet

THE POISONED ROCK

PROLOGUE
HOTEL MANDRAGO, GIBRALTAR TOWN, NOVEMBER 1942

MURDER

THE COUPLE LAY naked on the bed, the young woman's right arm and leg wrapped around the man's waist and thigh. Lovers at rest, a perfect post-coital scene.

The flash of a camera bulb made the woman start, her eyes opening wide. The man's eyes remained closed. From the shadows of the shabbily furnished hotel room, the photographer's stern voice ordered her to close them again. This she did. She had so little to do and was going to be paid so much that she would do whatever she was told. At first she'd thought the man on the bed was dead. That had alarmed her. But then she heard him breathing. Too much beer, she supposed.

As if dressing the room for the camera, the photographer had laid out the man's uniform along the bottom of the bed. It was an officer's tunic, Polish from its markings. Not that the young woman cared. She wanted the wretched business over and done with as quickly as possible.

She had taken it for granted that she would be asked to perform sexually – that was what usually happened – but not on this occasion. Instead, she was to remove all her clothes and then embrace the naked man lying unconscious on the bed. If it was supposed to be a joke, it would be an expensive one. Or was it supposed to be some form of artistic expression? She didn't care. She wasn't asking questions and the photographer wasn't offering any answers. Another camera flash. The job was done.

Three minutes later, the young woman stood at the bedroom door, placing the money she had just been given in her cheap silver-coloured purse. Looking across at the figure in the shadows, she smiled.

'Thanks.'

Don't be grateful, thought the photographer, as the woman slipped from the room. *Being grateful won't help you now.*

Behind the desk of the Hotel Mandrago's small reception area, its aged and dishevelled owner sat in drunken slumber. His feet were propped up on the desk and the spindly wooden chair he was sitting in was tilted back at a precarious angle. As the young woman crept down the stairs and passed him, she smelled the combined aroma of brandy and sweat hanging heavily in the air. Quickening her step, she crossed the narrow vestibule and was out of the main door before the man could stir.

As she reached the dark, narrow, cobbled street, the cool night air was like a cleansing elixir. She stopped for a moment to take a deep breath before slipping off her high heels and heading barefoot towards the harbour. It was after curfew and there'd be no return across the Spanish border to La Línea tonight. She would seek refuge at Izzo's Bar. The small, corpulent proprietor, Vittor Izzo, often let her stay in an unused box room at the top of the building. As her pimp, it was in his interests to look after her a little. Marisella's payment would have to be the usual sexual favour, but with any luck it was late enough in the evening for Vittor's total inebriation to be guaranteed. Sometimes, if she was lucky, Izzo's seven year-old son Oskar would awaken and plead with his father to let Marisella sleep in his room. The boy had no mother and was much neglected by his father. Marisella would often sing him gently to sleep and then pray that both she and the child would one day escape from Vittor's clutches.

Continuing on her path, Marisella concluded that the night had not been as bad as it might have been. She had experienced far more demanding and demeaning scenarios with punters. She now had a purse full of money and her precious baby was home and safe with its grandparents. They would all eat well this week. The shame of what she had been forced to do to achieve this was something she would not dwell on tonight. Since her husband had run off six months earlier, she had relied on her devoted parents. She had little choice. Thanks to Franco and his regime, poverty and deprivation surrounded her in the small Spanish town where she lived. Although Spain was officially neutral in the war, el Caudillo clearly admired Hitler and his aims. Life for those Spaniards who worked on Gibraltarian soil was not made easy by the dictator.

But for now, all Marisella could think of was sleep. Tomorrow she would turn up for her low-paid job at the fruit and vegetable warehouse near the harbour. Although menial, her day job was considered 'essential' work by the Gibraltar authorities, and every day she and several thousand other Spanish workers walked past the border post at Four Corners on their way to their labours. Their presence had become all the more important since the evacuation of the Rock's civilian population two years earlier. The war and Gibraltar's vulnerable strategic position in Europe had necessitated the moving of 13,500 citizens to French Morocco and then further afield to Madeira, Britain and the West Indies. By the summer of 1942, the Rock had become little more than a military garrison.

Most nights, Marisella would cross over to her Spanish homeland with genuine relief in her heart. An evening spent with her seven-month-old daughter Rosia in her arms was the goal of each working day. Her other 'occasional work' was a dark secret. A means to an end and hateful in the extreme.

Clasping her purse to her bosom, she continued down the lane, a passage made eerie by the lack of street lamps to light the way. Earlier that night, the sky above the Rock had been criss-crossed with the beams of powerful anti-aircraft searchlights. It had only been an exercise, but served as a reminder of the ever-present danger of aerial bombardment from enemy planes. A fellow worker had remarked to her earlier in the day, 'A blind man on a galloping horse can see that things are getting busy around here.' It was true. More ships, more equipment, tanks and planes were arriving daily. Provisions were being shipped in at a hugely increased rate. The fruit and vegetable warehouse in which she worked was operating at full capacity. On top of this, the Yanks were everywhere. Thousands of them. Something was brewing. Something big.

Marisella stopped for a moment to rub her foot. The pavement was cold and her toes were chilled. Apart from the constant, distant drone of work from the docks, the lane was silent and deserted. Moving off once more, she was suddenly aware of someone watching her. The hairs on the back of her neck stood on end and shivers, in no way related to the cold, shot down her spine. Turning her head to look behind, she glimpsed a fleeting shadow. Although she knew it was only her imagination, a rising animal fear possessed her. Quickening her pace, she reached a junction. Her choice was to take the longer route along Main Street – not clever after curfew – or the shortcut through a series of smaller passageways that led directly to the harbour. The passages were quicker and she could navigate them blindfolded. Quelling her nerves and cursing her imagination, she decided to take the first, safer route. Crossing the street as swiftly as she could, she disappeared into the darkness of the town.

Fifty metres on, Marisella turned a corner and descended a long flight of steps that would take her down to Main Street. As she did so, she saw at the bottom of the steps a man climbing up towards her. He was wearing a raincoat and a hat obscured his face. In an instant, Marisella was gripped by fear. Somehow she knew that, whoever the stranger might be, he wished her no good. Turning and retracing her steps up the stairway, she reached the top in moments. Almost running now, she turned the corner back onto the lane. Such was her haste, she had little time to see the figure standing directly in front of her. Stopping suddenly just inches from the stranger's face, Marisella let out a gasp of shock.

It took seconds to focus and steady herself before she could fully take in who it was that blocked her way. She saw – *Thank you, Mary, Mother of Jesus!* – a smiling woman's face framed by wisps of honey-coloured hair. Relief spread through Marisella and an embarrassed smile momentarily curled her lips. So pleased was she to see the person standing before her, she did not react when the woman reached out one arm towards her. Instead of the comforting pat she might have been expecting, the woman grabbed Marisella's hair in a vice like-grip. Pulling it sharply, she wrenched Marisella towards her. With a vicious yank, she snapped Marisella's head backwards as her other hand struck quickly at her throat. The blade she was holding cut deeply and expertly across the neck, severing the carotid artery and trachea with practised ease, slicing down almost to the bone. Marisella felt little pain as she fought for breath, her throat now filling with her own dark, hot blood and drowning her. In the eight seconds that remained of her life, she could not even cry out her beloved baby's name – Rosia.

Two Days Later

SHORT AND STOCKY Inspector Lorenz stood in what had once been the hallway of the ruined townhouse. It was almost impossible for the middle-aged officer of the Gibraltar Police Force to get a clear view through the darkness that permeated the old building. Torchlight was prohibited by the imposed night-time blackout. Not that it mattered. What he could see in the gloom gave him all the information he needed. It was a scene he had witnessed several times before. The body of a prostitute murdered either by her punter or her pimp. At least, that's what he supposed. She would be taken to the morgue and, he hoped, identified. The more likely scenario was that she would remain anonymous and disappear into oblivion. Numbered, catalogued and ultimately forgotten.

It was therefore a surprise to discover, in the woman's silver purse, a wad of crisp Gibraltarian pound notes. More surprising still was the discovery of a photograph of the woman, smiling to camera, holding a small baby in her arms. On the back of the picture, someone had handwritten 'Mama and Rosia'. The inspector raised an eyebrow. The identity of the young woman might prove easier to discover than he had supposed. As two ambulance men lifted the corpse onto a stretcher, Lorenz stepped out into the passageway to fill his lungs with fresh, clean air.

CHAPTER 1

THE UNION JACK rippled in the warm air that swirled around the upper reaches of the Rock, its vivid red, white and blue standing out against the azure sky above and beyond it. A bold banner, proudly positioned to fly high above the white, box-like military observation post more than 400 metres up on the northern slope of the Rock of Gibraltar.

From her position on the passenger balcony of the terminal of the new Gibraltar International Airport, Tamara Sullivan looked out across the runway, its short length sandwiched between the waters of the Bay of Gibraltar to the west and the Mediterranean to the east. Primarily designed for military aircraft during World War II, it still provided many challenges for modern-day commercial pilots. Not least among those the ever-changing up-currents and down-drafts caused by the Rock itself. That magnificent block of Jurassic limestone thrusting skywards before her had often created perilous and, at times, fatal conditions for take off and landing. Sullivan shivered and decided to turn her thoughts elsewhere.

It had been just six weeks since the thirty-one-year-old detective sergeant had arrived on the Rock. Back then, looking out of the cabin

THE POISONED ROCK

window of the incoming Monarch Airbus transporting her from a cold and wet London to the warmer shores of the Mediterranean, Sullivan had been thrilled at her first sight of the Rock's towering presence. It was a thrill that had survived intact during her month-and-a-half stay in Gibraltar Town – a vibrant and diverse place, with its mix of ancient and ultra-modern buildings hanging precipitously to the Rock's lower western slopes and built on reclaimed land taken from the Bay of Gibraltar. Living on one of the great wonders of the natural world had proved an unexpected pleasure for the tall detective with the dark hair and striking good looks that had been passed down to her from her mother's Irish gene pool.

Although only halfway through her three-month secondment with the Royal Gibraltar Police, Sullivan felt as though she had been on the Rock for much longer. Expecting a quiet and rather pedestrian time with the force, she had been surprised by the many challenges that had come her way. Some had been of the welcome variety, others terrifying and life threatening.

In another six weeks, she would be back at the airport, returning to London and the Metropolitan Police Service – and an uncertain future, her once-sure path to promotion and power within the Met blocked forever. But there was no use thinking about that now. Instead she would allow the heat of the morning sun to warm her face for a few minutes more, one last burst of sunlight before re-entering the sleek and beautifully designed terminal building behind her. Unexpectedly, Sullivan found herself not wanting to leave now, even for this short trip. Her journey today would take her to Manchester, then on to the Wirral and her old family home. It was to be a quick, twenty-four-hour visit to celebrate her mother's birthday and then a return to Gib to finish her secondment. It had always been part of the plan, but the nearer it came, the less Sullivan wanted to go.

Glancing to her right and over to Winston Churchill Avenue – the thoroughfare that crossed the short runway that separated the border with Spain from the Rock itself – Sullivan could see that the road barriers were down and the normally hectic traffic had been halted: a sure sign that an aircraft was about to land. In forty minutes, it would have refuelled and restocked and another 160 passengers would be on board for its return flight to Manchester. With a heavy heart, Tamara Sullivan prepared herself to join them.

CHAPTER 2

AMONG THE PASSENGERS aboard the Monarch flight about to land at Gibraltar was a gaunt, sallow, elderly gentleman. His patrician looks and air of authority marked him out from his fellow travellers. Sitting in row B, where the extra leg room afforded him the comfort he required, he had spent the flight lost in thoughts both troubling and comforting. Mostly he had been struggling to come to terms with how quickly time had passed. It astounded him. Was it really over a decade since he had received the call to his first meeting at the Cabinet Office in Whitehall?

That day, back in 2005, held more vivid recollections for him than far more recent events. Once more, he felt his apprehension – a feeling apparently not shared by his colleagues gathered in the room with him. Three elderly men, all familiar to Maugham, with distinguished academic careers in the fields of history and politics. His uneasiness now turned to surprise at the brief, curt introductions and the speed at which the Cabinet Secretary had risen and headed off, commanding the others to follow. He recalled again his astonishment at finding himself in a queue of suited bureaucrats descending a narrow staircase, accessed via a small door almost hidden in an alcove in the Cabinet Secretary's office. Moving down those stairs, behind the large frame of the Cabinet Secretary, Graeme Maugham had felt his heartbeat quicken and his cheeks flush, sensations rarely associated with the work of a civil servant archivist. Although his particular speciality was British secret services operations between and throughout the two world wars, his recent promotion had given him a brief that now encompassed most of the 20th century – Cold War, Northern Ireland and the rest. How this knowledge might be of help to the Cabinet Secretary, he thought as he journeyed towards the cellars, I can't imagine.

At the bottom of the staircase stood a formidable metal door. Standing beside it, awaiting their arrival, was a uniformed security guard. On a nod from the Cabinet Secretary, the man pulled the door open, allowing the small delegation to enter a large strong room stuffed full of filing cabinets, all crammed with files of varying colours and stacked with large bound bundles of paperwork. On the back wall of the room, an open door revealed another room beyond in a similar state of chaos. The effect of this unexpected sight of multitudinous records temporarily and uncharacteristically robbed Maugham of breath. This experience was, for a professional archivist like him, perhaps the equal of an archaeologist's first entry into a pharaoh's tomb, deep in the sun-blasted recesses of the Valley of the Kings.

'Well, this is it, team,' the Cabinet Secretary announced abruptly, turning towards them. 'My secret hoard. Well, not mine, exactly. The secret hoard of my many predecessors. Turns out that this stuff is my dodgy inheritance.'

With this, he laughed. The others followed suit, relieved by his levity and also by the apparent explanation of what they were all supposed to be – *a team.*

'This lot represents almost eighty years of Cabinet papers considered "too sensitive for public consumption", the CS continued. 'It no doubt also contains material my predecessors considered "too arduous to be arsed about". Such are the pressures of high office. And if this doesn't get your juices flowing, there's another hoard of similar immensity awaiting your expert perusals across at the Foreign and Commonwealth Office. The Permanent Under-Secretary's department will welcome you all with open arms.'

The CS reached for a file resting on an adjacent cabinet, the single motion causing a small cloud of dust to erupt into the air.

'You'll have to clear this lot up in more ways than one, I'm afraid,' the CS said. 'Getting cleaners to sign the Official Secrets Act is not an easy task these days. So I'd bring some dusters and rubber gloves along with you. All of these papers were considered toxic and top secret when they were hidden away. Your job will be to tell me how toxic they remain. It's my intention to have all these documents declassified. I want every one released into the public domain. Every document, that is, except the ones you tell me I can't possibly release. A toxicology report is what I require from you, gentlemen. I'll leave you down here for a little preliminary sniff around. As for the main body of the work, take as long as you need. Have fun!'

With that, the CS strode from the room and disappeared back up the staircase to address the more serious matters awaiting his attention above. The four men, all steeped in their particular areas of expertise, eyed each other momentarily and then without a word moved swiftly to the cabinets to begin a first reconnaissance of the terrain.

None of them would have guessed, as they carefully began their work, that it would be eleven years before No. 10 finally announced the results of the team's labours to the public. On a spring day in 2016, more than 900 files were made available to the public. Many of them shed light on embarrassing circumstances and incidents previously deemed to be 'not in the public interest'. Philandering politicians and members of the Royal family. Cross-dressing civil servants and orgy-inclined diplomats. Church ministers and television personalities with a penchant for underage girls (and boys). All included and meticulously documented.

But by far the most interesting revelations, as far as Maugham was concerned, were those detailing the more unsavoury aspects of British intelligence initiatives. War and peace-time skulduggery laid bare. Bribery, betrayals and double-crosses. State-ordered assassinations, both planned and realised, were now out in the open for all to see. A Pandora's box had been opened, its fascinating and damning contents given full transparency. Of the files still considered 'too toxic for release', there were surprisingly few. In fact, Maugham had kept back only one file from his area of interest, a slim volume found at the bottom of a drab grey filing cabinet. It contained information about intelligence and espionage operations carried out during World War II in the British Overseas Territory of Gibraltar. In particular, information about a single spy used to great effect by British intelligence from 1942 to 1944. It was not particularly ground-breaking information. Brutal and unpleasant reading, but of no real embarrassment to the UK now. Perhaps toxic enough to command a two-page spread about 'BRITAIN'S BLACK OPS SKELETONS' in the Daily Mail, but little more.

Maugham had thought long and hard about the file, deciding to keep it out of the mix only at the last minute. His reasons were almost, though not quite, personal. He had known as soon as he had read the file that its contents would be of huge interest to someone he had once met and greatly admired. A man whose story of loss and betrayal had affected Maugham more deeply than anything he had ever heard. With this in mind, the mild-mannered, by-the-book archivist had set about 'losing' the file in the hope of delivering it abroad to the old man in the south of Spain who would be grateful beyond words for the information it contained. *How truly out of character for me*, Maugham had thought as he had secreted the file. It would absolutely finish him if his deception were discovered. But at seventy years old, he no longer cared. This went against everything he had stood for during his long career, but somehow it seemed the right thing to do. As the Airbus 320 touched down at Gibraltar International Airport, Graeme Maugham felt proud that his unremarkable life was about to produce something of real worth.

CHAPTER 3

'AND ... ACTION!'

On the north side of Grand Casements Square, in the heart of Gibraltar Town, a young woman pulls the collar of her blouse up around her neck. It gives little protection from the chill of the evening air. In her high heels, she has to move carefully across the densely cobbled ground. Two US Army jeeps pass her at speed, the soldiers within them heading towards their garrison and a hot evening meal. Small groups of soldiers and sailors wander aimlessly in search of cheap bars and clubs. Some are pleasure-bent, knowing the coming days could find them in action once more against their Nazi foe. Perhaps realising this, the woman ignores the admiring wolf whistles that follow her and heads towards the meeting place under an arch on the square's east side. She has no desire to draw any more attention to herself than is absolutely necessary. The sudden flash of a cigarette lighter from beneath the arch alerts her to her contact.

Twenty metres further on, she stands face to face with the man she knows only as Diablo. He is younger than she expected, and sports a scar down the side of his right cheek.

'You have what I need?' he asks.

'Yes,' the woman replies, unable to hide the anxiety in her voice.

'Well?'

The woman removes an envelope from her bag and hands it to him. As he turns to go, the woman instinctively reaches out and grabs his arm.

'How is he?' she asks.

The man hesitates for a moment, looks around nervously and then pulls the woman to him, kissing her hard on the lips. The woman does not fight him. Pulling back, the man looks into her eyes.

'He told me to do that. From him, you understand?'

The woman smiles. 'Yes, I understand.'

'And ... CUT!'

The cry rang out across the square. An order that was echoed by the small army of assistant directors and runners whose job it was to set up and control the complex movie scene and its difficult, busy location ...

'We're going again!' the director called.

On this command, principal actors and supporting artists alike headed back to their beginners' marks. Wardrobe assistants and make-up artistes moved forward and checked and double-checked them for the camera before the call of 'ACTION!' filled the balmy July night air once more.

Director Jerry Callum-Forbes placed a baseball cap on top of his mass of grey, shoulder-length hair, then pulled its brim down low over his forehead. The glare from a huge light suspended more than twenty metres above the ground on a giant crane had momentarily blinded him. It was all the fiercer for being the only light shining in the square. As a film set in wartime, the lack of street lighting had to be authentic. The giant lamp created a moonlit glow across the square's cobbled surface. An effect that was perfect, but one achieved at the cost of much negotiation. Traders, residents and local government officials had all finally agreed to turn off street and building lights during the few hours that had been allotted to filming in the town centre.

Despite the late hour, hundreds of people had turned out to catch a possible glimpse of a Hollywood movie star and watch the machinations of film-making in their own backyard. Their presence had required some complicated and sensitive crowd control, a responsibility shared by the film's crew and the Royal Gibraltar Police. It had also cost a fair bit of money, a point not lost on the film's producer, Gabriel Isolde. Hunching his narrow shoulders and lighting yet another cigarette, the wiry film-maker paced nervously behind the director's chair and viewing monitor. The demeanour of the perfectly coiffured and immaculately dressed Gibraltarian was usually one of confidence and calm. Tonight it reflected stress and agitation. Although this was his third film as a producer, the massive pressures and never-ending list of responsibilities seemed only to increase, not lessen. The day had started with him firing his line producer. Until a replacement arrived, that individual's gruelling duties – preparation, scheduling, co-ordination, payments ad infinitum – would all fall to Isolde. Added to this, he was in his home town under the expectant stares of his family, friends and fellow Gibraltarians. The opportunities to cock up on a huge scale were many and varied. Only an endless supply of caffeine and cigarettes seemed to make the whole situation bearable.

Isolde's phone vibrated in his pocket. Taking it out, he could see a text message from Josh Cornwallis, the movie's young British screenwriter. Josh was supposed to have been there from the start of the night's filming, but had gone AWOL. His text message read: 'DELAYED. URGENT BUSINESS. NOTHING TO WORRY ABOUT. CATCH YOU TOMORROW.' Isolde sighed. He didn't like the sound of that. Josh had a tendency to take off for days on end, disappearing on spur-of-the-moment research trips and what he liked to describe as 'little adventures'. His timing was definitely out now, his absence taking its place on Isolde's ever-increasing list of anxieties.

To begin with, they were filming a winter scene in the middle of summer, during the Rock's busiest tourist period – a big ask. Isolde checked his watch, something he did so often that it had almost become a nervous tic. It was five minutes past one in the morning. With only five-and-a-half hours to go before daybreak and the end of the required darkness, the pressure was on for everyone to get the shots in the can.

'What the fuck are we waiting for?' Jerry hissed into his walkie-talkie. The rasp of the Scotsman's voice sounded even fiercer than usual.

Across the square, first assistant director Tommy Danes lifted his walkie-talkie to his mouth and replied to his director's question in a calm and reassuring manner. 'Just waiting for final checks on Miss Novacs. Sixty seconds, if you'd be so kind, guv?'

The lack of reply from Jerry meant that the director had decided to chomp on his cigar for the next minute instead of having a hissy fit. Tommy was feeling the heat, but his thirty years in the business had taught him that the gentle touch led to better results. He turned to watch the film's make-up designer, Tani Levitt, working her brush with professional ease over the face of one of the best-known and most beautiful women in the world. Julia Novacs, movie star and idol to millions, stood a few paces to Tommy's left, her hair, make-up and costume making her appear like a ghost from the 1940s, her face a picture of concentration as she waited to begin the scene once more.

'How we doing, luv?' Tommy gently asked Tani.

'We're cool,' Tani replied, giving one last look at her work.

'Thanks, Tani. Thank you, Miss Novacs. We're ready to go again if you are.'

The actress stared ahead into the distance, unwilling to break character.

Taking this as an affirmative, Tommy raised his walkie-talkie to his mouth once more. 'Okay, everyone. Set to go again?' He waited a few moments for any possible negative feedback from around the square. None came. 'Okay, guv,' he broadcast to Jerry. 'We're all clear. On your word.'

From across the square, Jerry's voice bellowed once more: 'Let's shoot this mother!'

Smiling, Tommy calmly gave the order.

'And ... ACTION!'

CHAPTER 4

A FEW KILOMETRES north of the Gibraltar peninsula, in the ancient Spanish town of San Roque, Josh Cornwallis was waiting in the shadows of the church of Santa María La Coronada in the Plaza de la Iglesia. Across from him was the white frontage of the old Palacio de los Gobernadores, now the home of the Municipal Art Gallery. Adjacent to the stone seat on which he was sitting was the Bar El Varal, its lights still on behind closed doors and blinds. *Some late-night brandy's being drunk*, Josh thought. Apart from whoever was in the bar, he was, as far as he could discern, alone in the centre of the town. The tall, olive-skinned and strikingly handsome young man had arrived half an hour earlier than the appointed time, eager not to miss a contact he was desperate to meet. Who the contact was, he had no idea, but their importance to the story he had been researching for the last five years was paramount.

Josh was both baffled and flattered that that story was now being made into a movie entitled *Queen of Diamonds*, a romance based on the supposed operations of a female spy operating in Gibraltar during World War II. The spy's real identity had never been discovered, but her exploits, thanks to Josh's discoveries, were now slowly coming to light. The tangle of fact and myth surrounding her had proved a most attractive proposition for a screenplay, a tale of espionage and treachery set on the Rock in the darkest days of the war. Although his script had taken much artistic licence with the truth, its basis, as far as he had ascertained through lengthy, methodical research, was as accurate as the limited facts allowed.

Five years earlier, the young screenwriter had been developing a film story based on the life of another legendary female spy, the self-named 'Queen of Hearts'. This brave thirty-year-old had offered her services to British intelligence officers based in Gibraltar in the early years of the war. Wife of the master of one of the harbours along the Bay of Gibraltar, she had helped foil the devastating 'human torpedo' attacks made by Italian commando frogmen on Allied shipping in the port of Gibraltar.

While on an early research trip to the Rock, Josh had received an anonymous handwritten letter. It had informed him of another woman agent recruited to British intelligence during the same period. No records had been released concerning this operative, and all knowledge of her was denied by the Ministry of Defence and Secret Intelligence Service. However, a further series of handwritten notes had given him information and a codename – 'Queen of Diamonds'. Only part of the information had proved verifiable at first, but it was enough for one old-time intelligence insider to say it had a 'whiff of truth about it'. Over a two-year period, Josh had accumulated enough intelligence – officially unconfirmed – to link the female spy with several successful secret British operations. Two national newspaper articles and a Wikipedia entry had brought both Josh and the mysterious espionage operative to public attention. With growing faith in his material, Josh had set about writing a screenplay based on his findings.

A chance meeting with Gabriel Isolde at a friend's party had led to a working and personal relationship with the passionate Gibraltar-born film producer. Isolde had taken the young man under his wing, even giving him the basement flat of his London house to live in, rent free. Now, three years later, everything had come together, their film fully financed and on location.

Principal photography had begun in the morning two days before, on the Rock's Eastern Beach, and tonight a large-scale night-shoot was taking place in the centre of Gibraltar Town itself.

The film was low budget by Hollywood standards, funded by a myriad of investors, broadcasters and financial institutions. A classic Euro-blend of art-house quality and tax-break investment, it still boasted a budget of several million pounds and had attracted Hollywood A-lister, Julia Novacs, to the leading role.

It had been a swift rise to prominence for the twenty-nine-year-old English writer, which had drawn much attention from the media. There had even been talk in the gossip columns of an affair between himself and the film's leading lady. Such rumours were not entirely unfounded.

After the film had been announced to the press, Josh's mysterious contact had gone quiet. Eighteen months had passed without so much as a whisper. But tonight, on the third day of the movie's seven-week shoot, the silence ended.

The letter he had found in his mailbox, bearing a La Línea postmark, had been direct to the point of bluntness.

YOU WANT THE TRUTH? COME TO THE SQUARE, SAN ROQUE, 1 AM. TONIGHT. ALONE ONLY. I MEAN THIS. WAIT.

That was all.

So Josh had come, and now he waited. Another five minutes passed. Looking up at the tall, silent bell tower of the church, he felt, for the very first time, a little vulnerable. Movement at the far end of the square caught his attention. From the shadows, a man appeared. He was wearing a dark jacket and trousers and moved slowly towards the front of the church, his perambulation aided by the use of a stick. In his other hand, he held a paper file. Josh did not move towards him but waited, watching all the while. The man was in his eighties at least. His slow progress across the square was determined and somehow dignified. Like an actor, Josh thought, making a grand entrance to an audience of just one.

At last the man arrived at his destination. Wisps of pure white hair hung from his balding head, and wrinkles were etched into the weathered skin of his face. He looked at Josh, but did not speak.

'*Buenas noches, señor,*' Josh offered in greeting.

The old man's eyes focused – taking Josh in, sizing him up. At last … '*Buenas noches,*' he replied.

'It's good to meet you at last,' Josh said. 'I want to thank you. For your help.'

The old man looked around the square. It was not clear to Josh if it was because he needed to make sure that they were alone, or if he had expected someone else to be there. His surveillance complete, the old man turned once more to the young man. For a moment he stared at Josh again, giving no sign of his thoughts.

Josh continued, in semi-fluent Spanish: 'What you've given me over these last few years has been invaluable, *señor*. You deserve credit for that. I know your "Queen of Diamonds" existed and, to some extent, the work she did to help the Allied forces and the people of Gibraltar. What I still don't know is who she was. Can you help me, *señor*? Can you tell me all you know?'

The man's gaze had not left Josh's face. For a moment, he seemed to hesitate. Whatever he might have to say would not be easily given. At last he nodded, but before he could speak, the doors of the nearby Bar El Varal opened. Three men fell out onto the square, all a little worse for drink. Before the old man could move to the anonymity of the shadows, one of the drunken *amigos* had spied him.

'Don Martínez!' the man called over, he and his colleagues stumbling towards them. 'Don Martínez!'

The drunks, on seeing Josh standing with the old man, looked concerned. 'Is all well, Don Martínez? You wish we walk you home, *sí*?'

The sound of his name was a clear irritation to the old man.

'All is well with me, my friends. Home to your beds. Your wives will not be pleased at this hour.'

The men acknowledged this with laughter and snorts, moving off in an unsteady chain and calling out 'Good night, Don Martínez!' as they left the square.

Josh and the old man were alone once more. Noticing indecision in the Spaniard's dark eyes, Josh pressed on quickly. He had waited too long to let this opportunity slip away.

'Don Martínez?' he asked. 'Finally. Your name.'

A flash of anger crossed the old man's face. 'It is,' he whispered, his voice rasping but strong. 'But that you must now forget. You do not know me and never will. Tonight, I will give you this.'

Don Martínez handed Josh the folder he had been carrying.

'This is all you need. Study with care and you will find what you need to know. Keep it safe. Yourself, too. But promise, on your life, that you will never look for me again. You understand?'

The intensity with which the old man spoke took Josh by surprise. The man was shaking, his eyes burning into his. Whatever secret this man had kept over the years had cost him dearly.

'I promise you,' Josh told him. 'Thank you.'

The old man's eyes sought confirmation of this promise in Josh's. Moments passed. At last the old man turned away. With the same steady dignity with which he had arrived, Don Martínez moved across the square and into the dark lanes beyond. He did not once turn back to see Josh heading for his car, the file held in a vice-like grip.

CHAPTER 5

DETECTIVE SERGEANT TAMARA SULLIVAN had begun her morning run a full hour earlier than usual. It had taken her some time to get used to the late rising sun of the Mediterranean dawn, and although it was 5.30 am and dark outside, she had got up and run. Outside the air would be fresher than at any other time of the day and the perfect antidote to the air-conditioned climate of her apartment.

Two days before, she had been on the Wirral celebrating her widowed mother's birthday. It had been a sad and tawdry affair. No other relatives had bothered to visit and the few friends her mother had managed to keep had not stayed long. A dry sherry and a Twiglet, exchanged for a card, some bath oils and a £20 Boots voucher. In the evening, Sullivan had treated her mum to a meal at a local Greek restaurant, after which they had returned to her mother's and gone straight to bed. The next morning, after breakfast, Sullivan had kissed her mum goodbye and headed for the station to board a train to Manchester airport. As she stood on the station platform, Sullivan realised that she would have felt a lot sadder had she not had a return air ticket to Gibraltar in her pocket.

She loved her new apartment – small but perfect for her needs – in a very pleasant building just fifty metres along from the main police headquarters on New Mole Parade. With a balcony looking out across the ship repair yard in the docks and then onwards to the sea beyond, it provided a welcome haven at the end of her working day. It was an obvious perk of being a Brit on secondment and the subject of constant ribbing from her fellow police officers in the RGP. Not that Sullivan cared. She could give as good as she got.

Leaving her apartment building, she had headed towards the centre of Gibraltar Town. Most days her morning run took her to Europa Point at the southernmost tip of the Rock. Passing the Mosque of the Custodian of the Two Holy Mosques and the impressive memorial to the wartime prime minister of the Polish Government in Exile, General Władysław Sikorski – killed in a plane crash in Gib in 1943 – Sullivan would pause briefly at the red-and-white striped Trinity Lighthouse. From there, she would look across the narrow strait to the coast of north Africa. It often felt as though she could reach out and touch the Moroccan mountains before her. Over recent weeks, she had found it the perfect spot to clear her mind and prepare for the day's work ahead.

This morning, however, she would head north to the Alameda Botanic Gardens. Passing them, she would run on and through the Referendum Gates to the Line Wall Road. This route would eventually bring her to Grand Casemates Square, where she would turn back for home along the pedestrianised, shop-lined Main Street. She had felt like a change and, if truth be told, wanted to check out where the filming had taken place the night before. She had already, two days before, driven out to Eastern Beach to see the barbed wire defences that the film's designers had produced to recreate the exact look of the location in 1942. Back in London, serving in the Met, she had come across countless locations being used for television and film productions. They had been of only passing interest to her – although a snatched autograph from Matt Damon had been fun to get. But here, six weeks into her enforced secondment to the Royal Gibraltar Police, she found the presence of Hollywood on her patch of the Mediterranean shore a little more glamorous.

A fifteen-minute hard push brought her to Grand Casemates Square in better than good time. What greeted her was the more unglamorous side of film-making. The stars had vanished into the night. All that remained were the scores of film people needed to return the square to normal in the quickest possible time. A legion of thick-set men shifting and loading equipment into trucks supervised by a team of location operatives and art department personnel. Intricately designed fake period façades were being pulled down to reveal the normal frontages of the buildings behind – a WHSmith, a betting shop and the Julian Lennon Beatles Memorabilia Exhibition, once more restored to their modern-day selves. Street lamps of 1940s vintage were being carried away, as the tables and chairs belonging to the square's many cafes were brought out in time for the morning's opening.

No glimpse of Julia Novacs, Sullivan thought, feeling a slight pang of embarrassment at having hoped otherwise. She knew she could have joined the crowds watching the proceedings through the night, but as some of her fellow police officers were going to be on duty to organise crowd and traffic control, she had thought it not the coolest thing to do.

Five minutes later, Sullivan was pounding down Main Street heading for home. A quick shower and a bowl of granola and Detective Sergeant Sullivan would be off to work. By 6.45 she'd be at her desk at police headquarters preparing for what the day ahead had to offer – a missing person, feared dead. She wanted to be on top of the details before her boss arrived. It was the least that Chief Inspector Gus Broderick would expect.

Had she not been in such a hurry, Sullivan might have noticed something odd back in Casemates.

A figure at the side of the square. The tall, somewhat dishevelled man would normally have caught Sullivan's eye, so out of place did he look. He stood alone, his gaze not directed at anything in particular and his eyes devoid of life. His bearded face creased with lines and darkened by shadows not normally found on a man in his early forties. Among the hectic industry of the organised throng around him, he seemed lost to the world, his mind focused on distant things. Only the constant clenching and unclenching of Lech Jasinski's fists gave a true sign of the turmoil that raged within him.

CHAPTER 6

ARRIVING AT NEW Mole House, the Royal Gibraltar Police headquarters, just a short way from her home, Sullivan looked across to the adjacent dry docks, occupied by two large commercial ships in need of repair. Gazing out above the ships and loading cranes, she enjoyed the view across the Bay of Gibraltar to the Spanish port of Algeciras. It was one of the many things she'd grown to love about Gibraltar – almost anywhere you looked, a rewarding vista greeted the eye. None more so than the views of the gigantic limestone Rock itself, towering hundreds of metres above the town. A mighty sentinel guarding the entrance to the Mediterranean Sea. Its pivotal position between sea and ocean and the two mighty continents of Europe and Africa had been coveted and fought over many times across the centuries. Even today, its loyalty to the British Crown was the cause of a major dispute between the UK and Spain, a situation that often triggered heated diplomatic discussions and frequent border delays. Gibraltarians were in no doubt where their continued loyalties lay. Ninety-nine per cent of them were more than happy for Gibraltar to remain a British Overseas Territory.

Entering the building, Sullivan strode past the duty officer's desk and headed for the stairs that would lead her up to her desk in a first-floor office. Before she could ascend, someone called her name. Turning, she was pleased to see the smiling face of Sergeant Aldarino. The tall, avuncular veteran police officer had been the first person to make her welcome after her arrival on the Rock. He had since been a source of considerable guidance to her as she had navigated the new terrain of the Royal Gibraltar Police, and had proved helpful in giving Sullivan the heads-up on her two immediate bosses – Chief Superintendent Harriet Massetti and CI Broderick.

'Early bird as usual,' the uniformed sergeant teased.

'Someone's got to work around here,' Sullivan smiled back.

'Just as well, though,' Aldarino continued, 'because on top of all your usual paperwork, the Chief Super wants to see you as soon as she gets in.'

This information wiped the smile from Sullivan's face. After an uneasy start, Chief Superintendent Massetti had left Sullivan alone. She had not been best pleased by her new arrival's three-month secondment and had made no bones about it. She knew it was a barely disguised punishment, imposed by Sullivan's London superiors after a rulebook-flouting but ultimately successful end to her last operation with the force. Sullivan's logical, 'means to an end' approach to a dangerous hostage situation had won the admiration of her colleagues, but not that of her commanding officer. Sullivan's secondment to the Royal Gibraltar Police had been conjured up as a face-saving way of allowing things to settle, and an opportunity for her to avoid severe disciplinary action – a procedure that would have completely wrecked the career of such an outstanding police officer. For Sullivan, it had been a humiliating blow. Her hopes of being promoted to become one of the youngest inspectors in the Met's history had been dashed at a stroke.

A cloud crossed Sullivan's face.

'I thought you'd be delighted,' Aldarino teased again.

'What do you think she wants?'

'I'd have thought it might be about going home,' the sergeant replied.

'Home?'

'You're only a visitor here, you know. Just five weeks left of your secondment, by my reckoning. All good things must come to end and all that.'

Smiling, Aldarino turned and left the room. Sullivan watched him go. *Only five weeks*, she thought. *That's what it will be*. But as she headed towards her office, she had to admit that the thought of leaving the Rock had unsettled her more than she might have expected.

CHAPTER 7

GUS BRODERICK WAS not in a good mood. Once again he had not slept well. As always, he had got off to sleep only to wake in the small hours of the morning. What followed were several more hours of restless anxiety, until sleep once more returned, just in time to render him impervious to his alarm clock's insistent bleeping. The pleading of his fourteen-year-old daughter Daisy – 'Get up, Daddy!' – at last raised him from the abyss.

He was up now and running late. A freezing cold shower and a shaving nick that refused to stop bleeding had not helped him to achieve a sense of ease with the world. A brief glimpse in the bathroom's full-length mirror gave the forty-eight-year-old no shock at all. He was looking older and beginning to lose his thick brown hair. His late mother's Gibraltarian DNA was now clearly visible in his face. But there the similarity ended. Below the neck he was starting to resemble his father's more haphazard Celtic form, with a stomach that could no longer be confined within the bounds of physical acceptability and a tan that was just a distant memory. So what was new? It was time to cover up this walking corpse.

Moments later, he was dressed. Attempting to knot his tie – *Why can't I ever get the length right?* – he looked out of the bedroom window. The sun was shining. *At least in summer you can rely on that*, he thought. Glancing down to check his old Mercedes in the townhouse's narrow driveway below, he could see that no harm had befallen it overnight. As a police officer, he had found himself victim to occasional acts of vandalism, usually directed at his car under cover of darkness.

Checking his watch, he headed out of the bedroom and down the stairs. Daisy was waiting for him in the kitchen.

'Porridge, Daddy,' she offered, placing a steaming bowl on the table for him. Although not in the least hungry, Broderick would eat it. His daughter had made it especially for him.

'Thanks, Princess,' he said and was immediately lifted by her radiant smile.

It was 7.45 now and Daisy would have been up for at least an hour and a half. Broderick would drop her at school this morning before heading in to work. It was a school Daisy loved, providing her with the perfect environment to learn and prosper. Born with Down's syndrome, her needs were always paramount in Broderick's mind. The school had proved a blessing and Daisy had thrived there.

'Penny's still in bed,' Daisy informed her father with a mock frown.

'No surprises there. When you're eighteen, we'll not be able to get you out of bed either, Princess.'

'No, never, never, never!' Daisy replied, shaking her head vigorously. 'Always first one out of bed. I'm the champion!' She raised her arms in the air and circled the kitchen table in a lap of triumph.

Broderick laughed out loud. As always, his youngest daughter could lift his spirits in the blink of an eye. It was nearly thirteen years since her mother had left Broderick and the girls, disappearing off the face of the earth, her depression and self-loathing finally taking her from their lives for good. Even with his police connections, Broderick had not been able to find her. Not a day went by without him wishing her back in their lives. For her to see her daughters happy and well. To know that they were loved.

It had been Broderick's elder sister who had come to the family's rescue. Unlike her brother – who had left Gib at the age of nineteen to join the London Met and live in the UK – she had stayed in Gibraltar. A happy but childless marriage had sadly ended in widowhood. Offering Gus and her nieces her home and love was, without question, the natural thing to do. And so brother and his daughters had come to stay on the Rock. Twelve years had now passed since Broderick had taken up a new job with the RGP, and his sister's three-storey townhouse had become a haven from the pain and despair of the past.

'Aunty Cath outside,' Daisy told her father as she looked out of the kitchen window to the small courtyard beyond. 'With Sister Clara.'

Broderick leaned forward to see his elder sister taking coffee with her friend and colleague. Sister Clara was Cath's boss, the president of the charity his sister worked for. The Rock of Ages Charitable Foundation had been set up decades before by Sister Clara's mother, but their friendship had made the 'boss' designation unacceptable. They were friends who worked and socialised happily together. Once a week, Sister Clara would come for breakfast, bringing her wonderful home-baked croissants and sweet marmalade. She loved Daisy and Penny and often brought them each a little gift, too. Despite having left her religious order some forty years before, she was still known as 'Sister Clara', which seemed to sit just fine with her. Privately, Broderick had long suspected her of trying to convert his sister to the Catholic faith, and Cath had once confirmed that she had flirted with the idea. Religious or not, as far as Broderick was concerned his sister was a saint already, her place in heaven most certainly guaranteed. If, of course, such a place as heaven actually existed. Broderick had his own ideas on that subject, but tried to show respect by not voicing them too often.

Minutes later he had finished his porridge, washed his bowl and handed it to Daisy to dry. Moving to the backdoor, he popped out his head to greet the breakfasting couple in the courtyard.

'Morning all,' he called. 'I'm in a rush, I'm afraid.'

'Daisy doing the honours?' Cath enquired.

'She is. Who says you can't get the staff these days? All well with you, Sister Clara?'

'Most well, thank you, Gus,' said the older woman with a smile. Her clear, unlined complexion showing little sign of her seventy-plus years.

'I like the dress, Sister Clara,' Broderick said. 'Very colourful.'

'Why, thank you, Gus.' Sister Clara smiled, running a hand down the folds of her long, brightly patterned summer dress. 'A gift from my friends in Sri Lanka. Quite vivid and very much to my taste, I'm glad to say.'

'Yeah. Nice. Anyway, I don't want to interrupt.' Broderick turned to leave.

'Join us,' Sister Clara invited. 'The coffee's hot. We're just discussing some rather exciting news about the orphanage in Kampala.'

'That and tonight's reception at the Governor's Residence. We're being presented with a cheque for the Foundation,' Cath added, barely hiding her excitement.

'Good, great,' Broderick mumbled as he checked his phone, his mind already elsewhere. 'Thanks anyway, but I've got to go and clean up the mean streets of Gib. I'll give Penny a nudge before I go. She'd sleep through to the weekend if given the chance.'

'She's not the only one, is she, brother of mine?' Cath teased.

'Don't make me swear with a nun present, Cath.'

'You should know better than to worry about that, Gus,' said Sister Clara. 'Oh, and I trust you'll be taking time out to concentrate on your costume choice for the Foundation's Fancy Dress Ball on Friday?'

'Ah, yes.' Broderick hesitated. 'It's quite a busy week for you, isn't it? Anyway, I'm, er ... sure I'll think of something to throw on.'

'Take a croissant,' Cath insisted, offering him the plate.

'I've just had my breakfast. But they do look delicious ...' Broderick hesitated for a split second, then reached over and helped himself to one of the warm buttery delights.

'Have a good day, Chief Inspector,' Sister Clara said. 'Oh ... and may your God go with you, et cetera and so forth.'

Broderick nodded, waved and left. The morning's banter was over, his working day about to begin.

THE POISONED ROCK

Chapter 8

AT PRECISELY ONE minute past eight, Sullivan's desk phone rang. It was Aldarino, informing her that Chief Superintendent Harriet Massetti was waiting to see her. The last hour had been a busy one, and Sullivan felt mildly irritated at having to leave her computer. She had been sifting through CCTV footage taken from a new apartment building on the east side of the Rock at Catalan Bay. An apartment had been rented by a young solicitor by the name of Krystle Changtai who had been reported missing by her firm two days ago after being absent from work for nearly a week. Broderick and Sullivan had set up a missing persons investigation. Checks on flights, boat departures and border crossings to Spain had thrown up nothing. Now there was little more to do than launch a public appeal for information. Changtai was a tall, handsome-looking woman. Someone must have seen her somewhere.

At 7.31, Sullivan had received a frantic call that had changed the parameters of the case. The call had come from the firm of solicitors that Changtai worked for as a junior partner: £1.5 million was missing from her client accounts. Monies transferred to untraceable offshore accounts over a period of two years. No real reason had been given by the firm for the time it had taken to discover this massive loss, and Sullivan's questioning about this had been met with embarrassed and unconvincing responses relating to client privacy and accounting software problems. With her meeting with Massetti pending, and neither Broderick nor DC Calbot through the door, Sullivan had decided to review the CCTV footage from Changtai's apartment building once again.

Now, half an hour later, she was downstairs knocking on her superior's door. Failing to get a response, Sullivan knocked once more and entered. Harriet Massetti sat at her desk engrossed in paperwork. She did not look up from her task.

'Take a seat, Sullivan,' she commanded.

Sullivan did as she was told and for the next two minutes waited patiently for Massetti to finish what she was doing. At last, the chief superintendent signed the bottom of a covering page and turned to look at the detective sergeant sitting in front of her.

'Hell of a day ahead. Lunch with my accountant, then this film reception thing this evening at the Governor's Residence. Canapés and fizzy wine and the chance for everyone to tell Julia Novacs how wonderful she is. It was the same when they filmed that James Bond thing over here. Everybody goes daft.'

'Except you, ma'am?' Sullivan asked.

'Someone has to keep a level head,' Massetti replied coldly.

'They do, ma'am,' Sullivan concurred, while noting her boss's new hairstyle and additional use of make-up for the day.

'To make matters ...' – Massetti checked herself quickly – '... a little more interesting, shall we say, Chief Inspector Broderick will be accompanying me.'

'Goodness!' was the only response Sullivan could muster at this intriguing news.

'It was a name-out-of-the-hat job. Aldarino managed to pull your boss's name out of the mix. Seemed to find that outcome most amusing,' Massetti added without amusement. 'Anyway, enough of that. The reason I want to see you is that you'll soon be coming to the end of your time here.'

'Five weeks, ma'am.'

'So I believe. It's not been an uneventful period for you. Your work on the Laytham murder case was impressive, but a little unorthodox for my liking.'

Sullivan let the barbed compliment go.

Massetti continued: 'You've fitted in *pretty well* on the whole. Pretty well. So here's the thing. It seems we have a vacant DS position to fill. As you know, we work organically here at the RGP, promoting from within the force. It so happens that Detective Sergeant Marquez has taken early retirement on health grounds. We thought it was a glandular infection, but the fact is, he lost the use of his voice after a drugs shoot-out last September. Shock, apparently. Anyway, it's still not come back and neither will he now. Shame, he was a fine officer.'

'I'm sure, ma'am.'

'Unfortunately it leaves us with a little problem. We promoted two officers to detective sergeant rank last month and for the moment there's nobody else ready.'

'What about DC Calbot, ma'am?'

'As I said, there's nobody else ready. So you've been suggested as a candidate. Subject to it being of interest. Which I'm sure it isn't. Am I right?'

Sullivan didn't know what to think. As out-of-left-field proposals went, this one had caught her well and truly off guard.

'Needless to say,' Massetti continued, 'as your return to London is imminent, a quick response would be appreciated.'

Massetti turned her attention to more papers awaiting inspection on her desk. The meeting, as far as she was concerned, was over.

'"Suggested"?' Sullivan interrupted.

'I beg your pardon?' Massetti responded, unable to disguise her irritation.

'"Suggested". Someone *suggested* me?' Sullivan asked warily. 'Which someone, may I ask?'

'No, you may not.' Massetti bristled.

'Permanent?' Sullivan continued. 'A permanent placement?'

'Obviously,' Massetti replied, as though talking to a child.

'With CI Broderick, ma'am?'

'That would be the general idea, Sullivan.'

'I need to think about it, ma'am.'

'That's what I just proposed, Sullivan. Don't take too long about it. Might appear rude.' With that, Massetti rose from her chair to signal the end of the meeting.

'Yes, ma'am,' replied Sullivan heading for the door. 'Oh, and by the way. Is that a new hairstyle? Very nice, ma'am.'

Massetti smiled at the compliment before she could stop herself. 'Yes, well, sometimes a change does one good, Sullivan,' she replied. 'On your way out, tell Aldarino to pop in, will you?'

'Yes, ma'am.'

Closing the office door behind her, Sullivan paused for a moment to think. Could it be Broderick who had 'suggested' that she stay? Surely not. Then again, who else could it possibly have been? Somehow, some way, she'd find out. More to the point, why was she hesitating giving Massetti an answer? A permanent posting to the Royal Gibraltar Police? That was definitely not part of her game plan. No way. No way, José.

CHAPTER 9

THE ATLANTIC MARINA Plaza towered over its large, yacht-filled marina in the north-west corner of the Gibraltar peninsula, its dynamic glass-and-concrete structure setting it apart from nearby apartment buildings of more conventional concept and design. In his luxurious open-plan apartment on the tenth floor, Josh Cornwallis had been toiling furiously for hours. Julia Novacs had left a long message on his mobile, checking he was okay. She was more than a little peeved to be without her screenwriter on such an important night. She reminded him that they were spending the weekend together in Marbella – she was staying in a villa in the hills above the town, lent to her by film star Antonio Banderas – and pleaded with him to phone her as soon as he could. Gabriel Isolde had also tried to contact him: three messages of increasing urgency. There had even been a tap on his apartment door an hour earlier. Most probably Isolde checking up on him, Josh presumed. The producer returning from the night-shoot and getting out of the lift two floors early, before heading up to his penthouse suite above. That both Isolde and Julia would now be asleep had given Josh a weak excuse not to reply.

Poring over the documents he had been given by Don Martínez several hours earlier, it had soon become clear to Josh that they were of major importance. As darkness had turned to dawn across his balcony, with its view of the marina and sea further out, he had read and reread the contents of the file. Aided by two cans of beer, a bottle of wine and the sugar rush from a half-eaten Snickers, he devoured the documents arrayed before him. Some of the information confirmed, in great detail, events Josh already knew about. The rest shocked him profoundly. The enormity of the revelations was such that he had been forced, several times, to stop and take in gulps of the fresh, chill air that flowed into the room from the wakening day outside.

This new and unwelcome information was a game changer of monumental dimensions. It turned on its head most of what he had believed he had known. As thought crowded in on thought, the growing panic made him reach for some whisky, anything to steady his nerves. All he had worked for, all he had achieved, the future of the movie itself could be ruined by the revelations in the file. How could he tell Gabriel? How would he explain it to Julia?

Downing the scotch, Josh moved out onto the balcony. Although the marina was still in the shadow of the Rock, the sea and distant Spanish coastline to the west were brightly bathed in morning sunlight. Steadying himself, he attempted to think rationally. How many people knew? How had this information remained hidden for so long? Was there any way it might work to his advantage? Could it, even at this impossibly late stage, be used in the movie? It would be a huge gamble, but it might just work if people didn't panic.

Encouraged by these new thoughts, Josh returned to the file. One thing remained unknown, he realised: the Queen of Diamond's real identity. Did Don Martínez know? If so, why hadn't it been included with the documents? The only note attached to the file was an address, written in the old man's shaky handwriting. Underneath the address was a scribbled message: 'I am old. I have not the strength or courage to visit this place. I trust you will be of stronger heart.'

Picking up a street map and his mobile, Josh left his apartment in search of answers, his heart pounding in his chest.

Chapter 10

THE MORNING WAS panning out a little better for Broderick than he had expected. Leaving Cath and Sister Clara to their breakfast planning session, he managed to raise his eldest daughter Penny from her slumber. On top of that – *Oh, sweet victory!* – he had gained a promise from her to spend the day looking for some part-time work. Penny had recently left school, and her year out before going to university had so far consisted of late nights and day-long naps.

In addition, the ride with Daisy to school had been far less traffic-bound than usual, resulting in him arriving at work ten minutes earlier than expected. Although still late, Broderick did not let that fact colour his unusually good spirits.

Entering his office at the police headquarters, he was greeted by the smiling face of Detective Constable John Calbot.

'Morning, sir. Bad traffic?' the young officer enquired.

'Yeah,' Broderick replied. 'Hellish.'

'Nice cup of coffee for you there, guv.' Calbot pointed to a take-away cup on a nearby desk.

The desk belonged to Sullivan and Broderick suspected that the coffee had not been intended for him. A suspicion that would not stop him drinking it. Calbot was after promotion and the confident twenty-seven-year-old was shameless in not hiding the fact.

'Right. Where's Sullivan?' Broderick asked.

'Downstairs with Massetti, guv.' Calbot shrugged his shoulders. 'No idea why.'

Broderick had no idea either. 'I see. So where are we on the Changtai disappearing act?'

'Got breaking news on that, sir.'

Both men turned to see Sullivan standing in the doorway.

'It seems Miss Changtai relieved Philips, Barton & Sholto of one-and-a-half million pounds before she disappeared,' Sullivan continued, moving to her computer and pushing a button. 'They called about an hour ago in quite a state.'

'I bet they bloody well were,' replied Broderick. 'How come they took so long to find out?'

'They gave unconvincing reasons, sir. My guess is they tried to track her down themselves. You know how these firms hate involving the police and making things public.'

'Should have thought of that before reporting her missing,' Calbot observed.

'Still nothing back from possible ports of exit?' Broderick asked.

'No sightings, sir,' Sullivan answered.

'What about phone and email contacts?'

'No communication from either since she left work, guv,' responded Calbot. 'No bank or credit card transactions either.'

'Thought I'd triple-check the CCTV footage from her apartment building before getting authorisation for a public appeal, sir,' Sullivan continued.

'Anything new?'

'Not really, sir. All other occupants accounted for. The evening she went missing, we see her enter the building but not leave it. To do so, she would have had to pass through reception and automatically be picked up by the camera.'

'Anyone on it that's yet to be accounted for?'

'Just one, sir.' Sullivan pointed to the screen where she had freeze-framed the figure of a suited gentleman passing the unstaffed reception desk on his way to the main door. The man sported a shaven head and carried a briefcase. His facial features were not particularly clear, but his general demeanour suggested nothing suspicious or untoward.

'Well, let's start with him ¬– the only person in the building on the evening of Changtai's disappearance we can't identify.'

'I'll check town and border CCTV with the Defence Police straight away,' Sullivan said.

Broderick moved to the door. 'In the meantime, I'll check in with Massetti about launching an appeal.'

Sullivan looked up from her computer, a slight gleam of mischief playing in her eyes. 'Looking forward to tonight, sir?'

Broderick stopped in the doorway as the phone on Calbot's desk rang. Calbot picked up as Sullivan continued: 'Envious myself, sir.'

'Of what, precisely?' Broderick asked.

'The film reception for *Queen of Diamonds*? Governor's Residence? Julia Novacs? Champagne and canapés?'

'Shit,' replied Broderick. 'That's tonight, isn't it?'

'I believe so, sir. As does the Chief Super.'

'Bollocks.' Broderick slumped in despair. 'Why does everything happen to me?'

Before Sullivan could bring herself to console her boss, Calbot interrupted. 'That was Marbella police on the line, guv. Seems they've found Miss Changtai. They want someone to go up there and identify her.'

'Identify her?' Broderick questioned.

'At the mortuary, sir. Apparently she's been dead for a week.'

Chapter 11

LECH JASINSKI HAD spent the night watching the filming in Grand Casemates Square. Upon wrap, as the detritus of filming was packed away and moved off, he stopped one of the film crew to ask how he might contact the movie's producer and writer. A moody-looking electrician told him to go to the unit base out at the old Royal Navy Dockyard, now known as Gibdock, or maybe the Atlantic Marina Plaza. All the big boys were staying there, except Julia Novacs. Apparently, the star of the movie was helicoptered off to her Marbella villa at the end of each filming session.

'Alright for some, innit, mate?' the spark added, loading another lighting stand onto a truck.

Yes, it was alright for some, Jasinski thought.

Earlier he had seen Gabriel Isolde from a distance, but had been unable to get close to him. Of the film's screenwriter, Josh Cornwallis, he had seen nothing. He knew both men from the internet and from the magazine articles he now carried in the rucksack on his back. The tall, formidable-looking Pole possessed a raft of information about the film and almost everyone of influence attached to it. Jasinski had only arrived on the Rock the previous night, having hitchhiked from his home town of Luboń in western Poland. He had come in search of answers to questions that had haunted him and his poor late father all their lives. Clenching and unclenching his fists and moving restlessly from one foot to the other, the Pole pondered his next move. Someone needed to help him. He was a man who needed help.

CHAPTER 12

THE LIFT DOORS opened onto the main reception of the Atlantic Marina Plaza apartment building and Josh stepped out. Although it was still early, the place was busy. A team of people were erecting big glossy promotion boards featuring glamorously clad and unclad men and women. As Josh passed the main desk, the doorman called to him.

'Sorry about all this, sir. A big PR launch this afternoon out on the Tropical Deck.' The man pointed towards the huge private pool and restaurant area that spread across the first-floor marina frontage of the building. 'It'll be over and gone by this evening.'

Josh nodded and moved to the main doors. Looking up at a promotion board he saw that the launch was for a new porn channel called 'Blue Job X'.

Nice, Josh thought wryly. *Another one of those is just what the world needs.*

As his taxi pulled away from the front of the Plaza, Josh checked the mysterious address scribbled on the notepaper held in his right hand – 'Sovereign Villa, Prince Edward's Road'. Whoever lived there had a bearing on the situation Josh was now facing.

Leaning forward, he gave the driver his instructions.

'Not filming today?' the driver responded.

Josh was momentarily perplexed.

'Picked you up a couple of days ago,' the man continued. 'Took you out to Eastern Beach. All that barbed wire and stuff. Very authentic. Very impressive.'

'Yes. It was.'

'So how's Julia finding Gib then? Staying up there in a penthouse with you, is she?' said the driver, laughing at his own little joke.

'Prince Edward's Road is at the top of the town, isn't it?' Josh asked, changing the subject.

'Thereabouts. Got a number?'

Something inside Josh made him disinclined to trust the driver with any more information than necessary. This instinct towards caution surprised him, but then everything recently had been surprising.

'Just the road, please. I know where I'm going from there,' he lied.

A few moments later the taxi was making its way along Line Wall Road, passing the City Hall on the left and the Gibraltar War Memorial on the right. The time was now just after 8 am and the town was getting busy. Following the one-way system alongside the old walled fortifications, they eventually passed the Inces Hall Theatre and the Trafalgar Cemetery, and then left and up onto Prince Edward's Road. It seemed the long way round to Josh, but he was in no mood to argue the issue.

'This will do, thanks,' Josh commanded. The cab pulled up. 'I'll walk from here, if you don't mind,' he told the driver, thrusting a £10 note into his hand and opening the passenger door.

'No worries,' replied the driver. 'Going to be a scorcher today. Bloody sunshine. I hate it.'

The driver's right, Josh agreed. *It's going to get very warm.* Wiping his brow, he walked along the road, checking each building's identity as he went. Some 150 metres on, as the road rose, he found what he was looking for. A small sign with an arrow pointing up a narrow flight of stairs. 'SOVEREIGN VILLA', it announced. Moving swiftly to the top of the steps, Josh finally reached an open cobbled courtyard. To his right, an iron gate set in a whitewashed wall protected a further set of steps leading upwards to a house and garden.

Once more wiping the sweat from his brow, Josh checked the nameplate on the wall before him. In simple lettering on a brass plate, it also read 'SOVEREIGN VILLA'. Turning the handle on the gate, Josh discovered it was securely locked. Stepping back across the courtyard for a better view of what lay above, Josh could see several palm trees and numerous displays of plumbago and bougainvillea rising above the parapet. The house beyond was almost entirely hidden from view by the foliage. Beside the gate, a narrow metal letterbox was set in the wall, next to which was a cream-coloured button, connected, Josh supposed, to a bell within the villa.

He pressed the button hard and long. Several minutes later, the door remained unopened. He was tempted to try scaling the wall, but he quickly thought better of it. Frustrated, Josh took the only course of action left open to him. Retrieving pen and paper from his jacket pocket, he wrote a brief note asking the villa's resident to contact him at the Atlantic Marina Plaza. He also mentioned his credentials as the screenwriter of the film being shot on the Rock, adding that he believed a meeting to be of the greatest importance and urgency – 'I have in my possession secrets and there are serious questions I need to ask.' Signing off with his name and his mobile and apartment numbers, he posted the note through the letter box, turned and descended the steps to the road below.

Chapter 13

AS THE NEAR empty toll road to Marbella opened before him, Broderick put his foot on the accelerator and let his old Mercedes' three-litre engine have its head. The thrill of speed was not something drivers on the Rock were used to as they navigated the myriad meanderings of the narrow lanes and steeply climbing roads, each with its own rigid and sensible speed limit in force. But now, as the speedometer hit 130 kilometres an hour, Broderick enjoyed another thrill –breaking the law. A nervous look from Sullivan sitting beside him made him lighten his touch on the pedal, but to no noticeable effect.

They had crossed the border into Spain with little delay. Their warrant cards took them to the front of the long four-lane traffic queue and through the passport checks with formal ease. Just the day before, the British prime minister had reprimanded the Madrid government for denying a reported shooting incident by Spanish police in the Gibraltarian waters surrounding the Rock. As usual, draconian checks by Spanish customs on all cross-border travellers to and from the Rock comprised Madrid's indignant response to the incident. The queues that Sullivan and

Broderick had jumped were a regular and unhappy result of failing diplomatic relations.

Once in Spain, Sullivan and Broderick went swiftly on their way. A smart and super-efficient toll motorway had been built in recent years to relieve pressure on the old coastal road that ran from Gib to Málaga and beyond. Once thought to be the most dangerous road in Europe, it had finally, after many years of lobbying, been relieved of major duties by its sister motorway. Cynics had observed that it was only the honour of Spain hosting the Ryder Cup at Valderrama that had finally shamed the government into constructing a decent road system to and from the main airports. Whatever the real reasons, it now provided a fast, if somewhat expensive drive to the main towns and cities of the Costa del Sol. Not that local Spaniards were impressed – refusing to pay the tolls, they mainly kept to the old road that snaked its way along the coast. As Broderick and Sullivan now bypassed the town of Estepona on their right and headed towards the Sierras towering above Marbella in the distance, they simply sat back and enjoyed the ride.

Forty minutes later, the two detectives had arrived at the police mortuary in the centre of Marbella old town. It had been a while since Broderick had visited the opulent seaside resort and he quietly marvelled at how much it had improved in both infrastructure and architectural flourishes. A visit to the majestic promenade and beach would have to wait for another day, but he had already decided that a family outing to the town was long overdue. Sullivan's reaction had been much the same. *It's just a shame*, she thought, *that my first visit to Marbella has be to a mortuary.*

They were met in the reception area of the sterile, characterless municipal building by Inspector Juan Córdobas. Broderick had

had dealings with the officer before and had found him to be both friendly and efficient. He also spoke excellent English.

After being introduced to Sullivan, Córdobas led them through to the main mortuary room. A technician was waiting beside a trolley that held a covered cadaver.

'This one has proved quite interesting,' Córdobas began. 'The victim of a brutal mugging down near the front in Alameda Park, which is, as you probably know, in a particularly pleasant and wealthy part of town.'

Broderick did know. It was a district of Marbella full of luxury apartment buildings and fine restaurants, which had long been fashionable for both Spaniards and foreign residents.

The inspector nodded to the technician to proceed. Pulling back the green sheet covering the body, he revealed the victim's head and shoulders. The woman's shaven head and badly bruised facial features came as a shock to the detectives.

'Dear God,' Sullivan gasped.

'This is an unusual assault in this part of the Costa,' Córdobas explained. 'Cash and jewellery were taken from the victim, but we traced her identity and address from what was left in the wallet.'

'This took place on the evening following her disappearance from Gibraltar,' Broderick commented. 'She'd embezzled one-and-a-half-million pounds. Can you be sure that this was just a random assault? Could it be linked to something else she might have been involved in?'

'Hard to say. That the mugger, or muggers, left a wallet full of credit cards and stole only cash and jewellery points to a random robbery. Wrong place at the wrong time, that sort of thing.'

'Not quite the dream she'd been hoping for,' Sullivan added.

'It was only by chance that we connected your missing-persons alert to the body,' the inspector continued. 'The name on the victim's credit cards and driving licence was that of Myrie Valeria. The address on the licence was for a luxury leased apartment overlooking the park itself ...'

'She'd changed identity,' Broderick interjected.

'... If we hadn't found another passport in the name of Changtai during our search of the apartment, we might never have made the connection. But that isn't all. There's another anomaly.'

Once more, Córdobas nodded to the technician. The man now pulled the green sheet away to reveal the body in its entirety. Sullivan and Broderick looked on in stunned surprise. Krystle Changtai was not only flat chested, but below her waist she sported a full set of above-average-sized male genitalia.

'A penis?' Sullivan asked incredulously.

Inspector Córdobas nodded.

'Fuck me!' Broderick heard himself exclaim. 'I didn't see that one coming.'

Nobody had.

The drive back to Gibraltar proved a more sombre affair for Sullivan and Broderick than their outward one. Krystle Changtai had conducted both a double and treble existence. Her escape to a luxury life in Marbella had been tragically short lived. Her ability to deceive over such a long time had been extraordinary. Sullivan had quickly concluded that Changtai had been the shaven-headed man seen on the CCTV leaving the apartment building on the night after the embezzlement.

'He must have taken off his dress, shaved his head and then changed into a suit before leaving the building,' she said, piecing it together. 'Changtai as a man being the perfect disguise. Far removed from the long-haired, glamorous woman he presented to the world as Krystle.'

Discovering Changtai's true identity and recovering the embezzled money would now be a joint investigation with the Spanish police.

'We can hand this one over to our fraud boys now,' Broderick told Sullivan, putting his foot down on the accelerator and enjoying the blast of air through the driver's window.

'And Córdobas continues to investigate Changtai's murder?' Sullivan asked.

'That's about the size of it.'

As the two detectives sped back along the toll road towards the Rock looming in the distance, the baking sun reached its midday height. Although it was only noon, both detectives felt as though they had done a full day's work already.

Chapter 14

SULLIVAN HAD PHONED through the developments in Marbella to Calbot half an hour before. Although originally irritated that Broderick had chosen Sullivan instead of him to go on the Costa del Sol expedition, he was now relieved not to have been part of it. He sipped his latte, freshly bought at the station's canteen, and scrolled through his mobile contacts list. *Who'll be the lucky girl tonight?* he wondered.

A moment later the door swung open and Chief Superintendent Massetti strode into the cramped office.

Calbot jumped up. 'Morning, ma'am,' he spluttered.

'Afternoon, Calbot,' Massetti corrected. 'Good to know you're alert and ready for action.'

Calbot looked at the chief super in surprise: Massetti was not wearing her usual uniform, but rather an attractive black dress and high heels – lunch with her accountant and the evening reception at the Governor's Residence did not necessitate formal uniform. It was the first time Calbot had seen his senior officer in civvies, and he was impressed by what he saw. Slender and with something of an Audrey Hepburn look, Massetti, in his opinion, scrubbed up well. The look he gave her did not go unnoticed.

'A busy day on the social front,' Massetti informed the detective constable, a faint blush spreading across her pale cheeks. 'Nice to be out of uniform for once.'

'I bet it is, ma'am.'

'I was passing, so I thought I'd drop in to see CI Broderick. Any idea where he is?'

'He's in Marbella, ma'am.'

'Marbella?'

Calbot thought he'd add a little more information. 'Took Sullivan with him, actually.'

Massetti focused her beady eyes on the young man. 'Please tell me it's on police business, Calbot.'

'Oh, absolutely, ma'am. It seems that the missing Krystle Changtai's turned up dead over the border. Only, when they found her, she wasn't a she, but a *he*.'

Massetti took a moment to take this in. Deciding that it was a conversation she no longer wanted to continue, she turned to go. 'Just tell Broderick I want to see him,' she ordered.

Before Calbot could answer, she had gone. Returning to his latte, Calbot put his feet up on his desk, pressed 'Apps' on his mobile and began his second game of *Angry Birds* that morning.

His concentration was immediately broken by a loud, piercing scream from the corridor outside. Jumping up, Calbot rushed out of the office. At the top of the stairs at the far end of the corridor, he saw Massetti slumped against the wall in agony. Running to her aid, he saw immediately that one of her heels had snapped and the chief super was nursing her ankle, which was clearly causing her a great deal of pain.

'Are you all right?' Calbot asked, ineffectually.

The look on Massetti's face told him all he needed to know,

and the expletive-laden tirade that followed introduced him to one or two swear words he had never encountered before. As a trained first-aider, the detective constable quickly established that Massetti's ankle was sprained and possibly broken. His prognosis was that the chief superintendent's day – with all its glamorous social appointments – was about to end, somewhat prematurely, in hospital.

CHAPTER 15

JOSH CORNWALLIS HAD not returned directly to the Atlantic Marina Plaza. After leaving his message at Sovereign Villa, he had paced the streets for almost two hours, stopping first at the House of Sacarello for some breakfast – an espresso and brandy – and then later at Jury's Cafe on Main Street, for a large piece of chocolate cake. He had even looked in at the Catholic Cathedral of St Mary the Crowned a little further up the street. Wandering around the cool interior, he had found himself lighting a candle and attempting a mumbled prayer. *Strange behaviour for an agnostic*, he had thought, *but any port in a storm ...*

Restless and impatient, he had twice returned to the villa in the hope of finding someone in. After pressing the bell button and banging on the wrought iron gate several times, he finally gave up. Before moving on, though, he knocked on two of the neighbours' doors to enquire about the identity of the villa's occupants. One door remained closed; the other was swiftly slammed in his face. He would have to be patient.

By the time he walked through the door of his apartment back at the marina, it was past midday. He had been religiously checking his mobile for messages. There were two more from Isolde – definitely pissed off by Josh's lack of communication – and none from Julia. No contact from Julia was either very good or very, *very* bad, Josh concluded. Isolde was already back in the production office out at the docks. There was no filming today, or indeed until the weekend – just a reception at the Governor's Residence, which Josh knew he had to attend – but there was still an impossible amount to do to prepare the filming schedules for the weeks to come.

Josh attempted to read the documents he had spread across the apartment's floor one more time, but the words no longer made sense to him. Suddenly overwhelmed with tiredness, he collapsed onto the large sofa and fell into a deep dreamless sleep.

A distant knocking brought Josh back to semi-consciousness. Waking slowly, he was at once aware of the sun's blindingly bright rays hitting his face through the open door of his balcony. Disorientated, and with a throbbing head, he turned towards the source of the knocking. As he walked to the apartment's front door, he attempted to pull himself together. Checking his watch, he was amazed to discover that nearly three-and-a-half hours had passed since his return to the Plaza.

Once again, the person on the other side of the door knocked gently. Josh slipped the lock and swung the door open to reveal his visitor.

CHAPTER 16

BRODERICK AND SULLIVAN pulled into a parking bay at the side of New Mole House, police headquarters. They were just in time to see an ambulance leaving from the front of the building. Sergeant Aldarino stood in front of the main entrance, as if waiting for them.

'Who's in the ice cream van?' Broderick asked.

'Our angry and sadly crippled leader, sir,' Aldarino answered dryly. The look of surprise on his fellow officers' faces prompted him to continue. 'Fell over in her high heels and is now off to A&E with a suspected fractured ankle.'

'Ouch,' responded Broderick.

'I'm afraid that "Ouch" doesn't come close to describing the Chief Super's thoughts on the incident, sir. The air's been blue around here for the last half an hour.'

'Poor Massetti,' said Sullivan.

'Spare a thought for poor Calbot, too. He's had to go along to the hospital with her.'

'Oh dear,' Sullivan said, with somewhat less sincerity.

'Come to think of it, you should spare a thought for yourself,' Aldarino said, turning towards her.

'Why's that?

'If Massetti's incapacitated, you'll be the one going to the governor's reception in her place.' Aldarino smiled knowingly. 'On the arm of Chief Inspector Broderick here.'

Sullivan and Broderick looked at one another.

'Sorry, guv,' said Sullivan, as she entered the building. 'Everything really does happen to you.'

CHAPTER 17

THE LAST HOUR had passed in a frenzy of explanations and questions for Josh. He had methodically taken his inquisitive visitor through each of the documents relating to the Queen of Diamonds. As they sat drinking tea together, it became clear to Josh that he was giving much more than he was receiving. He had even named Don Martínez as his intelligence source. The panic he had felt so acutely earlier in the day was returning. How had none of these revelations come to light before? Could they be fully believed? If true, who was the real Queen of Diamonds and what the hell had happened to her after the war? Why did Don Martínez give him the Sovereign Villa address and what was his visitor's connection to all this?

The only thing Josh knew for certain, as he sat surrounded by documents that could so easily lead to his ruin, was that he was feeling most unwell. He was still tired and had been drinking, but the sudden exhaustion and lightheadedness he was now experiencing was becoming more overpowering by the second. The room began to swim alarmingly around him. He reached out for some support but, finding none, collapsed backwards his legs giving way beneath him. The fall knocked the breath from his lungs, breath he now found increasingly difficult to retrieve.

Josh was suddenly aware of his visitor's face staring down at him. He tried to speak, to ask for help. No words came, only a swift and total darkness. He felt pressure on his face. He could not breathe. The weight bearing down on him increased. He could do nothing to stop it. Darkness and helplessness engulfed Josh Cornwallis, as death slowly and painfully came to claim him.

CHAPTER 18

TWO SOLDIERS FROM the Royal Gibraltar Regiment stood on sentry duty in front of the Governor's Residence at the southern end of Main Street. There would normally be just one stoic, unflinching and immaculately turned-out warrior on duty, but on state occasions or for civilian receptions such as the one taking place this evening, slightly more pomp and ceremony was deemed necessary.

It was now 5.45 pm and the guards were glad of the shade offered by the large, canopied main entrance of the imposing building. Its exterior – predominantly Georgian in style, updated over time with Victorian adornments – hid a building many centuries older. Once a Franciscan convent, the only remaining outward sign of its provenance was the ancient chapel that adjoined the building on its right side. The Convent – as the Residence had long been known – stood opposite the classic pillar-fronted and cannon-adorned Main Guard. Nearby was the equally distinguished building that housed many of the main departments and offices of the Gibraltar government.

As if adding some kind of relief to these centres of political and military power, the north and south sides of the enclave were lined with cafes, shops and, most prominently, the famous Angry Friar public house. For almost half an hour, Lech Jasinski had sat alone at one of the many tables that spilled out from the entrance to the old drinking establishment. Nursing a pint of once-chilled lager that had grown warm and flat in the late afternoon sun, he looked on as police officers closed the streets to traffic, and a large area in front of the Convent was cleared and ringed with metal barriers. This would be where the evening's more famous guests and dignitaries would arrive before being escorted indoors when the formalities commenced.

The reception for the *Queen of Diamonds* was to begin at 6.30, so the first of the guests would arrive soon after 6.00, Jasinski had concluded. The evening event had been so timed to allow Julia Novacs an early departure for Marbella. A stickler for early nights, she needed to be in bed at a reasonable hour. The gruelling shoot of the previous evening and morning had already upset her delicate metabolism. This, Jasinski wasn't to know. He was only too aware, however, that the star would arrive at this spot within the next thirty minutes.

Pulling his red baseball cap firmly down over his face and zipping up the light green jacket he was wearing in spite of the heat, Jasinski focused on the task at hand. Picking up his rucksack as he rose, he moved swiftly from his table at the front of the pub towards the newly cordoned-off area by the main entrance of the Convent. Assessing the best vantage point to see the incoming guests, Jasinski quickly positioned himself as close to the main doors as possible. He was not alone. Out of nowhere, several other people arrived at the same spot from different points around the enclave. Star spotters and autograph hunters who had been playing the same reconnaissance game as Jasinski now jostled for position. But the powerful Pole soon gained the best vantage spot by unceremoniously pushing a middle-aged woman to one side.

'Hey, watch it!' she cried out. 'That's my place.'

One look from Jasinski silenced not only the woman, but any others who might have considered challenging the brutish Pole. Backing away, the group let Jasinski take prime position without another word. Calming himself, Jasinski opened the zip of his rucksack and reached inside. He needed to check he had easy access to what was hidden there. There would be only one opportunity to do what needed to be done and he must not fail. Finally satisfied, he stood at ease and waited.

Not long now, Jasinski thought. *Not long now.*

Chapter 19

A LITTLE EARLIER, in the empty CID office at police headquarters, DC Calbot had sat thinking about the scene he had just witnessed. It was definitely a first, he had absolutely no doubt about that. The fact was that both his immediate superiors, Sullivan and Broderick, had left work early. This was unusual enough, but the fact they had both spent ten minutes prior to that complaining about having nothing to wear for the *Queen of Diamonds* reception was something that Calbot would relish for some time to come. How he wished he had been able to capture their panic for YouTube posterity.

What had made it all the more enjoyable was that Broderick had been worse than his female colleague. With the event coming a week before he had expected, the chief inspector had made several desperate calls in search of his sister. Apparently his only decent suit had a large ketchup stain on its right leg – the result of an exploding cheese burger – and he now had no time to get it to a dry cleaner before his enforced attendance at the early evening reception. He only hoped that Cath could work some magic with a cloth and washing-up liquid. Getting no reply to his calls for help,

Broderick had rushed off to attempt the task himself.

This display of male uselessness had not gone unnoticed by Sullivan.

'Isn't it strange that a man who regularly views bloody corpses with utter dispassion can so easily fall to pieces at the thought of a stray blotch of tomato condiment?'

The observation had been made safe in the knowledge that Broderick had just left the office. Moments later Sullivan herself had rushed off to the shops on a frantic last-minute quest to find 'Something in black. Or perhaps red. Or maybe even blue.'

Calbot had raised his hands in surrender as Sullivan had left him. Advice on ladies' formal wear being beyond his area of expertise, the detective constable concentrated on matters a little more serious – an unfinished cappuccino and a game of *Temple Run*.

CHAPTER 20

AT TWO MINUTES to six, the first guests arrived at the Convent. Not all came by limousine. Some had walked and others were dropped by taxi outside the crowded ring of tourists and celebrity watchers. On the other side of the metal barriers, several police officers were positioned for crowd duty and two of the governor's officials were at the door to greet the guests and guide them into the labyrinth that was the Convent. Added to this were several TV film crews and the ever-hungry paparazzi, eager for footage and images to splash across the night's news bulletins and the next day's papers.

Lech Jasinski had chosen his position well. He was to the right of the main entrance and the closest anyone could get to the arriving guests as they passed just a metre or so away. He could reach out and touch them if he wanted. But alone among the gathered throng, Jasinski found himself with no desire to do so. His aims were different. Most people in the crowd had cameras on standby, while others had pieces of paper ready to thrust into the faces of a passing star or two. The main focus of their attention was undoubtedly Julia Novacs' imminent arrival, but many of the movie's supporting cast were turning up and they were famous

THE POISONED ROCK

enough in their own right to merit a scream and an outstretched hand to shake. Jasinski knew them all. In recent months, he had carefully documented the growing cast of actors after the film had been announced to the press. The Pole even knew the names of many of the technicians working on the other side of the camera. He had made it his personal business to become informed about every aspect of the *Queen of Diamonds* enterprise.

Another limo pulled up and the American actor Ryan Grace emerged. The crowd erupted with applause and shouts of appreciation. The handsome star of the film version of the TV western Rawhide waved languidly to the crowd before reaching into the limousine to offer a hand to the beautiful young Australian actress and model, Estelle McCormack. Stopping briefly to sign autographs and pose for snaps, the couple passed right in front of Jasinski. The Pole let them go without so much as a smile. Grace and McCormack were not who he was waiting for.

Jasinski's glazed expression hid a growing inner discomfort. He was feeling sick to his stomach. It was due to nerves, but also because he had not taken his medication. This discomfort was the price he had to pay to maintain mental clarity. His drugs would subdue and distance him from what was happening. That was unacceptable. It was imperative he remained alert and in the moment.

CHAPTER 21

SULLIVAN AND BRODERICK had agreed to meet outside The Angry Friar at 6.15.

'No need to be too bloody early,' Broderick had insisted.

Not that there had ever been any real chance of that happening. Returning home, Broderick had nearly gone insane searching for his sauce-stained suit. It was nowhere to be found. Cursing the whole business, he had finally cobbled together a jacket and trouser combination that, though far from ideal, would have to suffice. Having ironed himself a shirt and buffed up his shoes, he changed into the mismatched outfit and briefly caught a glimpse of himself in the hallway mirror.

Jesus, I look like the man who got chucked out of the Rotary Club, he thought as he saw his dismal reflection.

Fighting off the desire to pour himself a scotch and run up the white flag, Broderick was distracted by his sister entering via the back door holding aloft his newly dry-cleaned suit.

'I put it in yesterday,' Cath announced. 'I knew you'd forget.'

Grabbing the suit and moving to the stairs, Broderick mumbled some thanks to his sister.

'Now I've got to get ready, too,' Cath called after him. 'Sister Clara's got a tummy bug, so it's just you and me.'

Broderick stopped in his tracks. 'What are you talking about?'

'The governor's reception? The film company is making donations to various charities in Gib, the Foundation among them. Sister Clara and I were supposed to be picking up a rather generous cheque from Julia Novacs. Now it's just me doing it.'

'You didn't say.'

'Yes, I did,' Cath replied firmly, passing him on her way upstairs. 'I mentioned it last at breakfast this morning. I knew you weren't listening. Now get your glad rags on and we'll walk down to the Convent together.'

As usual with matters concerning his sister, Broderick simply decided to obey orders.

Chapter 22

WEARING A NEWLY bought dark blue dress, a rainbow-coloured clutch bag and her Jimmy Choo shoes – an entirely out-of-character Christmas present to herself the previous year – Sullivan arrived outside The Angry Friar right on time. The crowd that stood before the Convent now numbered in the hundreds, and an air of excitement and expectation filled the street as Sullivan looked around for a sign of the absent Broderick. A few moments later, he and Cath strolled around the corner of the Main Guard and made their way over to her. Broderick, Sullivan could not help noticing, looked more uncomfortable than she had ever seen him. At his side, Cath was calm, smiling and very pretty in her simple white summer dress and sandals.

Cath beamed at Sullivan. 'You look perfectly lovely, Tamara.'

'And so do you, Cath. What a nice dress,' Sullivan replied before looking at her boss. 'Nice flute, guv. Not a stain in sight.'

Broderick grunted in reply.

'Time to go in, I think,' Cath continued. 'Don't want to miss anything.'

The three moved towards the opening in the barriers and the

main doors beyond. About to pass through the check point, they were beaten to it by a large limousine. The silver Bentley glided almost silently past them before coming to a gentle halt a few metres from the entrance. Because it was bigger and shinier than the previous cars, the crowd had no doubt who it belonged to and they gave a huge cheer. The police officers at the entrance were now forced to stop the two senior officers from proceeding further.

'Sorry, Chief Inspector,' one of the constables said. 'We've been told to hold at the barrier until this one's cleared.'

Broderick glowered. 'So much for power and influence, eh?'

Meanwhile, the limo's chauffeur had slipped out of the driver's seat and briskly walked around to open one of the car's rear doors. After a pause to achieve maximum dramatic effect, Julia Novacs appeared, rising from the limousine and out into the sunlight as if she were walking on air. The star was dressed in a pink, floor-length, off-the-shoulder creation that clung to her beautiful body like a delicate mist.

Alexander McQueen, Sullivan thought. Or perhaps *Stella McCartney* ...

'Bloody ridiculous' was the phrase on the tip of Broderick's tongue.

It was the diamond necklace that had caught Cath's attention. It had to be worth several hundreds of thousands of pounds. *Enough to run our African hospices for years*, she thought without judgement or anger.

Just yards away, Lech Jasinski was having much darker thoughts. It was immediately clear that Julia was not going to engage on a one-to-one basis with her adoring crowd. No autographs and handshaking for her. Just a regal wave and a flash of the smile that had helped her achieve stardom. Having also emerged from the back of the limo, Gabriel Isolde now stood respectfully to one side of his leading lady. His job was to escort Julia Novacs but in no way suggest that the two might be a couple. A delicate balance between personal space and etiquette had to be observed, and Isolde was a master at accomplishing that. Smiling admiringly at Novacs, he politely gestured towards the main door of the building. Novacs needed no second invitation. With a last wave to the crowd, she moved to the entrance as quickly as she could.

Standing in readiness, the front of his cap pulled down low to disguise his face, Jasinski realised that his chance had finally come. As the star approached him, the Pole reached into his rucksack and pulled out a gun. Novacs was now only about a metre from him, but moving swiftly. With precision honed from his years in military service, Jasinski took aim and squeezed the trigger. The spray of red paint that erupted from the end of the gun hit Jasinski's target with some force, covering Novac's face, hair and most of her upper torso. The movie star's screams were soon lost among the cacophony erupting from the shocked crowd and police.

Dropping the paint-gun onto the ground, Jasinski reached again into his rucksack for some paper flyers, throwing a large number of them into the arena. On each was printed in bold red letters: 'QUEEN OF DIAMONDS – MURDERER.' The effect of these actions temporarily paralysed those around the Pole. Only the police officers beyond the barriers moved swiftly to apprehend the aggressor. Turning quickly, Jasinski looked for his escape route. The terrified crowd now in front of him automatically cleared a passage, thus facilitating his getaway. One or two people tried in vain to stop him, but the huge Pole effortlessly brushed them to one side. Then, as quickly as it had parted, the crowd closed behind him, innocently hampering the attempts of the police to cross the barriers and give chase. Just as he was nearly clear, a man from the crowd leapt at Jasinski, bringing him to the ground in a rugby tackle. In the scuffle that followed, Jasinski's cap and rucksack fell to the ground. Desperate to keep his face covered, the Pole kicked away his assailant and reached for the hat lying on the cobblestones. Rising, he replaced it on his head and escaped north towards Main Street. Running as fast as his legs would carry him, it took several seconds for him to realise that his rucksack had been pulled from him and was his no more.

Having passed the Law Courts on his right, he had to swerve suddenly to avoid running into a mother and child as they left a small gift shop. Jasinski instinctively muttered an apology to the shocked woman and her little boy. Checking over his shoulder to make sure he was not being followed, he once again set off at a run along the busy pedestrianised street. Had he checked more thoroughly, Jasinski might have spotted the fast-approaching young woman who was attempting to catch up with him.

At the first sign of the assault, Broderick had moved forward into the cordon to support his fellow police officers. Sullivan had decided on another approach. Thrusting her clutch bag into Cath's hands, she had skirted around the outside of the crowd just in time to see Jasinski take off down the street. Tearing off her Jimmy Choos and holding one in each hand, she pursued him alone, her colleagues helplessly trapped within the cordon.

The man is fast, Sullivan thought, but she knew she stood a chance of catching him, even running in bare feet.

Continuing along Main Street, passing George's Lane on his right and the C of E cathedral on his left, Jasinski was now beginning to breathe heavily. The spike of adrenalin of a few moments before had dipped and the sheer energy needed to move his considerable bulk at speed was diminishing. Turning his head for a second time, he noticed her, the dark-haired woman running determinedly towards him, gaining by the second. Her speed and the fact that she was holding her shoes like hand-weapons suggested she was not an ordinary member of the public. Plain-clothes police officer? Army? Navy? It did not matter which – he had to outrun her. Even if she was a trained professional, she would not stand a chance against his mastery of the brutal art of combat. For her own sake, he had to shake her off.

Taking a sharp right into Library Street, Jasinski ran uphill. Fifty metres on, he entered the tree-shaded plaza overlooked by the Garrison Library and the old offices of the Gibraltar Chronicle. Turning left, he moved swiftly past the modern frontage of the O'Callaghan Eliott Hotel, with its cafe bar tables full of early evening drinkers, finally coming to a standstill in front of a large building site. It was a dead end. Glancing behind him, he saw his relentless pursuer turn the corner into the plaza and immediately fix him in her sights. Summoning up whatever strength he had left, Jasinski scaled the perimeter fence of the site, falling heavily on the other side. Pulling himself up, he staggered further on into the maze of half-built walls, mechanical diggers and cement mixers. The ground underfoot was uneven and treacherous, but although he slipped several times, he soon found himself on the other side of the fenced site. Climbing onto a large mobile generator, Jasinski scaled the fence and fell to the ground at the entrance to a narrow, dark alleyway. Picking himself up once more, the exhausted Pole moved off into the cooling shadows of the town.

CHAPTER 23

ON THE OTHER side of the building site, Sullivan came to a frustrated halt. With the sound of approaching police sirens in her ears, she was forced to abandon any idea of following the man over the fence. The ground would have cut her feet to shreds, and not for the first time in her life, she cursed designer heels.

Moving to her right and left, Sullivan tried to find a way around the seemingly impenetrable dead end. It was impossible. She would either have to retrace her steps down to Main Street or attempt a circumnavigation of the site by way of Governor's Street in the other direction. Not knowing the direction the man had taken after she had lost sight of him beyond the far fence, Sullivan realised that the chase was over. For her, at least.

Moments later, police motorcycle officers Tarrento and Bartlett pulled up beside her. Quickly showing them the direction in which Jasinski had escaped, Sullivan ordered them to search the streets and passageways beyond.

'He's a big man. Red cap and green jacket.' Sullivan told the officers. 'I'm afraid that, in my present state of dress, I'm of no use to you.'

As the officers sped off, Sullivan looked down at her sore and swollen feet.

No chance of getting my Jimmy Choo's back on this evening, she thought.

Feeling less than glamorous, she turned to retrace her steps back to the Convent. At least she might be of some help there.

CHAPTER 24

SEVERAL HUNDRED METRES beyond the building site, Jasinski was back on Main Street. Turning down a lane, he stuffed his cap and jacket in a nearby refuse bin and continued on past a small cafe and a busy tattoo parlour. The sound of an approaching motorcycle prompted him to quickly enter the parlour to hide. The customers within were all intent on watching the artist at work and took little notice of the large, slightly breathless Pole. A young woman with a pronounced Birmingham accent was chatting inanely as the tattooist's needle etched a likeness of Beyoncé on her shoulder.

Seconds later PC Tarrento and his motorcycle passed the front of the shop at low speed. Glancing into the parlour and seeing nothing untoward, the officer continued on his way. After a few moments, Jasinski stuck his head out into the lane to check that all was clear. Leaving the shop and walking quickly down to the main road, he cautiously turned the corner to find a large red and white Gib bus waiting at a stop immediately in front of him. Slipping through its doors, which swiftly closed behind him, Jasinski paid his fare and took a seat at the back.

Furious at the loss of his rucksack, the Pole consoled himself with the fact he still had his passports – one in his own name and another with a forged identity. He also had his money and cards tucked away in the small travel bag fastened around his waist. As the bus headed north towards the frontier, Jasinski estimated that he would cross the border into Spain in about fifteen minutes. Then he would have to find himself a knife. A hunting knife would be best, but anything with weight and precision sharpness would do. Once he had acquired that, he would make preparations for the second stage of his plan.

CHAPTER 25

FROM THE MOMENT of the Julia Novacs attack, Broderick had found himself at the centre of a maelstrom. His first concern was to get Novacs inside the building and clear of any possible further harm. Although she appeared to be covered in red paint, Broderick had to establish that the substance wasn't of a more sinister nature.

'Get an ambulance here ASAP' was his first order, sharply directed to one of the crowd control officers.

Rushing to Novacs' aid, he and another police officer helped her to her feet. The actress was in great distress, crying and hitting out at those who were attempting to protect her. Gabriel Isolde was the first to get punched in the face for his trouble. Matters were further complicated by the sudden appearance of a rogue paparazzo. The photographer had breached the cordon and was now intent on getting the best shots he could, clicking away just inches from Novacs' face with almost criminal insensitivity. Broderick was having none of this. Reaching across to the photographer with both hands, he lifted him off his feet and threw him to the ground. Before the man could recover, two other police officers grabbed him and pulled him from the scene.

Returning to Novacs, Broderick began questioning her. 'Miss Novacs, the substance you've just been sprayed with – is it causing you any discomfort? A burning sensation perhaps?'

Novacs shook her head.

Broderick continued: 'I realise you're in shock, Miss Novacs, and maybe you're in some pain, but is there anything to suggest that the substance covering you is causing any further harm?'

Once again the actress shook her head.

'Thank you, Miss Novacs.' Broderick turned to the officers at her side. 'Get her inside please. Quick as you like lads.'

As the policemen led her into the Convent, the governor's personal security officer, John Manasco, appeared at the door. Having followed procedure and ensured that the governor and chief minister were secure within the building, he now took control of the developing situation. Although Broderick was the senior officer at the scene, he knew he would have to defer to Manasco while in the governor's domain.

Acknowledging Broderick's presence with a nod, the forty-two-year-old ex-soldier got straight to business: 'What the hell happened?'

'Paint attack from someone in the crowd positioned to the right of the archway,' Broderick informed him. 'One lone perpetrator by the look of things. He escaped towards the centre of town. How are things inside?'

'Governor's secure in the ballroom. So are the rest of the guests. The great and good of Gibraltar. All in there waiting to meet Miss Novacs.'

'I bet they are,' said Broderick.

As Manasco headed inside, a police constable appeared at Broderick's shoulder holding a rucksack.

'Excuse me, sir. The attacker left this behind.'

THE POISONED ROCK

Broderick raised his eyebrows in concern.

'Oh, not to worry, sir. We've checked it for devices,' the constable reassured him. 'Just a load of papers, an old photo and several packets of medication. No name on the packets. There's also a guide book to Gibraltar. It's in Polish.'

'Thank you, constable.' Broderick said, taking the bag. 'Names and addresses of those closest to the incident, please. We'll need statements.'

'Sir.'

Reaching into the rucksack, Broderick took out an old and faded black and white photograph. It showed a couple on a bed. Although asleep, there was little doubt what they had recently been up to. After glancing quickly through the rest of the bag's contents, Broderick moved into the Convent.

Once inside, he saw Novacs sitting in the shaded hallway out of harm's way. One of the governor's people was attempting to wipe the paint from her arms, while Gabriel Isolde stood by her side holding a glass of water. Novacs had calmed down a little, but it was clear the assault had affected her deeply.

Broderick sought out Manasco.

'The minister of justice is locked in the ballroom, too,' Manasco informed the chief inspector. 'Mad as hell not to be out here, but I had to secure the whole room when the alarm went up. No exceptions. You never know what it might be these days.'

Broderick nodded and handed Manasco a leaflet from the rucksack.

'"QUEEN OF DIAMONDS – MURDERER" – looks as though whoever did this has an issue with the subject of the film.'

'Or with the actress playing the starring role,' Manasco replied, heading over to check on Novacs.

Or with the actress? Broderick considered this for a moment and then accepted that an answer to that question would have to wait. For now, a major world celebrity had been assaulted on Gibraltar soil. With the siren of the approaching ambulance ringing in his ears, Broderick realised that the repercussions of the incident could well be huge.

Moving out to the front of the Convent, Broderick scanned the crowd for signs of his sister. Cath was where he had left her, at the entrance to the cordoned-off area. As he strode towards her, the ambulance was waved through the barriers and came to a halt beside the still waiting limousine. Within seconds, the paramedics from St Bernard's Hospital were on their way into the building to check on Julia Novacs.

'How is she?' Cath asked her brother as he reached the barrier.

'In shock, but okay, I think.'

'Poor thing. Why would anyone want to do that?'

'Who knows? Some lunatic. One thing's for sure, though,' Broderick observed. 'There'll be no reception here this evening.'

'Looks as if I'll be off home for an early bath then,' Cath replied. 'I take it you might be working late?'

'Looks likely.'

'Oh, and by the way – could you give this to Tamara, please?'

Cath handed her brother Sullivan's rainbow-hued clutch bag.

'There'll be something to eat in the fridge when you get in. Take care of yourself, Gus.'

With that, Cath headed off, leaving her brother holding Sullivan's bag as if it were a hot potato.

'Suits you, guv,' a voice announced from the crowd.

Looking up, Broderick saw his DS making her way to the barrier entrance.

'Where the hell have you been? Things kick off here and you bugger off.'

Gaining entry to the area, Sullivan quickly removed the clutch bag from her boss's hands.

'I haven't exactly been idle, sir. Got a sighting of the guy and tried to chase him down. Lost him up by the Eliott unfortunately.'

'Bugger.'

'Got a description out though, so hopefully he'll be picked up.'

'Get another one out. There's a strong possibility our man's Polish.'

'Yes, sir. How are things here?'

'Julia Novacs is covered in red paint. The governor, the chief minister and the minister of justice have been locked in the ballroom and are pissed off as hell. And somewhere out there is a lunatic who needs catching. So put your shoes on, will you? You're a police officer, remember?'

Without waiting for a reply, Broderick headed back inside the Convent, leaving Sullivan to experience the agony of pushing her swollen feet back into her Jimmy Choos.

CHAPTER 26

HAVING FOUND THAT no actual physical harm had befallen Ms Novacs and recommending complete rest and a check-up within twenty-four hours, the paramedics left the Convent. An hour had now passed since the attack and the crowd outside the Governor's Residence was showing no signs of diminishing; if anything, it had grown. An increased media presence also guaranteed that the news was going global. The BBC, ITV, Sky and CNN were all running the story in their bulletins, and that was just the tip of the iceberg. Simon Granger, the dapper and highly skilled press officer for the Gibraltar government, was at the centre of the scene, fighting off a mountain of requests for updates.

'It's trending on bloody Twitter now,' he groaned. 'Never get this kind of coverage when you're promoting good news, do you?'

Getting positive spin out of the incident was clearly going to take every bit of his considerable skills.

The dilemma was one that had not escaped Gabriel Isolde's attention. Going into damage limitation mode, the producer had decided that his main energy should be focused on getting his star performer away from the press and safely back to her villa in Marbella. Pleading Novacs' special needs, he had requested and been granted safe passage for the star back to the unit's base at the old Royal Navy Dockyard. Tani Levitt would be standing by in the star's Winnebago to tend to her make-up, and her PA and entourage had been put on standby to assist. Isolde had even demanded that Novacs' helicopter be able to land at the docks to facilitate a quick get-away for the star and himself to the Costa del Sol. John Manasco had been quick to agree to the plan. Broderick was to follow them to the docks to ask the shaken actress a few more brief but necessary questions.

'I'll need to question you as well, sir, I'm afraid,' Broderick had told the producer.

'By all means, Chief Inspector,' Isolde had replied with charming ease. 'Whatever I can do to assist.'

Helping Novacs to her feet, Isolde and Manasco led the star – her ruined dress having been replaced with a dark grey blanket that enveloped her – out of the hallway and along a passageway towards the rear of the building. Stopping along the way to receive heartfelt apologies from the governor and the chief minister – 'A complete and unprecedented outrage, dear lady' – Novacs was swiftly taken to the back door of the Convent. Reunited once more with her limousine and chauffeur, the bedraggled star was whisked away in seconds.

CHAPTER 27

A POLICE SQUAD car had taken Sullivan and Broderick back to HQ, where they transferred to Broderick's Mercedes and drove the short distance to the old Royal Navy Dockyard. The vast area of warehouses, engineering shops and dry docks had been run by commercial companies since the downsizing of British military activity on the Rock a decade earlier. Only a small percentage of the docks was now used in any meaningful way, resulting in a lot of dormant space. Some bright spark in government had seen its potential for the *Queen of Diamonds* unit base for the duration of the filming in Gib, offering both size and security. Gabriel Isolde had jumped at the chance to use it.

Presenting their warrant cards for inspection at the main entrance to the dockyard, Sullivan and Broderick were efficiently waved through by the security guards.

The arrow-shaped direction signs, tied to lamp posts and attached to buildings along the way, soon guided them to a massive hangar close to the harbour's edge. Parking outside, the two detectives were once more asked for identification by the film company's own security guards at the entrance.

'Mr Isolde has asked me to escort you through,' the largest of the guards informed them. 'Follow me, please.'

Entering the cavernous building, both Sullivan and Broderick were stunned by what they found within. A great number of Winnebagos and other trailers, at least one for each of the film's main departments. Make-up, wardrobe, crew and production staff facilities stood alongside dining buses, generators and mobile lavatories. It was a small town engulfed in the shadows of the former engineering hangar.

'Bloody hell,' Broderick said. 'No wonder this filming lark costs an arm and a leg.'

The security guard led the officers to the far end of the building, to the largest Winnebago on the site. This was where Ms Novacs resided while at work.

Broderick stopped for a moment to take it all in. 'You could get half of police HQ in that thing.'

'That would suit me fine,' Sullivan replied.

Outside the main door of the trailer, several staff were standing by to accommodate the star's immediate needs. Two of them were glued to their mobiles, fending off the many enquiries concerning Julia Novacs' health and state of mind. Walking past them, the security guard knocked gently on the door. After a wait of at least a minute, it finally opened and Isolde appeared in a state of some consternation. He ushered Sullivan and Broderick into what was obviously considered a hallowed domain – a luxurious lounge area, replete with reclining chairs, sofas, a bar and a huge television on the far wall. Isolde gestured for the detectives to sit.

'Ms Novacs is not in a good place at the moment,' the producer whispered. 'As I'm sure you can imagine, this has been a traumatic experience for her.'

'Of course,' Sullivan said.

'She's with her PA, Wendall, and make-up designer, Tani,' Isolde continued. 'There was real concern that the red paint used in the attack was oil based, with the horrendous possibility that Ms Novacs would have to have it cut out of her hair. Tani now believes it will wash out and cause no further problems. I don't need to tell you what a relief that has been for everyone concerned.'

'No, you don't,' Broderick replied. 'Will it be possible to see Ms Novacs any time soon?'

'Wendall will let us know as soon as she's ready, Chief Inspector.'

'I see,' Broderick continued. 'So let's start with you, shall we, sir?'

'By all means.' Isolde sat down on the sofa opposite the detectives.

'Can you think of any reason why this assault took place, sir?'

'Nothing specific, I'm afraid,' Isolde answered. 'The world is full of lunatics and stalkers, as I'm sure you're only too aware. As far as I know, there have been no threats made to Ms Novacs prior to the commencement of the shoot.'

'What about threats made about the making of the film?' Broderick continued. 'After all, this may not have been specifically aimed at Ms Novacs. The literature the assailant left behind seems to be about the real so-called "Queen of Diamonds".'

'There have been no threats to myself or my production company, Chief Inspector,' Isolde said. 'As you probably know, the film is a fictionalised account of the Queen of Diamonds war-time spying operations. No one has raised the slightest objection to that, as far as I'm aware.'

'Am I right in saying that the Queen of Diamonds is a fictional character?' Broderick questioned.

'"Mythical" is the description most often used, Chief Inspector. But we believe she very much existed.' Isolde became defensive. 'We have no definitive proof, but our extensive research has led us to believe that the myth of the Queen of Diamonds was based on a real-life operative. No smoke without fire, et cetera. Our film may involve a certain amount of artistic licence, but we think it will prove a fitting tribute to a brave and sadly unsung war heroine.'

'That's as may be, sir, but it seems that someone out there isn't too happy about it. I'd ask you to make a thorough check of both your records and your memory. Even the smallest detail may prove useful. The assailant avoided capture, Mr Isolde, and may even now be planning something more unsettling than a change to the colour of Ms Novacs' hair.'

Before Isolde could respond, Wendall Phillips entered the room. The tall, flamboyant New Yorker presented himself with an air of cultivated self-importance. A one-time model and would-be actor, the forty-two-year-old had been with Novacs for the best part of five years and protected her as though she were his baby sister. Sullivan's first thought was that he bore a striking resemblance to Denzel Washington.

'This is Chief Inspector Broderick and Detective Sergeant Sullivan, Wendall,' Isolde informed him. 'They're here to ask Julia a few gentle questions.'

'She's just taking a shower. You'll have to wait,' Wendall told the detectives, then turned to Isolde. 'Her hair will be fine, Gabriel, but she's exhausted. She just wants to know what the assault was all about.'

'We all do, Mr Phillips,' Sullivan said. 'We won't keep Ms Novacs longer than we have to.'

'She also wants to know where the hell Josh has got to,' Wendall continued, ignoring Sullivan's interjection.

'Me, too,' Isolde replied. 'Me, too.'

Broderick's mobile phone sprang to life, playing its old-fashioned ring tone. The name on the screen was 'Massetti'.

'Excuse me,' he said, taking the call. 'Yes? ... We're waiting to interview Ms Novacs, ma'am ... I see. Where? ... Of course, we're on our way. I thought you were in hospital, ma'am ... I see. Understood.'

The call ended, Broderick stood to go.

'We have to leave, I'm afraid, Mr Isolde. If you could ask Ms Novacs the same questions we put to you, I'd be grateful. Sorry about this, but something's come up.'

'Something that's more important than what's just happened to Julia, Chief Inspector?'

'No, sir, but it may be related. I can't say any more at this stage, I'm afraid.'

Seconds later the detectives were out of the Winnebago and being escorted from the unit base.

'What's going on, guv?' Sullivan whispered to her boss.

'A body's been discovered at one of the Atlantic Marina Plaza apartments. Massetti's having a fit. Even discharged herself from St Bernard's. She wants us on it straight away.'

'I'll get to meet Julia Novacs some other time, I suppose,' Sullivan mused.

'Probably sooner than you think, Sullivan. The body belongs to the film's screenwriter, Josh Cornwallis.'

CHAPTER 28

BY THE TIME Sullivan and Broderick arrived on the tenth floor of the Atlantic Marina Plaza, Josh Cornwallis' apartment was already a full crime scene. Putting on protective gloves and overshoes, both moved through the small hallway and into the large open-plan sitting-room. The first thing to greet their eyes was the young man's body stretched out on the large sofa in the centre of the room. On the small table in front of it was a near-empty wine glass and two tea cups. Next to this, a movie magazine lay open with a half-eaten piece of cake carelessly left on its centre pages. A police photographer was going about his business, recording the scene with the methodical precision of a professional. Nothing visible to the naked eye would be left out of his pictures.

Detective Inspector Ed Mintoff, the first senior officer to arrive, had already interviewed the distraught young maid who had discovered the body during her late afternoon rounds. Massetti had called soon after to tell him that Broderick would be arriving to take over the scene. Already working alongside Mintoff were two crime scene investigators in white overalls, both collecting and logging possible evidence from around the room. Standing at the large dining table on the right side of the room was Police Surgeon Hannah Portillo, the RGP's new forensic medical examiner. Having finished her initial examination of Cornwallis, she had then expressed her concerns about the cause of Cornwallis's death, thus setting in motion the current procedures. She now reconfirmed her worries to Broderick and Sullivan.

'Unusual this one,' the thirty-eight-year-old Gibraltarian doctor informed the duo. 'He appears to have been asphyxiated sometime this afternoon. Within the last four or five hours, I'd say. Looks like whoever did it used the purple cushion that's beside the body. The victim has fibres from it in his mouth. Something's not right, though. No real bruising or signs of struggle. Almost as if he was asleep when it happened. He'd clearly been drinking, and his pupils suggest some chemical intake. I'll know more when the blood tests and tox screen come back.'

'But definitely not suicide, you think?' Broderick asked.

'I'd be most surprised if it was. I think you have a murder on your hands here.'

'Thank you,' Broderick replied, with unusual formal courtesy. 'Settling in okay, I hope?'

Portillo smiled warmly. 'Just fine, thank you, Gus.'

The highly regarded doctor had taken to her new position well. Even Broderick treated her with respect. Sullivan suspected he had a soft spot for her – something she did not feel able to tease him about. Not yet, anyway.

Both Sullivan and Broderick began their own walk-through of the scene, methodically taking notes about the corpse and then working outwards in sections to take in the whole room. From there, they moved further afield, checking the two bedrooms, the kitchen and the main bathroom. At first sight, nothing seemed to be out of place, but Sullivan had a question for the crime scene investigators.

'Have you found a mobile or a laptop of any kind?'

They hadn't.

Moving out onto the balcony, both detectives compared notes.

'No phone and no lap top. Strange that, for a writer whose film has just started production,' Sullivan observed.

'Other than that, nothing stands out as being particularly out of place. In fact, it looks as though the apartment's been cleaned up a bit,' Broderick replied.

Their attention was suddenly drawn to a low-flying helicopter close to the marina and then climbing northwards.

'That'll be Novacs and Isolde, I should imagine,' Broderick said. 'Marbella bound.'

'Shouldn't we notify them about this, guv?' Sullivan asked.

'Apparently not,' Broderick replied. 'Masetti wants this kept under wraps for as long as possible. Give us a chance to find some answers ahead of the press frenzy.'

Mintoff stuck his head out of the balcony door. 'We've got CCTV footage from the cameras in reception and the basement car park, sir. I've just spoken with the daytime receptionist. He says a foreign-sounding gentleman was making enquiries about both Cornwallis and Mr Isolde earlier today.'

'Get a description?' asked Sullivan.

'Big man. Red baseball cap –'

'That's our guy,' Sullivan interrupted.

'Should have him on camera then,' Mintoff continued. 'They're ready to review downstairs. One other thing: the guys found this in the pocket of a jacket hanging by the main door of the apartment.'

Mintoff handed Broderick an envelope addressed to Cornwallis. Inside was a handwritten note instructing the young man to meet someone outside the church of Santa María La Coronada in San Roque at one in the morning.

'The postmark shows that it was sent the day before yesterday in La Línea, but the note's unsigned,' Broderick observed. 'We need to find out who sent this and if they met. In the meantime, Sullivan, you go down and check the tapes. We need an image of our suspect for circulation ASAP. Massetti's got no choice but to go public with this. The man who attacked Novacs is most probably responsible for what's happened up here, too. He could easily strike again and soon.'

CHAPTER 29

TEN MINUTES LATER, Sullivan was in reception, looking at the playback of the security tapes. The daytime receptionist had said that the foreigner had come in after 9.00 in the morning and asked to speak with Mr Cornwallis or Mr Isolde. He had been informed by the receptionist that both gentlemen were out of the building. It took Sullivan just a few minutes to find what she was looking for.

The computer screen showed clearly the very busy reception area, with several PR people preparing for the afternoon launch of the porn channel Blue Job X. At 9.17 on the clock, a tall man wearing a light green zip-up jacket and red baseball cap entered the building and walked directly to the reception desk. Sullivan's heart immediately quickened as she recognised him as the man she had chased from the Convent to the building site a couple of hours before. Zooming in on his face, she took a shot of it with her phone camera. The result wasn't perfect, but at least it was a good enough likeness to email across to police HQ and circulate from there. That done, she began the longer task of checking for the man later in the day. If he had been Josh Cornwallis's murderer, he would have to have returned to the apartment building at some point. Finding him would involve her methodically checking through hours of surveillance footage. It would have been easier to use the facilities at New Mole House, but as time was of the essence, she had no choice but to buckle down to the job on site. A few minutes into the task, she was interrupted by Broderick.

'Leave that for Mintoff,' he ordered. 'We've just got a possible ID of our man on the other side of the border. Someone from the crowd this afternoon has spotted him over in La Línea. We need to get over there right away.'

Minutes later, both officers were back in Broderick's Mercedes and speeding across the airport runway towards the frontier crossing to Spain.

CHAPTER 30

COLIN AND EILEEN Hoare had been waiting nervously in their Renault Clio for the best part of an hour and three quarters. Most of that time had been taken up with Eileen persuading her reluctant husband to go along with her plan. Once agreed, Colin trudged back over the border and reported to the Gibraltar police officers on duty there.

It was now nearly 9.00 in the evening, and the light was fading from the sky. They had parked outside the Kang Fu Chinese restaurant, directly opposite the border crossing from La Línea to Gibraltar. The Spanish town, although much safer than it had once been, was still feared by a certain generation of British ex-pats who remembered the bad old days. The Hoares had lived in Spain for nearly twenty years, and tales of drug wars, muggings and murder were still vivid in their imagination. This meant that the couple, now in their mid-sixties, rarely ventured from their apartment villa complex after dark. The last eight years of their ex-pat lives had seen them enjoying an increasingly insular life in a gated luxury 'urbanisation' twenty minutes up the coast near Duquesa. It was run and mostly occupied by Germans, which, to their great surprise, suited them perfectly: 'The place is so much cleaner than Estepona, where we were before. And the Germans speak such good English.'

As they waited for officers from the Royal Gibraltar Police, the Hoares asked each other if it might have been better to have kept quiet about what they had seen earlier. If only they had not chosen today to visit the Rock, Colin reasoned, they would now be safely back on their patio, sipping the remains of a bottle of Chardonnay and reading the latest Danielle Steel novel or Jeremy Clarkson anthology. If only they hadn't been passing the Convent at the exact moment Julia Novacs had been sprayed from head to toe with paint, they lamented. If only they hadn't found themselves directly in the path of the man who had subjected the star to such an attack.

But they had been.

Only fate, they concluded, could have contrived for Eileen to have recognised the same man an hour later – minus cap and jacket – crossing the dual carriageway on the Spanish side of the border. And Eileen being Eileen, she had felt it her public duty to notify the authorities. If she had not insisted on that, Colin argued, they would most definitely not be waiting nervously in La Línea now. She had embroiled them in a search for a fugitive on the run. The initial excitement had prompted them to action – well, it had prompted Eileen at any rate – and now there was no escaping the situation.

'What in God's name have you done?' Colin asked his wife accusingly.

Help finally arrived for the couple in the shape of Sullivan and Broderick. The detectives had left their car by the airport and crossed the frontier on foot. Within seconds, Sullivan had spotted the Hoares' parked Renault. After approaching the couple and identifying themselves, they took them to a nearby cafe.

'I knew it was him straight away,' Eileen Hoare launched enthusiastically. 'Even without his cap. It was his eyes. A bit mad. Not quite right.'

'And the way he walked. Like he was about to bump into something all the time,' Colin added, not wishing to be left out now that things were becoming exciting. 'Not drunk, you understand. Just a bit off centre.'

Eileen pointed to the grass verge that separated the dual carriage way that ran alongside the border fence. 'Walked right past us over there, he did, out of the blue,' she continued. 'We'd only just got over from Gib ourselves. Bit shocked by all the bother with Julia Novacs, to tell the truth. We were heading for the car and there he was. Walked by and stopped for a bottle of water at that newsagent place just over there.'

'Cool as a cucumber, if you please,' Colin said. 'Next thing I know, Eileen here has got her Samsung phone thingy out and is filming the blighter.'

'"Stop that!" Colin tells me,' Eileen said. '"Don't want him catching on he's being spied on. We've seen what the brute's capable of." But I said, "No, Colin, no! I have to have proof that it's him or nobody will believe me."'

'Quite right,' Sullivan assured her. 'May we see it?'

'Of course you can, my dear.'

Playing the recording back, Sullivan saw for the third time that day the bulky figure of their suspect. Enlarging the image to the maximum, both she and Broderick could see that the man had close-cropped hair and a rugged and bearded but not unhandsome face.

'All a bit exciting for us really,' Eileen said. 'Felt as though I was one of you chaps. Gone all undercover and everything –'

'Well, you've been very helpful,' Sullivan interrupted before her boss could respond to the woman's last comment.

'Nearly three hours ago now, though. God knows where he might have got to,' Eileen said. 'We should have followed him really ...'

'No, we shouldn't!' her husband blurted out in alarm. 'We'd be dead in an alleyway by now if we'd done that.'

'We're glad you didn't pursue him, Mrs Hoare,' Broderick said. 'You've given us valuable information, however. We now know he's in Spain, for one thing. We can focus on that and allocate resources accordingly.'

Eileen Hoare blushed with pleasure at this endorsement of her actions.

'Well, if there's anything else I can do to help you, Chief Inspector ...'

'We'll be sure to let you know,' Sullivan swiftly interjected.

After making sure that Eileen's video recording had been sent successfully to Sullivan's phone, the detectives paid for the coffees and escorted the couple back to their car.

'Thank you, officers!' Eileen called to them through the open car window as her husband drove them away. 'One of the most exciting nights of our lives!'

'I can well believe that,' Broderick observed as the Hoares disappeared from view. '"Gone all undercover", my arse.'

CHAPTER 31

MASSETTI HAD BEEN back at her desk for nearly an hour. With a fractured ankle and enough painkillers inside her to numb an angry rhino, she was desperately trying to co-ordinate the latest developments and placate the press that was hounding the force at the doors of police HQ.

'The Rock's only two kilometres square! How many places are there for a mad Pole to hide, for God's sake?' she had screamed at Aldarino.

Added to this was the inevitable pressure from above, delivered with increasing regularity by phone from the commissioner of police – inconveniently at an international conference in New York – and locally from the minister of justice.

Calbot and Aldarino were doing their best to keep her up to date, but the tide of information had turned into a flood since the discovery of Cornwallis's body on the other side of town.

The news from Broderick, that the suspect was now believed to be in Spain, had come as some relief. At least the manhunt could be called off on the Rock. However, it now meant co-ordinating operations with the Spanish police and that could prove a slow and frustrating exercise.

As soon as they arrived back at New Mole House, he and Sullivan were summoned by Massetti for an update.

'This thing is huge,' Massetti barked the moment they came through her door. 'Even Obama's sent Novacs best wishes for a speedy recovery. The pope will be onto it next.'

'I'm not sure that Ms Novacs is a Catholic,' Sullivan ventured.

'Since when did the Vatican give a shit about that? If it's good PR for Washington, it's good PR for Rome. The only place it's bad PR is here in Gib. Any suggestions?'

'Some observations,' Broderick began cautiously. 'If our man has crossed into Spain, there's a chance he's still after Novacs. We should therefore notify both her and Isolde and make sure the Spanish police offer immediate security backup. They will, of course, also have to be told about Cornwallis.'

'You'd better leave that to me,' Massetti replied, her attention suddenly diverted by a tap on the door. Calbot entered the office.

'Sorry to interrupt, ma'am, but you need to know this ...'

Massetti nodded for him to continue.

'We found a banker's card receipt in a pocket of the man's rucksack. We traced it to a Lech Jasinski, a Polish national living in Luboń, most recently as a patient in its top psychiatric hospital. He's an ex-Polish army special forces operative, retired ten years ago with a severe schizophrenic disorder. Father died a few months back – apparently Jasinski went missing from the hospital not long after.'

'Dear God,' Massetti sighed. 'Well, that's who he is and where he's come from. Now all we have to do is find out where he's gone.'

'We've also had Cornwallis's mobile phone records checked,' said Calbot. 'His last calls were made just after lunch on the afternoon he died. Just checking his messages, by the look of things. However, he sent two texts to Novacs and Isolde from the San Roque area in the small hours of the previous night.'

'Okay. Thank you, Calbot.' The young police officer left the room. Massetti turned to the two detectives. 'Any more thoughts?'

'Obviously we have no jurisdiction over the border,' Sullivan now took over. 'But it doesn't mean we have to wait for the Guardia Civil and Cuerpo to give us the nod, ma'am. What if he isn't after Novacs? What if Jasinski's just biding his time or maybe even on the run for good? An anonymous letter to Cornwallis was found in his apartment. An invitation to meet its author in San Roque that same night. What if the letter was from Jasinski? What if San Roque is where he's been staying and where he's gone now?'

'You think it's worth checking out?'

'Better to be doing something than waiting for a whole lot of nada from the Guardia, ma'am.'

'Okay,' Massetti decided. 'Get photos of both Cornwallis and Jasinski and get across to San Roque and ask questions. Be discreet, though. I didn't order you to do it, understood? You both went on your own accord. If the Spanish police find you, tell them you're on holiday. And I didn't tell you to tell them that either, okay?'

'Yes, ma'am,' Sullivan and Broderick replied in unison as they headed for the door.

Chapter 32

THE OLD MAN poured the fine Rioja into two sparkling glasses, his steady hand and his eye for a generous measure belying his age and frailty. For two days, Don Martínez had played host to his friend from England. His beautiful ancient townhouse in the centre of San Roque was proving an oasis of sanity to the elderly archivist on the first leg of a long overdue touring holiday of Europe. The secret file that Graeme Maugham had delivered to his Spanish friend two days earlier had been so gratefully received that he had known at once that his decision to smuggle it out of the UK had been the right one.

For three hours, Don Martínez had studied the documents before him, reading and rereading entire sections. When he had finally finished, a single tear had fallen down his cheek.

'Thank you, my friend,' he had said to Maugham. 'I promise I will deliver this to where it will do only good. The ghosts of many good men and women will then be able to rest in peace for ever. May God bless you.'

The following night, Don Martínez had slipped out of his home with the file in his hands. An hour later, he returned without it.

Maugham had asked no questions and Don Martínez had given no explanations. To both men's great relief, nothing more was said on the subject.

Now, as they raised their glasses in a toast to absent loved ones, both men felt strangely complete. An aura of tranquillity surrounded them, an atmosphere enhanced by their steady drinking through the late afternoon and evening. As they sat in the flower-bedecked courtyard at the centre of the house and gazed up towards the darkening sky, all seemed well and secure within the thick, cooling walls that protected them. All, no doubt, would have continued in such harmony, both men drinking and musing till the need for sleep moved them to their beds, except for the sharp knocking on the back door.

It came as something of a shock. *It must be Aina*, Martínez thought. His housekeeper had gone home a good hour before, but must have returned to pick up something or attend to a forgotten chore. *Unlike her to forget her keys*, Martínez thought with a little irritation.

Struggling to his feet, the old man shrugged his shoulders at his guest and moved towards the long hallway that would take him to the kitchen and back door of the house. This, in turn, opened onto an ornamental courtyard, off which another door led to a passageway that ran between his and the neighbouring house.

Slipping back the large bolt and opening the door to the passageway, his eyes met something both intriguing and unsettling. A surprise visitor who could not be turned away.

Chapter 33

THE VILLA SANTA Monica lay hidden in the hills above Marbella. Its position, in a small valley protected on three sides by steep inclines and a sheer drop at its front, offered its occupants a sense of isolated safety in an idyll of natural beauty. A full kilometre from the main road, the villa's winding driveway was guarded by two separate security checkpoints, the second of which allowed entry through a two-metre-high perimeter fence. A magnificent example of modernist architecture – glass, water, light and landscape blended together in effortless harmony – the villa offered the finest luxuries that money could buy. Two swimming pools, gardens, tennis courts, a helicopter pad – and a separate six-bedroom annexe for staff and security operatives discreetly and elegantly located alongside the main building. All was unique, beautiful and safe. Julia Novacs had fallen in love with the Villa Santa Monica at first sight. Antonio Banderas had been such a sweetheart to offer it to her for her stay on the Costa.

The helicopter carrying Isolde, the star and her entourage had dropped off its precious cargo just before 8.30 pm and departed towards Málaga. Novacs was swiftly taken to her suite at the far end of the villa, while Isolde prepared to head back to Gibraltar by car, the helicopter being too expensive to justify single passenger occupancy back to the Rock.

Novacs had calmed down a little and Isolde considered his further presence to be pointless. Taking Wendall Phillips to one side, he had told him that there was still a movie to be shot and that the level of his responsibility for it had doubled the moment he had sacked his incompetent line producer the day before. A replacement would be flying out from the UK in two days, but until then, he would have to deal with every aspect of keeping the film on schedule and on budget. With all these things on his mind, Isolde decided to stop off down the coast at La Alcaidesa to check out a beach location that urgently needed to be confirmed by the director and location manager.

As Isolde left the villa, he had became immersed in a heated phone conversation with one of the film's main backers – a locally based Russian steel magnate. On hearing the news of the assault on Novacs, the man had developed the jitters. As Isolde drove away from the Villa Santa Monica, he clicked his mobile onto hands-free mode and desperately tried to pour balm on worried Russian nerves.

CHAPTER 34

IN NOVACS' SUITE, a doctor was waiting to check on her and offer sedatives to help her sleep. Forty minutes after arrival, the star had bathed, meditated and taken her prescribed medication. She now slept fitfully beneath the silk sheets of her enormous bed.

Wendall Phillips closed the door to the suite as softly as he could and moved silently across the small plant-filled atrium into the main body of the villa. There was an urgency in his pace driven by his need to speak to the villa's head of security, Dag Liskard, as quickly as possible. He had spent the last fifteen minutes in a growing spiral of alarm. An alarm he had not allowed the distressed and vulnerable Novacs to detect.

While his employer had been taking her bath, Wendall had noticed that something was different about the suite. Although they had been in residence there for only a week, Wendall knew every detail of the rooms. Novacs' obsession with neatness and order was one that her PA shared in spades. If a book or cushion was so much as a millimetre out of its usual position, both would know at once and set about correcting the aberration. This was why, although everything appeared to be in perfect order, Wendall

Phillips knew that it wasn't. The chair by the French windows was slightly crooked. The remote control for the television was on the wrong shelf and the bottom drawer of the dressing table slightly open. In the dressing room itself, the skirt of one of Novacs' many dresses was caught in the sliding door of the wardrobe. Wendall knew that the housekeeper would never have left the suite in that condition. Someone else had been in there during their absence. Someone had been taking a good look around.

Moving across the villa's huge central living-room, with its automated ceiling retracted and open to the star-filled sky, Wendall felt the warm night air on his face. He would have liked nothing more than to pour himself a night cap from the well-stocked bar at one end of the room and sit and stare at the Milky Way for an hour or two. But that would have to wait for another night.

Making his way down the passage that led to the kitchen at the rear of the villa, Wendall entered the state-of-the-art culinary centre. Sitting at a huge central table, with an array of walkie-talkies and mobiles and a mug of steaming coffee in front of him, was Liskard. The lean, hard-faced Dutchman took one look at Wendall and knew at once all was not well.

'What's up? You look as if you've seen a ghost.'

'I need to check the villa's surveillance tapes for the last forty-eight hours,' Wendall ordered. 'I think we've had a visitor.'

Chapter 35

THREE MINUTES LATER, both men were huddled around the multi-screened monitoring console in the small security room beside the main entrance to the villa. Each screen kept a separate area of the residence and its grounds under surveillance, each one skipping from one location to another at ten-second intervals. When the villa was occupied by Novacs and her people, the screens were monitored by security guards around the clock. When she was not there, a more relaxed regime was put in place. Wendall and Liskard quickly reviewed the facts and possibilities.

The star had left for the night-shoot the previous afternoon at 3 pm. The housekeeper had immediately attended to Novacs' suite after her departure, finishing her work just past 4 pm. In the unlikely event that an intruder had managed to breach the villa's security net and enter the star's rooms, it must have been some time after that.

After twenty minutes forwarding through the CCTV recordings, something caught Liskard's eye. The time on the monitor's digital clock was 20.57 the previous evening. Movement in the foliage within the main garden made both men stare even more intently at the screen. Suddenly, in the top right-hand side of the picture, a figure moved quickly from the bushes and ran towards the far end of the villa. Switching to the internal cameras positioned in that part of the building, they saw a man wearing a baseball cap and carrying a rucksack enter the villa through a window that had been carelessly left open. Once inside, he took his bearings for a moment, before moving down the hallway towards the door to Novacs' suite. Turning once to look directly at the security camera above him, the man opened the door and entered the rooms.

'Jesus Christ!' Liskard exclaimed. 'Who the fuck is that?'

Wendall did not answer. He was already on the phone trying to reach Isolde. Although he had never seen the man on the screen before, he knew it had to be the same person who had assaulted Novacs in Gibraltar just a few hours before. How he had got into the villa the previous day was something to be explained at a later point. All that mattered now was that every effort was made to ensure he didn't get close to Novacs again. Isolde's mobile returned an engaged signal.

Shit, Wendall thought with growing alarm. He would now have no choice but to carry out the agreed protocol. Isolde had made it clear that on no account were the Spanish police to become involved further. Everything had to be kept in-house. The Guardia had doubled their patrol at the main entrance and that is where they would remain. Phillips would now wake the rest of the guards asleep in the annexe. With the active bodyguard protection doubled on-site, he would oversee a full search of the villa and grounds.

At this precise moment, another possibility occurred to him. 'What if the bastard's already here?'

CHAPTER 36

AT JUST AFTER 10.30 pm, Sullivan and Broderick drove across
the border with Spain and took a left along the Avenue Principe
de Austurias. Five minutes later they were on the CA-34 passing
the gigantic CEPSA oil refinery on their left and heading north
towards San Roque. Behind the wheel of his Mercedes, Broderick
broke into fluent Spanish.

'*Muy noble y muy leal ciudad de San Roque, donde reside la de
Gibraltar.*'

Sullivan looked askance at him. 'Well, well. Very impressive.
The San Roque and Gibraltar bit I got. As for the rest ...?'

'It's the town's motto: "Very noble and very loyal city of San
Roque, where Gibraltar lives on",' Broderick explained.

'"Gibraltar lives on"? I don't understand.'

Broderick gave her his patient look. 'San Roque was established
by the former Spanish citizens of Gibraltar, after the majority fled
following the takeover by the Anglo-Dutch in 1704. The Spanish
king Philip V was so chuffed that they had stayed loyal to him that
he established the new town of San Roque in 1706. The town has

retained the motto and some of its people maintain strong feelings about the Rock.'

'Eat your heart out, Simon Schama,' Sullivan teased.

'I like my history, Sullivan. Comes in handy at times.'

'Very impressive, guv. Are we nearly there yet?'

A minute later the Mercedes entered the lower reaches of San Roque. Sullivan noticed that they appeared to be on a small ring road circling the town. Off this road many smaller streets and passages climbed upwards to the centre. Broderick parked the car at the bottom of one of them and both detectives got out.

'What's wrong with driving up there, guv?' Sullivan asked.

'The one-way system here is hell. People drive in there and aren't seen again for weeks. Thought we'd do better wearing out some shoe leather.'

With that, Broderick took off on foot up the narrow street with its many-coloured townhouses rising on both sides of the steep incline. Sullivan followed close behind, wondering how the middle-aged, full-bellied, gym-allergic Broderick could move so quickly when the need demanded.

At the top of the street, they took a left and followed a lane with a less challenging incline. After a few hundred metres they entered a square. Sullivan looked up to see the name Plaza de la Iglesia on the wall of a large white townhouse.

'"Plaza of the English",' she announced. 'So not everyone here dislikes us.'

Ignoring this, Broderick headed towards the Bar El Varel situated to the right of the plaza. Sullivan followed, taking in the impressive sights of the Governor's Palace to her left and the Church of Santa María La Coronada, with its bell tower and high terracotta roof dominating the area before her.

Although it was fast approaching 11 pm, the town was still gently busy as people wandered to and fro between homes, bars and restaurants. A lorry full of empty orange boxes had rattled past Sullivan and Broderick as they had climbed towards the plaza, and the sight of a nun riding an old motorcycle had brought a smile to their faces. Now, as they moved towards the Bar El Varel, a small rental car with two tourists inside entered the plaza. Its presence animated several of the locals sitting outside the bar. Rising from the bright red 'Coca Cola'-emblazoned plastic chairs on which they were seated, they waved their arms and called out for the driver to stop. Despite their furious efforts, the car continued on and up a one-way street in the wrong direction.

One of the locals shrugged his shoulders as the two detectives arrived outside the bar. *'Alemán,'* he muttered, looking in the direction of the rogue car. *'Alemán.'*

Broderick looked at Sullivan. 'Germans,' he said. 'You can spot German tourists by the clothes they wear.'

'What about British tourists?' Sullivan asked.

'You can spot Brits at a hundred metres,' Broderick replied. 'Hear them, too. Go down to the port when the cruise ships are coming into Gib. It can be a terrifying assault on both eye and ear.'

Inside the Bar El Veral, business was good. Most evenings found it packed full of locals. One or two non-Spanish couples sat at tables. *Tourists*, Sullivan deduced. This observation being based entirely on the way the couples were dressed.

Broderick moved directly to the bar and caught the barman's attention. The man smiled broadly and moved swiftly around the bar to shake hands with the chief inspector.

'Señor Gus!' he exclaimed. 'Long time, no?'

'It is,' Broderick replied. 'You look well, Pablo.'

'And happy, my friend, in spite of these difficult times.'

Broderick quickly introduced Sullivan to the well-built, charming Spanish barman. Sullivan shook his hand and then showed him the image of Jasinski on her mobile. 'Have you seen this man recently by any chance?

'Ah, so you two are here only on official business, *sí*?' Pablo asked with a twinkle in his eye.

'*Unofficial* official business, my friend,' Broderick quickly replied.

'Of course,' Pablo replied tapping the side of his nose with his forefinger. '*A buen entendedor, pocas palabras.*'

Sullivan looked to Broderick for translation.

'It's an old Spanish saying. It sort of means he *gets* it.'

'Nod's as good as a wink sort of thing?' Sullivan asked.

'No, that's another saying, but along those lines,' Broderick replied, showing that his patience was being tested.

'I get it!' Pablo interrupted triumphantly. 'Let me see.'

Pablo put on the glasses that hung on a chain around his neck and peered at the image on Sullivan's phone. 'No. Never seen this man,' he announced.

'What about this one?' Broderick asked as he showed him a picture of Josh Cornwallis. The Spaniard inspected it closely.

'No. This man also I have never seen, but let me ask Miguel.'

Before Broderick could stop him, Pablo had taken the phone and thrust it in the face of a large and rather ugly man sitting further along the bar.

'Miguel? You seen this man?'

The Spaniard took a moment to sip his brandy before applying his attention to the image before him. He looked long and hard at it.

'*Sí*, I see him last night. When you throw us out of here. The man was talking with Don Martínez. We ask if Don Martínez is okay. He tell us to go home to our wives and so ... we did.'

Broderick interrupted the man. 'Last night you say?'

'*Sí,*' Miguel replied. 'Late.'

'How late?' Sullivan asked.

'I throw them out at maybe one, one-thirty,' said Pablo.

Broderick shook his friend's hand. 'Thank you, Pablo. Now can you please tell us where Don Martínez lives?'

Chapter 37

THE TWO DETECTIVES heard the first scream as they crossed the Plaza de Armas, just seconds away from the Bar El Varal. It was distant, but unmistakably that of a woman in some distress. That it came from the direction in which Sullivan and Broderick were heading made them increase their pace. As they passed Don Benito's restaurant at the far end of the plaza, a second scream, followed by a high-pitched wail, emanated from the street directly beyond. Exiting the plaza at its southern end, they paused to look along the street that sloped down in front of them. Halfway along the *calle*, a small crowd had gathered outside the open door of a rather grand-looking townhouse. Approaching now at a run, Sullivan and Broderick could see an elderly woman at the centre of the gathering. She was hysterical and in much need of the comfort being offered to her by the neighbours. Three of them broke away and entered the building. Both detectives instinctively followed them into the main hallway. The cause of the woman's distress was soon obvious.

Following those that had gone before them into the darkness of the ancient building, they soon came to the courtyard at its heart.

The horrific scene there was both shocking and all too familiar to Sullivan and Broderick. Two elderly men lay dead at the centre of the courtyard. One sat sprawled across a chair, his head bent back, jaw slack, eyes bloodshot and open wide. The other man lay face down in a pool of blood on the hard stone floor, the back of his head smashed open, his hair covered with blood, bone and brain matter.

On the large rosewood *mesa baja* before them, half-full brandy glasses, coffee cups and slices of *bizcocho* seemed to suggest that an orderly evening had preceded the assaults. It occurred to both detectives that an element of surprise may have been involved.

'Don Martínez. *Santa Madre de Dios!*' one of the neighbours gasped.

'*Ambulancia! Ambulancia!*' Broderick barked as he and Sullivan moved closer to check the bodies.

Taking this as their cue to get out of the house, the neighbours headed back outside leaving the two RGP officers to examine the scene more fully.

'I'd say this one met his end in exactly the same way as Cornwallis,' Broderick observed, nodding towards the dead Spaniard in the chair.

'Unlike his colleague here,' Sullivan replied, kneeling down beside the body on the floor. 'This one's skull's almost completely caved in. Smashed over the head from behind by the looks of it.'

'And not that long ago, I'd say.'

'What do we do?' Sullivan asked.

'Get out as quick as we can. If the Guardia arrive and start asking questions, we'll be here for days.'

'But we can't just leave!' Sullivan protested. 'We're police officers!'

'Police officers who are out of their jurisdiction and for the bloody high jump if the Spanish authorities find out. We live in awkward political times, Sullivan.'

'But ...'

'And don't think Massetti will come to the rescue. She doesn't even know we're here. Remember?'

As Broderick headed for the hallway, Sullivan checked through the pockets of the dead man beside her.

'Did you hear what I said, Sullivan?' Broderick hissed.

'We can't just leave with nothing, guv.'

With skilled ease, Sullivan gently prised a slim wallet from the inside pocket of the man's jacket.

'Jesus Christ, Sullivan!'

Checking its contents, Sullivan found a driving licence. 'His name is Graeme Maugham,' she read. 'UK citizen. Lives in Shrewsbury, apparently.' She swiftly wiped the wallet free of her fingerprints and returned it to the man's pocket. As she did so, the sound of voices and approaching footsteps came from the hallway. A moment later, an elderly man carrying a small doctor's bag entered the courtyard, followed by a horde of emboldened neighbours.

'*Yoy soy medico,*' the man announced. '*Separar, por favor.*'

As the doctor set about checking the two bodies for signs of life, Sullivan and Broderick withdrew into the crowd of onlookers. None of the people newly gathered there spared a glance at them. Taking this chance to escape, both officers quickly made their way to the main door and out onto the street. The sound of a distant police siren greeted them. Without a backward look, they headed quickly down the steep *calle* towards the main road at the bottom. As they stopped for a moment, Broderick glared daggers at his detective sergeant.

'Sorry, guv,' Sullivan responded. 'I had to do *something*.'

'I'm not angry with you, Sullivan.'

'Really?'

'Just pissed off I didn't do it myself.'

'Thank you, sir.'

'Don't thank me, Sullivan. Disobey a direct order again and you'll be on the next plane back to London. Understood?'

Sullivan understood, but knew that on this occasion Broderick didn't really mean it.

'Yes, sir. So what do we do now?'

'We call in and tell Massetti and Calbot about the mess back there,' Broderick replied, taking out his mobile.

'Looks like it has to be Jasinski, guv.'

'It bloody well better be, Sullivan. If it's not, we really are up shit creek without a paddle.'

CHAPTER 38

TEN MINUTES TO the south of San Roque, on the beach to the northeast of La Línea de la Concepción, drug dealers were selling their wares. Business was slow tonight along the promenade and amid the sand dunes covered in marram grass and sand reeds. Two or three backpacking couples had innocently made camp on the beach, unaware of the trade in crack and marijuana going on around them. Most of the beachside properties in this part of town were top-end developments built during the boom years on the Costa del Sol. Some had been bought recently at knock-down prices by foreigners, others belonged to the drug dealers themselves, while still more stood empty and would remain so, slowly rotting in the sun. If you wanted a hit of any kind, this was the neighbourhood you came to at night. The local police kept away from it for the most part, a fact that Lech Jasinski appreciated only too well.

Having ditched his baseball cap and jacket immediately after crossing the border earlier in the evening, he had headed straight to the centre of La Línea. Stopping off in a bar, he had viewed the news bulletins that were covering the attack on the movie star. Although his Spanish was only basic, Jasinski figured out that the description given by the newsreader mentioned just the attacker's nationality, size, beard and colour of jacket. Surprisingly, given how popular Julia Novacs was, there seemed to be no clear pictures of the attack, just a few blurred images. There was also no mention of his protest about the *Queen of Diamonds* film. The report's conclusion was that the attack was the act of a deranged stalker. This was not what Jasinski had intended at all. His message had been ignored.

Finishing his brandy with a furious gulp, Jasinski had left the bar. Finding a large Supermercado, the Pole had bought a razor and shaved off his beard in the gentlemen's toilets. The face that stared back at him from the mirror looked younger but no less haggard. Leaving the shop and moving along the street, he found a large sports and outdoor recreations store open. Ten minutes later he had purchased a new T-shirt, a brown fisherman's waistcoat and a brightly patterned bandana – a look very far from the one in the description that the authorities had given out. He also purchased a new rucksack and a small hunting knife. A new plan was forming in his mind and the knife would be essential to its success.

The loss of the rucksack and its contents was a setback. His identity would now have been traced. The medications discovered in the bag would also have given the police a clear indication of his troubled mental health. He had been rationing his drug intake to make his limited provisions last as long as possible and had already experienced three blackouts of varying lengths. They had left him, as they always did, disorientated and unable to recollect his movements or actions. He knew that, in these time lapses, his behaviour was unpredictable: sometimes he would curl up into a ball and hide; other times, massive and violent mood swings would leave him raging. For now Jasinski felt fine, but that wouldn't last

THE POISONED ROCK

without his medications. This was not what he had planned. There was now less time to achieve his aims. Less time to be in control of his thoughts and actions.

Now, moving between the grassy dunes, Jasinski found a quiet spot to dig in for the night. He would sleep for a few hours, lulled into unconsciousness by the rhythm of the waves rolling onto the shore nearby. He would rise before dawn and once again cross into Gibraltar, this time on his false passport. Something more had to be done. Something dangerous. People would have to be made to listen.

CHAPTER 39

After a day of escalating dramas, Harriet Massetti could hardly believe her ears when Broderick phoned HQ to tell her about the deaths in San Roque. Apart from her continued relief that the murderer was off her patch and no doubt holed up on the other side of the border, a different can of worms had now been opened.

It probably would not take the Guardia long to discover that two RGP officers had been making enquiries in the town and had also turned up at the crime scene. Broderick had suggested she send details of the Cornwallis murder and all information pertaining to Jasinski across to the Spanish police. It might help to defuse any complaints from that quarter. It was also imperative that the Spanish police begin a full-scale manhunt for the Pole.

Broderick had just reported all this to his superior when his mobile lost signal. Or, as Massetti saw it, the chief inspector had pulled off a very convenient ploy to stop her bawling him out there and then. That pleasure would have to wait until he and Sullivan got back. Meanwhile, she would grudgingly set about doing all the things CI Broderick had suggested. *His methods might be a pain in the arse,* she thought, *but he's rarely wrong about what needs to be done.*

CHAPTER 40

A few minutes after midnight, Sullivan and Broderick arrived back at New Mole House. Calbot met them at the gate.

'Massetti calmed down yet?' Broderick asked as they moved across the central quad.

'She's just left,' Calbot informed them. 'Her husband's away, so her son picked her up. Aldarino and I had to carry her out to the car. Her ankle's the size of a pumpkin.'

'She needs rest,' Sullivan responded sympathetically.

'We should be so lucky,' Broderick observed. 'With the amount of shit that's hit the fan today, she'll be back in tomorrow ready to take us apart.'

'She's on enough painkillers to paralyse a bull on heat,' Calbot continued. 'Still capable of inflicting damage, though. Aldarino persuaded her go home, but she wasn't happy.'

'I imagine she was looking forward to seeing us,' Broderick said with a raised eyebrow.

'She was looking forward to expressing her thoughts on your Spanish excursion, guv,' Calbot replied with a smirk. 'But there's someone else here who needs to see you.'

'Oh, yes?'

'Isolde turned up half an hour ago in a hell of a state. He got back to the Atlantic Marina Plaza this evening and went looking for Cornwallis at his apartment. Found our boys there instead. He's furious that he wasn't informed earlier. We put him in one of the interview rooms to cool down.'

'While you got Massetti out of the building,' Broderick observed.

'If you like, guv. You want to see him?'

'I'll do it, sir,' Sullivan interjected. 'Give you and Calbot a chance to catch up.'

Broderick nodded his head wearily as all three entered the building. A long day was turning into a long night.

CHAPTER 41

ISOLDE WAS PACING up and down when Sullivan entered the interview room, in one of several refurbished additions to the police HQ, on the ground floor of the northern side of the quad. Not that the refurb had made it anything more than just a plain room with a table and four chairs at its centre.

'At last!' Isolde exclaimed on seeing Sullivan. 'I was thinking that you'd be locking me up next.'

'Sorry to keep you, Mr Isolde,' Sullivan replied calmly, gesturing towards the chairs. 'Please take a seat.'

Isolde hesitated for a moment and then moved to the table and sat on the far side of it. Sullivan took her place opposite him.

'I understand you must be upset, Mr Isolde ...'

'Upset? Upset!' Isolde replied with mounting anger. '"Upset" doesn't come close to describing what I'm feeling right now. Josh and I were close. He was like a brother to me, you understand? I should have been told immediately about his death. Instead I turn up at his apartment and your people tell me to come over here. Jesus Christ, do you have any idea how that feels?'

'Mr Isolde, I understand your distress.'

'Apart from my feelings, have you any understanding of the possible repercussions of all this?'

'We do, Mr Isolde, and you would have been one of the first to have been informed once it was wise to do so.'

'"Wise"? Are you insane? There's obviously a killer out there and it doesn't take an Einstein to figure out who it might be. Miss Novacs was assaulted by a man this evening and now I'm told Josh has died in mysterious circumstances ...'

'Who told you that, sir?'

'Your colleague, Calbot, told me when I arrived here. Don't you people talk to each other, for God's sake?'

'We do, sir, and again, I'm sorry. Things have been developing at a rapid pace, but I'm sure that from now on you'll be informed in an appropriate manner.'

Isolde fixed his eyes on Sullivan's. 'Catch the bastard. No fucking about, okay?'

'If it's the same man who assaulted Ms Novacs, we'll get him, sir.' Sullivan stood to signal the end of the conversation.

'He's planned it all, you know. He was even at her villa yesterday. Thank God, Julia was here on the Rock doing the night-shoot.'

Sullivan stared at the producer, who had remained seated. 'I beg your pardon?'

Isolde looked up at her. He had not planned on saying quite so much. 'My phone ran out of juice on the way back from Marbella. I was out of contact till I arrived back at my apartment. I've only just found out from my head of security at Ms Novacs' villa that a surveillance recording of a man fitting the description of her assailant has been discovered. It shows him inside the villa yesterday evening. He somehow breached our security systems.'

Sullivan could hardly believe her ears. 'When were you informed of this, Mr Isolde?'

Isolde shifted in his chair uncomfortably. 'About ... about an hour ago. When I got back and charged my mobile. It was the first message up.'

'And it's taken you this long to tell us?' Sullivan demanded, unable to keep the fury out of her voice.

'I'm sorry.' Isolde squirmed. 'You'll understand that it's imperative not to alarm Ms Novacs further. The future of the film depends on it. My security team have procedures they must adhere to and ...'

'So perhaps you weren't going to tell us at all?'

'Of course I was. I don't know why I didn't earlier. I've just been too upset to think straight ...'

Before he could finish, Sullivan strode to the door and left the room. Isolde sat alone staring after her. Suddenly the dam holding back his emotions burst and a series of deep, heaving sobs erupted into the silent room.

CHAPTER 42

AS A SQUAD car left New Mole House to drive Isolde back to his apartment across town, a light burned brightly in the ground-floor incident room occupied by the Royal Gibraltar Police CID. Inside, several officers were hard at work. Broderick sat in his section, phone in hand.

'*Sí*, Inspector Benitas. If there's anything else we can do, please let us know right away. Buenos noches.'

Broderick put the phone down and turned to his colleagues. 'Well, that went down like a cup of cold sick. However, the Guardia will be circulating the Jasinski photograph and they've also sent more officers to Novacs' villa at Marbella.'

'So it's a joint operation, guv?' Calbot asked.

'Of course.'

'Shouldn't you have fessed up to our being in San Roque tonight?' Sullivan asked, her eyes trained on her computer screen.

'No need to upset them about that,' Broderick said. 'If the Guardia find out about it, Massetti can spin a story as and when. The important thing is that our Spanish compadres are hunting for Jasinski. Where are we on the rest, Calbot?'

'Forensics are going to be working through the night, guv. The chief minister put in a word, apparently. Hopefully they'll have something for us in the morning. Same with pathology. Portillo says she'll get us what she can as soon as possible.'

'What about the dead men in San Roque?' Broderick asked.

'Only been able to do basic checks so far,' Sullivan said. 'Don Martínez seems to have been a respected businessman. Property mostly, widowed, ex-mayor, et cetera. The Englishman is more interesting. Graeme Maugham MBE. Retired civil servant. An archivist specialising in the history of the British Secret Intelligence Service and, in particular, its activities during World War II. Spent the last decade as part of a team set up to declassify British Cabinet secrets. Possible link between that and Cornwallis and his film. Source of sensitive information, perhaps?'

'More than a "perhaps", I think,' said Broderick. 'We know Jasinski's view of the person known as the Queen of Diamonds, even if we don't understand his reasons. If he was willing to murder Cornwallis, it would make sense that he might have been prepared to punish those associated with him in a similar manner.'

'But why not do the same to Novacs?' Sullivan ventured. 'He had the opportunity.'

'Maybe he would have done if he'd found her at the villa the other afternoon. And maybe that's where he's heading tonight. Let's hope the Guardia have that possibility covered.'

'Massetti has just texted,' Sullivan interrupted. 'She's going to brief the press on Cornwallis first thing tomorrow. She'd appreciate your presence at the conference, sir.'

'I bet she would,' Broderick sighed and stood up to stretch his back. The office clock read 1.20 am. 'I suggest we call it a night. What with Changtai this morning and three more bodies tonight, I think we need a little rest from the carnage.'

CHAPTER 43

TEN MINUTES LATER Sullivan was surprised to find herself alone with Calbot on the steps of her apartment block. The young officer lived in the opposite direction, but seemingly determined to engage her in conversation about the day's events, he had insisted on walking her home.

There was little doubt that they had plenty to talk about, but she sensed an all-too-obvious ulterior motive for the late-night perambulation. His attraction to her had been apparent from their first meeting, but his attempts to communicate it had either been awkward or dressed up in the cocky banter of the workplace. He was not unpleasant on the eye – *Far from it*, Sullivan thought – it was just his infuriating over-confidence and lack of grace that drove her crazy. Besides which, a workplace relationship was not something she was prepared to countenance. She had been badly burned the last time it had occurred, and she was not going to lay herself open to it again. Or at least, she hoped not.

'I don't suppose I can tempt you to a little late-night tipple?' Calbot eventually got around to asking. 'Jimmy's Bar is open till two.'

'You must be kidding,' Sullivan said. 'We're only going to get three hours' sleep as it is.'

'All the more reason to keep going, I say.'

'No thanks. I'm done for,' she replied, reaching into her pocket for her key.

'And so to bed?' Calbot asked.

'Is that a leading question, Detective Constable?' Sullivan smiled back, amused by Calbot's unsubtle flirtation.

'It's a question, certainly.'

'And here's an answer: bugger off, get some kip and stop being a naughty boy.'

Calbot raised his hands in the air. 'I'm going quietly, Sarge. I know when I'm not appreciated.'

'Oh, you're appreciated, Calbot,' Sullivan said as she opened the communal door to the entrance lobby. 'Just not particularly wanted.'

'Well, that's charming.'

Sullivan entered the building and the door closed in her colleague's face.

'But I'm made of sterner stuff!' Calbot called through the glass at her in mock outrage.

Stepping back onto the pavement, he smiled to himself and headed south along Rosia Road, towards his lodgings near the old barracks.

'Never give up, never give up, never give up,' he muttered under his breath.

CHAPTER 44

FOR A MOMENT, Jasinski had imagined he was back in the desert, an illusion heightened by the gritty feeling of sand in his mouth and the slight chill of a pre-dawn morning. Even before opening his eyes, he could feel his adrenalin levels rising dramatically – a response to potential danger. A soldier's instinctive readiness for fight or flight. Twelve years earlier, it would have been real. Guarding oil platforms in Iraq or carrying out special seek-and-destroy missions. Jasinski had seen things in Iraq that he had never witnessed during his time as a Polish soldier. Working in the Middle East as a 'contractor' for a security firm, he had seen things that would never leave him. Living nightmares that played out in his mind on a constant loop. Hell on earth.

It was the sound of the sea that brought him safely into the present. Opening his eyes, he took in his surroundings: the dunes, the sand, the ambient light of the street lights fifty metres behind him. He had slept deeply and dreamed little, but that would change if he went another day without his medication. The madness had already begun and it would soon spiral out of control, with him a hostage to paranoia and hallucinations so real he could almost touch and taste them. He would lose control and all his efforts during the last few days would be in vain. His mission would be aborted due to the lack of mental capacity to achieve them. That could not happen. He had sworn to his dying father that he would take revenge on those who had harmed their family, be they living or dead. He would not fail him now.

Stretching his long muscular arms, Jasinski stood and checked his watch: 0500 hours. Sunrise was still hours away, but he would now move to the border and cross into Gib with the first Spanish workers soon after 0600. Confident in his new disguise and with his false UK passport in hand, he would head back to finish what he had begun the previous day.

Along the shoreline to the south, the huge presence of the Rock loomed out of the dark. Checking his bandana and adjusting his hip belt, Jasinski took a deep breath of the ozone-sweet Mediterranean air. Turning towards the lights of La Línea, he began to jog purposefully across the sands.

CHAPTER 45

THE ELECTRONIC THROB of Sullivan's alarm awoke her at 5.45 am precisely. Uncharacteristically, she dallied for a few moments beneath the comforting sheet that covered her. She had drifted off to sleep three hours earlier with thoughts of Calbot. At the time, the notion had been pleasurable, but now the lack of another physical presence in her bed flooded her with relief. She knew that a relationship with a junior officer would be misguided and such a thing would undoubtedly diminish her career prospects even further. The advice given by a female colleague in the Met many years before came back to her: *Never fuck below your rank, sweetheart. Always ends in tears.* Harsh words, but bitter experience had taught her that a relationship with any rank ended with much the same result.

This morning she felt tired, a deep exhaustion brought about by the frenetic developments of the last two days. Lack of sleep and the effects of adrenalin crash were taking their toll. The images of the dead she had seen the day before had also played vividly upon her mind. Grotesque, distorted faces and crushed skulls. Sullivan shuddered and rose from her bed to escape the ghosts.

THE POISONED ROCK

The desire to forego her morning run was strong but one she would override. Her one concession would be to give the more arduous route out to Europa Point a miss and instead take the shorter town circuit. Within minutes of rising, she was dressed and on her way. Across the road in the dry docks, lights were still blazing as work continued around the clock on a container ship in for repairs. Across the bay, a giant cruise liner was on its way out to the Strait, bound for its next port of call in the Balearic Islands. *Life goes steadily on*, Sullivan thought. Setting herself a fast pace, she headed north along Rosia Road, hoping the day ahead would bring better results and no deaths.

Minutes later, she passed the HM Naval Base and Dockyards, and reached the tiny Trafalgar Cemetery beside the Referendum Gates that led onto Main Street and the town proper. On recent runs, she had turned left at this point onto Line Wall Road and run along the old Bastion fortifications, but not today. Something had caught her attention fifty metres ahead on Main Street, usually quiet at this hour.

Sullivan could see a small group of people removing large sacks from a shop in the parade opposite John Mackintosh Hall. From her position, it looked as if they were looting the place. Closing the distance between them in seconds, she realised that the group contained some familiar faces. At the centre of the operation at the front of the Rock of Ages charity shop stood Cath and Daisy Broderick and Sister Clara, all heaving sacks into Gus Broderick's old Mercedes.

'The question is, should I be arresting you or helping you?' Sullivan said, catching the group by surprise.

'Good morning to you, my dear,' Sister Clara replied with a smile. 'I'm afraid it's all hands to the pump this morning.'

'More like all hands to *stop* the pump,' Cath continued. 'Bit of a panic. Burst pipe in the apartment above the shop. Water's pouring into our storeroom at the back. Our dear landlord's upstairs trying to stem the flow, but he's not having much success.'

Sister Clara nodded. 'So here we all are trying to save as much as we can,' she said, placing a bag into the back of the car.

'Not that you should be here,' Cath admonished her elderly friend. 'You should be home in your sick bed. You're still not a hundred per cent.'

'Thanks for your concern, but I'm feeling quite well enough for this. Rather exciting really.'

'Yes, exciting!' Daisy confirmed triumphantly and marched back into the shop for more bags.

'Well, that's stopped it for now.'

All heads turned to see a sprightly and trim-looking octogenarian emerging from the front door of the building. He carried a bag of tools in one hand and a large bunch of keys in the other.

'My maintenance guys are on their way to fix things properly,' the old man continued. 'I can only apologise. The apartment has been empty for over a month and it obviously needs some care and attention.'

'Thank you, Oskar,' said Cath. 'So sorry to have got you out of bed. I didn't know who else to call.'

'I'm glad you did. It's always a pleasure to see you, my dear.' His eyes twinkled flirtatiously. 'And after all, it *is* my responsibility.'

Putting his tool bag down on the pavement, he turned and noticed Sullivan for the first time. 'And who is this new addition to the tribe?' he asked.

'This is Tamara Sullivan,' Cath answered. 'A friend. She was just passing. Tamara, this is Oskar Izzo.'

Izzo reached over and, with practised ease, took Sullivan's hand. 'It is a pleasure to meet you, my dear.' The old man smiled, raising her hand to his lips and kissing it. Taken off guard, Sullivan could only smile back weakly.

'Now, let me assist with this temporary evacuation,' Izzo said. 'Daisy, will you help me?'

'Yes! I'm the best at helping!' Daisy replied, jumping with excitement.

'Then let's get to it.'

Daisy and Oskar Izzo moved swiftly back into the building. A bewildered Sullivan turned to the others. 'Your landlord, I presume?'

'Indeed,' Sister Clara replied. 'Although he is much more than that. Oskar owns quite a bit of property here on the Rock. And much, much more across the border. He's a very wealthy man. As he often says about himself, "Not bad for the son of a crooked bar owner from Malta." He's also a very generous man. Apart from giving us our premises rent free, he is a major contributor to the charity.'

'He's also a terrible flirt,' Cath added, 'and always has been.' The older women laughed.

'Well, looks as if you've still got a bit to do,' Sullivan observed. 'I can spare twenty minutes or so before heading into work, if that's any help.'

'Certainly more help than my brother,' Cath replied. 'Didn't even make it to bed last night. Fast asleep in an armchair as I left the house. A plate of cheese and biscuits on his lap.'

'We had a busy time of it yesterday,' Sullivan informed her, grabbing a box from the ground and squeezing it into the back of the car. 'And I've got a feeling today's going to prove even more challenging.'

Chapter 46

FROM HIS POSITION on a park bench eighty metres from the border, Jasinski waited for the number of people crossing over to the Rock to increase. Soon after 6 am, the Pole felt safe enough to join the migration and become just another anonymous face in the flow of workers and visitors moving towards and through the custom gates. Minutes later, he was in Gibraltar once more, passing the old airport terminal on his left and heading onwards across the runway to the town. As hoped, his passage had gone unchallenged by the border guards, who gave only a cursory glance at his passport.

Thoughts of his father filled his mind once more. *How proud he'd be of me now*, Jasinski told himself. *After all the years of pain, frustration and impotence he went through, something is being done.*

Buoyed up by these thoughts, he quickened his pace, a sense of clarity and purpose moving him forward. He would at least have the element of surprise on his side. As an ex-soldier, he appreciated the huge advantage that gave him. In fifteen minutes, he would be in position and then it would be a waiting game. Once more he checked off his list of actions. Once again he glanced over his shoulder to make sure that he was not being followed. Not that he would be able to tell if he was. There were too many people travelling on foot both behind and ahead of him. None of them stood out as suspicious or in any way interested in him. Why, then, did he feel as though he was being watched?

Pulling his new rucksack tighter to him, Jasinski passed the Victoria Stadium on his right and glanced fleetingly at the 'Cross of Sacrifice' war memorial on the opposite side of the road. A sharp jab of pain crossed his forehead. The headaches would soon begin. He prayed that time would be on his side.

CHAPTER 47

SEVERAL LINES OF coke had fuelled Gabriel Isolde's attempts to remain conscious through the night. Events had moved so swiftly over the past twenty-four hours, he felt helpless in the face of them. Julia Novacs had been assaulted by a madman, her Marbella villa trespassed, and the *Queen of Diamond's* backers were now terrified that the star would walk out on the movie. In the morning, the cast, crew and production team, numbering nearly two hundred, would demand answers to questions that Isolde could barely comprehend, let alone respond to. The media attention, already at a frenzy, would no doubt reach new levels of intrusive hell. Above all else was the still unimaginable truth that Josh was dead. Josh, who Isolde had loved and adored. Josh, to whom he had so often been cruel. Josh, his handsome, talented friend, was gone for ever. Murdered most horribly, just a few hundred metres from where Isolde now sat with his head in his hands and tears still falling down his cheeks.

A moment later, Isolde forced himself to take several deep breaths.

Feeling a little calmer, he checked his watch. To his horror, the time on the dial read 6 am. In half an hour, he would have to be in the production offices out at the docks. His mobile was full to bursting with messages from the hundred and one people demanding to know what was going on. With shooting scheduled to recommence in just over twenty-four hours, and news of Josh's death yet to be announced, the best he could hope for was a delay. His main challenge was to keep Novacs on board. That she and Josh had recently become lovers was not going to make things any easier. Julia would also have to be told that security at the villa had been breached in her absence. It would not take her long to figure out what might have occurred had she been at home the previous evening. Given her volatile nature and obsession with personal safety, Isolde realised that calming her down was going to take every ounce of his considerable negotiation skills.

Deciding to take one step at a time, he put in a call to his production co-ordinator, Tracy Gavin. Having sacked his line producer, Isolde had had to place more responsibility on her shoulders. Instructing her to have the director and department heads ready for a briefing, he then requested a helicopter to be on standby to fly him up to Marbella to meet Julia Novacs for breakfast. Knowing the seriousness of the situation, Tracy took her instructions without question. Relieved that he had made a start, Isolde showered and dressed, grabbed his car keys and headed for the door. Minutes later, a lift had taken him to the basement. Exiting, he moved across the small lobby and pressed the green release button to unlock the door to the car park. Feeling the chill of the early morning air, sea fresh and awaiting the warmth of first sun, Isolde moved to his car parked close to the exit ramp. Slowly, very slowly, his head was clearing.

There must be a way through this shit, he thought. *There has to be.*

Caught up in his fevered thoughts, the producer failed to notice the fast-approaching figure following him to the parked BMW.

Reaching for the car door handle, Isolde was violently pulled backwards as a hand covered his mouth and a fist smashed a mighty blow to his kidneys, sending a searing pain racing through his upper body. As his knees gave way, he felt the razor sharp blade of a knife pressed close against his throat.

'Do not fight me,' a voice hissed fiercely in Isolde's right ear. 'If you fight me, you will die.'

Chapter 48

THE ROPE BINDING Isolde's wrists together was tight, but not to the point of cutting into his skin. The tape that covered his mouth had been bound twice around his head, making breathing – solely through his cocaine-infused sinuses – very uncomfortable. Bound and gagged, the producer had been placed on a chair in the middle of his own sitting-room. Isolde calculated that it had been an hour since his assailant had forced him at knife point up the emergency stairs of the apartment building to the penthouse overlooking the marina below. Through the balcony window, he could see morning light break across the bay beyond. That meant it was least 7 am.

His mobile phone had buzzed several times before the man sitting silently before him had removed it from Isolde's pocket and turned it off. For much of the time before that, his assailant had methodically searched the apartment. It had produced nothing of interest and so the man now sat unmoving, staring at his hostage, the stillness of his features disturbed only by his eyes blinking and the short, tense rhythm of his breathing. Isolde was in no doubt as to the identity of his captor. Although now clean shaven and in a different set of clothes from those in the police photograph, his build was unmistakable and his accent Polish. Isolde's heart raced as he sat looking into the face of Josh's murderer.

Jasinski's thoughts, however, were not of murder. He had other things to achieve. So far, all had gone better than expected. On approaching the front of the Atlantic Marina Plaza, he had been surprised to see the two uniformed police officers standing in the reception area. He was equally surprised, on moving to the back of the building, to find no police presence at the entrance to the basement car park. During his brief visit the previous day, he had noted the CCTV monitors in the room behind the reception desk. Now, walking down to the parking level, he took great care to identify the camera positions and avoid their field of vision. Moving stealthily between the parking bays and hiding behind the concrete pillars that lined the car park lanes, he gained a position that allowed him a clear view of all persons leaving or entering the building.

His plan was simple. Most of the main people involved in *Queen of Diamonds* were staying in rented apartments within the building. All Jasinski needed was to get his hands on one of them, and the next stage of his plan could commence. What he had not expected, or dared hope for, was that the first person through the doors would be the film's producer. With Isolde, he had struck gold on his first try.

Rising from his chair, Jasinski found a sheet of clean paper on Isolde's desk and quickly wrote a message on it. Picking up Isolde's mobile from the coffee table, he now moved back to the Gibraltarian and removed the tape covering his mouth.

'Do not say a word until I tell you,' he threatened.

Isolde nodded and tried with difficulty to swallow. His mouth and throat felt as dry as sandpaper.

Jasinski pressed the mobile's camera symbol and pointed the phone directly at his captive's face. Holding up the paper and its message for Isolde to see, the Pole fixed him with a cold and terrifying stare.

'Read this out loud,' he ordered. 'Now.'

CHAPTER 49

THE NUMBER OF reporters and cameramen waiting to enter the newly scheduled 8 am press briefing at New Mole House police headquarters was on a scale usually associated with royal visits. For the last hour, Chief Superintendent Harriet Massetti had been barking orders to all and sundry. Moving from room to room on crutches and still in some considerable pain from her ankle, the diminutive police officer was firing on all cylinders. The decision to bring the media briefing forward by an hour had been made minutes after she had arrived at HQ. The murder of Josh Cornwallis had to be announced, plus the subsequent deaths of Martínez and Maugham on the previous evening. Spanish police officers would soon be in Gibraltar and all details regarding the Gibraltar cases handed to them in the spirit of joint investigation. The prime suspect was Lech Jasinski, and the manhunt for him – already begun – needed maximum publicity.

Chief Inspector Broderick and his team had already established an incident room on the ground floor, and the whole HQ was alive with adrenalin and anticipation. None felt it more keenly than Sullivan and Calbot. Having helped out at the flooded charity shop for nearly half an hour, Sullivan had rushed home to shower, dress and get into work on time. Both she and an unusually sheepish Calbot had subsequently been working flat out to set up the incident room. They had also been pushing both Forensics and Pathology for any results from the Cornwallis murder scene. So far Forensics had drawn a blank, but Portillo had come through with initial findings from the path. lab. Armed with these, both officers approached Broderick and Massetti.

'Initial pathology has just come through from Portillo,' Calbot announced, placing several pages of printed material before his commanding officers.

'High levels of Rohypnol in Cornwallis's blood,' Sullivan confirmed.

'Rohypnol?' Massetti asked incredulously.

'Enough to pretty much wipe him out, ma'am,' Calbot said. 'Cornwallis would have been completely helpless.'

'But that may not have been the cause of death,' Sullivan continued. 'The purple and red spots that we saw on his face are petechiae. They're also present in his eyes and lungs. All typical of death by asphyxiation.'

'Suffocation?' Broderick queried.

'Yes, sir.'

'Sounds like someone was pretty determined to kill the poor fellow,' Massetti observed.

'Or intent on rendering him helpless enough so he wouldn't put up a fight when they smothered him, ma'am.'

'Anything from our Spanish colleagues?' Broderick asked, taking a sip from a cold cup of coffee.

'Afraid not, sir.'

'Although from what I saw of Martínez and Maugham, I'd say there's little doubt that the Spaniard was asphyxiated in the same way as Cornwallis,' Sullivan ventured, looking to Broderick for confirmation. The chief inspector nodded in support.

'But as that's not confirmed, we'll side-step questions on it for now,' Massetti said as she rose and, leaning on her crutches, moved with great effort towards the door. 'Apparently we're having to set up shop for the press briefing outside in the quad. Nowhere else is big enough.'

'You going to do this on your own, ma'am?' Broderick asked.

'I'll do the talking, but I want you and Sullivan out there with me, okay?'

Both officers nodded.

'So let's get it over with, shall we?' Massetti said as she reached the door and waited for one of them to open it for her. 'If someone would be so kind ...?'

Chapter 50

WAITING OUTSIDE IN the quad was a posse of news gatherers. Sullivan counted at least five TV cameras plus reporters whose number was well into double figures. They had been corralled by uniformed police constables into a section of the quad to the right of the custody suite doors. This meant that Massetti could address them from just outside the entrance to the building and quickly disappear inside at the briefing's end. Entering the quad with Broderick and Sullivan at either shoulder, the chief superintendent swiftly quelled the gaggle of questions fired at her from the throng.

'Ladies and gentleman, my name is Chief Superintendent Massetti and I'd like to thank you for being here this morning.'

'Is it true that Julia Novacs has pulled out of *Queen of Diamonds* due to concerns about her safety?' a reporter yelled from the back of the press corp.

'Ms Novacs was the victim of an assault outside the Convent yesterday evening. We understand that she's safely at her villa in Marbella. We don't know the position regarding her filming commitments here on the Rock. There have, however, been several very important developments following yesterday's attack which I would now like to brief you on.'

'Spanish police have released a statement saying they're also looking for her assailant. Does this mean he's gone after Novacs in Marbella?' a female reporter shouted.

'Is he a stalker? Has he contacted Novacs in the past?' queried another.

'As I said, there have been several other developments that you need to be made aware of. Ms Novacs' attacker has been identified as a Polish national called Lech Jasinski. Enquiries have led us to believe ...'

Massetti was suddenly aware that mobile ringtones had begun to sound among the assembled journalists. At first, it was just one or two, but within seconds the number had increased considerably. To Massetti's consternation, almost her entire audience was now speaking into their mobiles or checking their messages.

Turning to Broderick, she hissed: 'What the hell's going on?'

'Looks like something's broken, ma'am.'

Massetti turned to the group once more. 'Ladies and gentleman, if I might continue ...' Her words died out as she watched helplessly as the entire press contingent headed out of the quad and back towards the street. 'Where are you going?' she called after them, somewhat desperately.

'The Polish stalker's holding Gabriel Isolde hostage over at the Atlantic Marina Plaza,' one of the reporters called back. 'Check your messages!'

A furious Massetti pivoted on her crutches to confront Broderick and Sullivan. She was alone. A glimpse of Sullivan's back through the custody suite door told her all she needed to know. Both detectives were heading to the incident room without her. Across the now press-free quad, several uniformed police constables stood uncomfortably. Spying them over her shoulder, Massetti finally flipped.

'Don't just stand there. Help me inside, for God's sake!'

CHAPTER 51

BY THE TIME Massetti reached the incident room, Broderick, Sullivan and Calbot were on their way out.

'Will someone tell me exactly what's happening?' Massetti demanded, stamping the ground with one of her crutches.

'Sorry, ma'am,' Broderick begun. 'Officers Thompson and Basco called in a few minutes back. Jasinski is holding Isolde hostage in the main reception at the Atlantic.'

'Jasinski also contacted several news agencies, GBC Radio and the *Chronicle*, alerting them of his whereabouts,' Sullivan said.

'And he's uploaded a message from Isolde onto YouTube,' added Calbot.

'Firearms are on their way to the scene and we should be, too, ma'am,' Broderick insisted.

'On your way,' Massetti consented, swallowing back the desire to question why she was the last person to find out.

As they left, she moved to Sergeant Aldarino sitting at a computer on the far side of the room.

'I've got Isolde's message online, ma'am.'

'Play it,' she ordered.

Both officers looked at the image before them. Isolde's face, pale with fear, stared at them from the screen. Falteringly he spoke:

'My name is Gabriel Isolde. I am the producer of the film *Queen of Diamonds*. It is the story of a spy known as the "Queen of Diamonds" – a British agent working in Gibraltar during World War II. In my film, I have been attempting to depict her as a heroine. She was not this. The Queen of Diamonds was a murderer and a traitor. A destroyer of families and a servant of evil. The world must now know the truth. My film is a lie.'

The screen went blank. To Massetti's horror, she noticed that the message had already received several thousand views.

CHAPTER 52

BY THE TIME the three officers arrived at the Atlantic Marina Plaza, a major 'situation' had developed. Uniformed policemen were struggling to cordon off the area at the front of the building from a growing crowd, news of the hostage situation having spread rapidly through social media and online outlets.

The curse of the internet, Sullivan thought.

The main road that passed the building had been closed by RGP patrol cars, and traffic police were now focusing on the massive logistical problem of redirecting rush hour traffic.

The Plaza building stood outside the Old Town fortifications, on land reclaimed from the sea. A massive hi-tech apartment complex of coloured glass and steel with a balconied frontage – a clear architectural expression of luxury and grandeur. It was the face of the new Gibraltar and its hopes for the future. Its current role as a place of murder and hostage-taking was definitely not part of its carefully marketed image.

At the scene, the first to greet Broderick, Sullivan and Calbot was Inspector Pérez, head of the RGP's Firearms Unit, a huge bear of a man with a reputation for calmness and professionalism under pressure.

'Jacket up,' he commanded, handing them all bullet-proof vests. 'PCs Thompson and Basco were confronted by Jasinski and forced to leave the building. He has subsequently taken a position behind the desk in the main reception area and is holding the man at knife-point. However, we can't be sure that he hasn't got a firearm as well.'

'Understood,' replied Broderick, taking off his jacket and slipping on the protective vest. Beside him, Sullivan and Calbot followed suit.

'I have three police marksmen in place. None has a clear shot of Jasinski. He's chosen his position well,' said Pérez.

'Ex-Polish Special Forces,' Sullivan contributed. 'Most probably covered every angle.'

'Thank you,' Pérez bridled slightly. 'I'm aware of that. I have three more officers covering the rear car park exit and six more ready to go in at the front if given the order.'

'Anyone made contact with him yet?' Broderick asked.

'No, sir. We tried to contact Inspector Gomez, our principal negotiator, but he's in Madrid.'

'Doing what?' Broderick asked.

'He's at an international symposium for police negotiators,' Pérez replied.

'Is that supposed to be joke, Pérez?'

'I wish it was, sir.'

'Looks like *I'll* be speaking to Jasinski then,' Broderick continued. 'How do I do that?'

'He told Thompson and Basco that he had Isolde's mobile phone. We'll connect you to that, sir.'

'I also want him to have visual contact with me,' Broderick added. 'I'll start outside the main entrance and persuade him to let me into the reception area to talk face to face.'

'So long as you keep your distance, sir,' Pérez advised.

'I have no intention of being a hero, Inspector. I leave that sort of thing to you guys.'

Pérez handed Broderick a head-set. 'You'll be connected to Jasinski once you're in position. I'll be listening in and can interrupt without Jasinski hearing. If I do, it'll most probably be to tell you to back off. Understood, sir?'

'Understood.'

'I suggest you take up position five metres from the main entrance,' Pérez continued. 'You should have clear sight of him from there. The rest of us will stay in view but further back. I'll be following the conversation on my own head-set. Good luck.'

Broderick nodded. 'Thanks.'

With Pérez leading the way, the police officers crossed the road and moved into position at the front of the building – Broderick near the main doors and Sullivan and Calbot ten metres directly behind him. Pérez crouched behind a police patrol car with a view of the whole scene. Looking into the building through the huge windows that fronted the street, Broderick could see both Jasinski and Isolde. The Pole had Isolde in a tight grip and held him in the doorway of the monitoring room immediately behind the reception desk. Broderick's earpiece clicked and Pérez's voice came through, calm and clear.

'Connecting you now, sir.'

Three rings later and Broderick was through.

'Yes,' the harsh voice at the end of the line answered.

'Lech Jasinski?' Broderick asked, knowing full well the voice could belong to no one else.

'Who do think?' was the terse reply.

Broderick continued. 'My name is Chief Inspector Gus Broderick. I'm the senior officer here. I need you to listen carefully,

Lech. You're aware of the situation you're in and the response you've forced us to make. I need to ask you to lay down your weapon, release Mr Isolde and give yourself up.'

Silence greeted Broderick's words.

'Did you hear me, Lech?'

'I hear you. Now you will hear me. There is a woman standing directly behind you. I can see her. I will speak with her now.'

Looking over his shoulder, Broderick realised that the Pole was referring to Sullivan. 'I'm afraid that is not possible, Lech. I am the person you need to talk to and I hope you understand fully what I've just asked you to do.'

'I will speak with the woman or I will speak with no one. Don't mess with me or you will regret it. I hope you understand fully what I have just asked you to do, Chief Inspector.'

As Broderick looked across to Pérez, the channel on his head-set clicked. 'Pérez here, sir. I don't know why he should want Sullivan, but I see no reason to refuse him at this stage. Would you agree?'

Broderick thought for a moment. Sullivan had arrived on the Rock with the stigma of a difficult hostage case behind her. Her actions had resulted in the successful release of the hostage, but she had disobeyed direct orders from her commanding officer. She had been considered a loose cannon at the Met. Was she really the person needed at this juncture?

'Perhaps best not to aggravate him too much at this stage, sir,' Perez suggested.

'Okay,' Broderick decided. 'I'll let her talk to him.'

Turning to Sullivan, he waved her over.

'What is it, sir?' she asked, arriving at Broderick's side.

'Jasinski has asked to speak to you. Christ knows why, but I think we should find out.' Broderick handed his head-set to her. 'In view of your past experience in these matters, I would request that at all times you take orders from me and under no circumstances fuck up. Is that clear, Detective Sergeant?'

'As day, sir.'

'I'll get another head-set from Pérez,' Broderick said as he moved off. 'Don't engage him until I'm back in the loop.'

Turning to view the scene within the reception area, Sullivan took a deep breath. *Why would Jasinski ask to speak to me? If he's hoping I'll be a soft touch, then he's in for a shock*, she told herself, placing the head-set over her ears.

The channel clicked. It was Broderick. 'Okay. I'm here and I can hear everything. Stick to the book and reel the bugger in, Sullivan.'

'I'll do my best, guv.'

The channel clicked again and to Sullivan's surprise she could now hear breathing at the other end. Short, sharp exhalations. It was Jasinski and he sounded every bit as tense as she had imagined he would be.

'Mr Jasinski ...?' she began.

'Ah, good,' the man replied. 'I will speak with you.'

'That's good. That's very good, Mr Jasinski.'

'I recognised you. From yesterday. You are very fast. You almost caught me.'

'But I didn't, Mr Jasinski.'

'No. I'm glad. I would not have wished to have been forced to hurt you.'

'There is no need for you to hurt anyone, Mr Jasinski.'

'Call me Lech.'

Sullivan could hear a slight change in the man's tone. Softer. More engaging.

'If you wish,' she replied. 'My name is Tamara, Lech. It's good to be talking with you.'

'Can I trust you, Tamara?' Jasinski asked.

'Yes. Yes, you can, Lech.'

'That is good. I need you to know that I do not wish to harm anyone.'

'That's good, Lech. That's very good. I can assure you that, if you let Mr Isolde go free, no harm will come to you either.'

'I have your word?'

'You have my word, Lech. All you have to do is put down your weapon and release Mr Isolde.'

'Cameras?'

'I'm sorry? What cameras, Lech?' Sullivan asked.

'Where are the cameras? TV? I need to know. I cannot see them.'

Momentarily thrown by this, Sullivan looked across to Broderick and Pérez.

'I can find out for you, Lech. Please give me a moment.'

The channel changed on Sullivan's head-set. Broderick spoke: 'The press and TV crews are being held back beyond the cordon, Sullivan. Find out what the hell he's asking for.'

The channel changed and Sullivan was once more through to Isolde's captor.

'At present the cameras are being held back, Lech. I'm sure you understand why.'

'I understand,' Jasinski replied, the hard edge returning to his voice. 'Bring them close. I need them closer.'

'I'll have to check if that's possible, Lech.'

'Bring them close and I will release Isolde. You hear me?'

This was not what Sullivan had expected. The click in her earpiece brought Broderick's voice to her.

'Tell him we'll bring the cameras closer. He can have a bloody close-up if he wants. Just get him to release Isolde.'

'Sir.' Sullivan turned towards the building as the channel cleared. Once again she could hear Jasinski breathing.

'We're letting the cameras through, Lech,' Sullivan told him as she glanced to her left. The press were being allowed through the cordon and were being positioned approximately twenty metres from where she stood. 'Now will you let Mr Isolde go free?'

'This is what will happen,' Jasinski replied. 'I will come outside with him. When I see the cameras, I will throw down my knife. I will release Isolde and put my hands in the air. I will kneel slowly and lie on the ground with my arms out beside me. Understand?'

'I understand, Lech.'

'Then your men will approach, search and bring me to my feet. But – and this is important – you Tamara will be the one to handcuff me and make the arrest. You and you only. I must have your word that it will be so.'

The channel changed on Sullivan's head-set. Pérez spoke.

'Once he's released Isolde, we can do what we like, Sullivan. For a start, we need to check he has no other devices on him.'

'May I request that, if your men find him unarmed, we do as he asks. Allow me to arrest him. If I give my word, I like to keep it, sir.'

Silence. Finally Broderick's voice: 'Tell him it's a go, Sullivan.'

'Yes, sir.'

Checking that the press had moved to their new position and had their cameras in place, Sullivan re-engaged with the Pole.

'Lech, your request has been granted. Exit the building and follow the actions exactly as you described them, and I'll arrest you in person. You have my word.'

'We're coming out,' the Pole replied.

Moments later, Jasinski and Isolde emerged from the main entrance of the Atlantic Marina Plaza. Isolde's face was ashen and pale, his expression one of pure fear. Jasinski, too, was showing signs of great stress. As a soldier, he knew he was now at his most vulnerable. Flicking his eyes from one side to the other, he kept

Isolde at knife-point and as close to himself as possible. He was only too aware that the police marksmen would attempt to get a clear shot of him. Whether they took it or not was up to fate now. He had to trust that the police would honour their word and allow him to release his hostage without violence.

Ahead of him, he could see Tamara and, further on, several police vehicles with officers behind them. To the side of these he could see the press and TV reporters with their cameras pointed in his direction, recording the event that was unfolding. The time had come. Lifting the hand in which he held the knife high in the air, Jasinski drew it back and threw it several metres to his right. Releasing Isolde from his grip, he stepped backwards and raised his other arm in the air. Slowly lowering himself to his knees he watched as Isolde stumbled and ran towards the police officers before him. Simultaneously, several armed officers left the cover of their vehicles and rushed towards him as he slowly lowered his head and chest to the ground and stretched out both arms at his sides. On reaching him, two of the police officers searched Jasinski's prostrate body while the others stood to the side, their weapons trained on the Pole.

'All clear!' one of the officers announced, while he and a colleague reached down and hauled Jasinski back onto his feet. Holding his arms forcibly behind his back, the same officer looked across to Sullivan and nodded. Without hesitation, Sullivan moved towards them, removing a pair of steel handcuffs from her pocket as she did so. Seconds later she had handcuffed Jasinski and was escorting him towards a waiting patrol car. Turning his head to see his female police captor, Jasinski's face broke into a wide smile.

'Thank you, Tamara,' he said. '*Dziekuje.*'

CHAPTER 53

'THE FORENSIC MEDICAL examiner's taking a look at Jasinski now,' Calbot reported as Broderick and Sullivan sat sipping coffee in the police canteen. 'She's already given me the nod to get a psychiatrist and a mental health officer over from St Bernard's. You'll have to wait till they give us the green light before you can interview him, guv.'

'Get yourself a coffee, son, and we'll see you back in the incident room. The hard work's just about to begin,' Broderick replied.

The previous hour and a half had seen Broderick briefing both the commissioner of police – via a conference call to New York – and Harriet Massetti about the events leading up to Jasinski's arrest. Massetti had been less than happy that the Pole's request for Sullivan to get involved had been granted. The detective sergeant's lack of seniority and her turbulent history should, in Massetti's opinion, have kept her direct involvement in the negotiations for Isolde's release to a minimum. This was especially true in light of the subsequent media coverage.

'Jasinski's a clever bastard,' Massetti had told her colleagues. 'He made sure the cameras were on him and then, to maximise potential exposure, he gets a good-looking female police officer to arrest him. It's a news editor's dream. Have you seen the bulletins? Sky? CNN? Top story. They're calling them "Beauty and the Beast".'

Broderick had argued that, to effect a safe and quick conclusion to a dangerous situation, he had considered co-operation the best course of action. Fortunately the commissioner had sided with Broderick and both had left Massetti to stew on the matter and nurse her injured ankle.

'By the way, how was Massetti?' an unknowing Sullivan asked as she and Broderick headed out of the canteen.

'Pissed off that you're in the limelight.'

'I didn't ask to be, guv.'

'Take no notice of her. She's probably worried that someone will want to make a movie about you next.'

'I could be the next Julia Novacs,' Sullivan replied smugly.

'Pig-headed and temperamental, you mean?' Broderick countered. 'I'd say you're typecast already, Detective Sergeant.'

As they walked down the corridor together, Sullivan smiled at what she hoped had been one of Broderick's rare jokes.

CHAPTER 54

BACK IN THE incident room, Broderick and Sullivan's first job was to liaise with the two Spanish police officers from the Cuerpo Nacional de Policía. To their great surprise, neither of their Spanish counterparts mentioned any reports of the duo's presence at the scene of the previous night's murders in San Roque. Either nobody had mentioned them or, if they had, nobody had considered that they might be foreigners. This is good, Sullivan thought. *Relations between Spain and Gibraltar are bad enough without me and Broderick adding to them.*

The Spanish officers reported that forensics from the crime scene across the border would take time. They did, however, possess an initial pathology report on the bodies of Martínez and Maugham. As with Cornwallis, large doses of Rohypnol had been found in the dead men's blood. Petechial haemorrhages were also present in Martínez, indicating asphyxiation as the principal cause of death. Several blows to the head were the more obvious cause of Maugham's demise. The conclusion was that all three men were most probably murdered by the same person. The job now was to prove that the murderer was Lech Jasinski.

As he had been arrested on the Rock, it had been agreed that the main thrust of the investigation would be carried out by the RGP. On this understanding, and taking with them all the relevant facts pertaining to the cases, the Spanish detectives left to return to Algeciras.

'While we wait on both sets of forensics,' Broderick told his team, 'Sullivan and I will do our best to get a confession out of Jasinski.'

'He gave himself up pretty easily,' Calbot noted. 'Maybe he'll just continue to give it all up.'

'Well, it ain't over till the big Pole sings, Calbot. Let's hope the psychiatrist considers him competent enough to be interviewed.'

'I wouldn't worry, guv,' Calbot said. 'Jasinski will be back on his medication by now, so hopefully he won't be too *Cuckoo's Nest*.'

A local news bulletin was running silently on one of the computer screens next to where Sullivan was standing. More footage of her taking Jasinski into custody, Sullivan's name standing out in bold letters in the news story running on a loop at the bottom of the screen. The description of her as a 'police heroine' made her feel both uncomfortable and angry. Ribbing from her fellow colleagues had begun almost immediately. Most of it had been good humoured, one or two gibes less so. Massetti was not alone in her disdain for Sullivan's ubiquitous media presence.

Jasinski was being held in a cell adjoining the custody suite. For the best part of two hours, he had been examined by a psychiatrist, Allana Cosquieri. After consultation with a mental health officer, Cosquieri gave the all-clear for him to be interviewed.

'Mr Jasinski has been experiencing negative symptoms associated with his condition, symptoms exacerbated by a pattern of reduced medication,' the psychiatrist told Broderick and Sullivan. 'He's also complained of increased headaches and occasional blackouts, some lasting for several hours. Without your recent intervention, he could have expected increased paranoia and dramatic shifts in his emotional state, leading to erratic and violent behaviour. He remains a severe schizophrenic and a possible risk to others and himself. I've renewed his medication and believe that that will bring some immediate relief. Therefore I consider him able to sustain interview, but of strictly limited intensity and duration.'

'How would he act during his blackouts?' Sullivan asked. 'Would he be unaware of his actions during those periods?'

'His history would suggest that to be the case,' Cosquieri replied. 'It is a form of amnesia.'

'You mean he could've carried out crimes and then have no recollection of them?' Broderick pressed.

'It's possible. No doubt your questioning will reveal exactly how much he remembers or not.'

'Or perhaps exactly how much he chooses to remember,' Broderick added with a touch of irritation. 'He's chosen not to have a lawyer present, which suggests he may be confident of proving diminished responsibility for his actions.'

'If they were his actions, Chief Inspector,' countered the psychiatrist, moving to the door. 'Remember, he's a sick man, and you'll have to treat him as such, irrespective of the crimes you think he may have perpetrated.'

After Cosquieri left, the two detectives stood in silence for a few moments. Eventually Broderick spoke. 'I thought things were going too well.'

'You know what they say, guv – if a case seems to be going too well, it's usually 'cause it ain't.'

CHAPTER 55

WITHIN MINUTES OF the medical examiner's departure, Jasinski was escorted across the central quad to one of the newly remodelled interview rooms on the other side of police HQ. Handcuffed to the single table that stood in the centre of the room and watched over by two uniformed police constables, he waited impassively for the next stage of the proceedings to begin.

Broderick and Sullivan did not keep him long. After they took their seats opposite their suspect, the chief inspector switched on the recording apparatus on the table before him and began the interview.

'Eleven twenty-three am. Interview with Lech Jasinski. Presiding officers Chief Inspector Gus Broderick and Detective Sergeant Tamara Sullivan. Mr Jasinski, you weren't cautioned at the scene of your arrest due to the heightened precautions surrounding it. I must now tell you that you are under arrest on suspicion of assault against Ms Julia Novacs, the kidnapping of Mr Gabriel Isolde and the murders of Joshua Cornwallis, Eduard Martínez and Graeme Maugham. You do not have to say anything. But it may harm your defence if you do not ...'

As Broderick continued to caution, Sullivan became aware of a sudden shift in Jasinski's mood. The blood had drained from his features and the pupils of his eyes had dilated to mere pinpricks. His breathing had once again become intense and rasping.

'... rely on in court. Anything you do say can be given ...'

Suddenly Jasinski slammed his fists down hard upon the table and exploded in a rage of indignation. 'You are lying, no? Murder? Murder! I kill no one. You hear me? I kill no one! Nobody!'

The two police constables sprang forward to restrain the furious Jasinski, but Broderick waved them back. The handcuffs securing the Pole to the table were enough to limit the man's potential to cause harm. Broderick calmly finished his caution and continued.

'Mr Jasinski, you have chosen not to seek legal representation. In the light of your latest reaction, you may wish to reconsider this.'

Jasinski stopped for a moment, his chest heaving and his eyes ablaze.

'Get me a lawyer. Now.'

CHAPTER 56

THREE HOURS LATER, in the presence of an appointed legal representative and with a psychiatric nurse on standby outside the room, the interview continued.

'While admitting the charges of assault and kidnap,' Jasinski's rather young and profusely sweating lawyer began, 'my ... er ... client most strongly denies any ... er ... involvement in the deaths of Cornwallis, Martínez and ... er ... the Englishman.'

'Maugham?' Sullivan prompted.

'Yes ... er ... Maugham. The Englishman,' the young man added, puffing out his chest to suggest competence.

'Yes, he made that clear to us earlier,' Broderick observed. 'However, you'll understand that we must ask Mr Jasinski to account for his whereabouts both yesterday afternoon in Gibraltar and across the border in Spain last night?'

Jasinski's lawyer nodded his consent.

'Yesterday afternoon I was here in Gibraltar,' Jasinski began, flexing the fingers of his large manacled hands. 'I had come over from Spain the previous night and watched the filming in Casemates Square. I needed to make contact with someone important. Important with the film. I wanted them to know about its lies.'

'Is that why you broke into Ms Novacs' villa in Marbella the previous day?' Broderick questioned.

'Of course,' Jasinski replied. 'I needed to speak to her. To tell her that the film is lies and more lies. She would have understood. I know she would not have been able to continue.'

'But she wasn't there, and so you came in search of her here on the Rock,' Sullivan said.

'I did not know she was to have a night-shoot. If I could have spoken to her before, she would have helped me. I know.'

'So why didn't you approach her at the square?' Broderick asked.

'I could not get near her. Or anyone. Police. Security. So when they finish, I ask where the important people go. I am told they are at the Atlantic Marina and so I walk there.'

'With a view to doing what?' Sullivan enquired.

'So I can tell them the truth. Speak to them face to face. Make them understand.'

'And so you went to find them at the Atlantic Marina Plaza. We have you on CCTV that morning, visiting the main reception and checking out the rear entrance and car park,' Broderick told the Pole.

'What did you do for the rest of the day up until your attack on Ms Novacs at the Convent?' Sullivan asked.

'Walked. Everywhere. I have never been here before, there was much I wanted to see.'

'Where specifically did you spend your time?' Sullivan persisted.

'Main Street. Irish Town. The Botanic Gardens. Everywhere. I drink coffee in cafes. I learn from a waitress at a cafe about the reception for the film people last evening. Then I plan.'

'You plan what exactly?' Broderick asked.

'I plan to get Ms Novacs' attention. If I cannot speak to her, I decide I must find other ways of telling the world about the lies.'

'So you decided to assault her?'

'Of course. I have printed leaflets in my bag that tell the truth. I see a paint-gun in a shop and buy it. I then go to the Governor's Residence and pick my spot. All afternoon I guard it.'

'You say you were outside the Convent all afternoon?' Sullivan asked.

'Yes, which is why I could not kill anyone. Wherever you think I must have been, I wasn't. I was waiting outside the Convent for Ms Novacs to arrive.'

'And obviously just out of view of the CCTV positioned there.'

'Of course. I could see the cameras. I know how not to be seen by them. I am trained in such things.'

'You did not return to the Atlantic Marina Plaza. Is that what you're saying?' Sullivan continued.

'Not till today. I came back because I had no choice. Nobody hears my message. The news people say I am just a stalker. They do not tell the truth. It is just more lies.'

'And yesterday evening? You crossed back into Spain?' Broderick asked, anxious to move things on.

'After my escape ... from *you*, Tamara ...' Jasinski said, smiling at Sullivan.

'Detective Sergeant Sullivan,' Broderick corrected.

'From the *detective sergeant*,' Jasinski continued playfully. 'I take a bus and go to the border.'

'And then?'

'I sleep, then shave my beard. Then I go shopping.'

'And when did you head out to San Roque?' Sullivan asked.

'That's a leading question, Detective Sergeant,' Jasinski's lawyer interrupted. 'My client, I think, denies ever being in San Roque.'

'Well, he hasn't denied it to us,' Broderick snapped back.

'You deny it, don't you?' asked the lawyer, turning nervously to his client.

'I did not go to San Roque,' Jasinski confirmed with a smile. 'I have never been. Last night I went to beach and stay there till dawn. Then I returned here to finish what I started.'

'And at no point yesterday did you experience what you describe as "blackouts". Loss of time and so on?' Sullivan asked, looking Jasinski straight in the eye.

'Not that I remember,' Jasinski replied. 'But then again, I can never be sure.'

'I don't believe you,' Broderick interjected, his patience waning.

'About the blackouts or about everything I tell you?' Jasinski replied, mischief playing in his eyes.

'Pretty much everything. I think your plans went far beyond assaulting Novacs and taking Isolde. I think you murdered Cornwallis yesterday afternoon and then went on to the Covent. After your assault on Ms Novacs, you crossed back over to Spain and found your way to San Roque with the express purpose of killing both Martínez and Maugham. I don't believe you experienced your so-called "blackouts" either. I think you were fully in control of all your actions and carried out your plans to the letter.'

'Interesting,' Jasinski replied.

'In what way interesting?' Sullivan asked.

'Interesting neither of you ask me why I would do such things. You have not asked me about the lies.'

Broderick and Sullivan glanced at one another. It was true.

'We've only just begun, Mr Jasinski,' Broderick informed the man. 'We're just warming up.'

'Well, I am sorry to have to tell you that I am tired now, Chief

Inspector. I need a break,' Jasinski replied coldly.

'Well, of course you do.' Broderick responded. 'Of course you do.'

'Lucky for me you are both excellent police officers,' Jasinski added.

'Meaning what exactly?' Broderick bridled, his voice dropping in pitch.

'Meaning I am innocent of murdering these people and I trust you will prove it so.' Jasinski now turned to his lawyer. 'You, I do not trust to help me. I demand another lawyer.'

The young man opened his mouth to reply, but words failed him.

'We'll see what we can do,' Broderick said, frustrated by the two of them.

'Thank you,' Jasinski replied. 'And now I must rest.'

CHAPTER 57

'HE WON'T BE fit for interview for at least an hour, his nurse says,' Broderick announced, exiting the building and making his way across to where Sullivan was sitting on a bench beneath a palm tree in the central quad.

'If you ask me, Jasinski's using his condition to call the shots on this,' he continued. 'He doesn't appear to be particularly mentally disturbed to me.'

'Just because he's not twitching doesn't mean he's not a lunatic, guv,' Sullivan observed.

'I suppose not. But I'm not having him lead us a merry dance. If we have to get tough, we'll get tough. He's not crying out for a nurse every time things get uncomfortable for him.'

Sullivan sat looking into the middle distance.

'I know that face,' Broderick continued as he sat down beside her. 'Usually means you're working up to a good one.'

'I'm just not sure.'

'Here we go!' Broderick exclaimed, raising his hands in exasperation. '"Our Lady of the Met" is on one. What's the problem? Got anyone else in mind for our triple murder?'

Sullivan shrugged her shoulders.

'Didn't think so. You don't have to be a fancy-pants profiler to put this one together, Sullivan. Jasinski's means and opportunity are rock solid. His ability to kill with ease, not in question. He says he wasn't at either murder scene. We have only his word for that. I've got the team checking through every witness statement from outside the Convent. See if anyone saw Jasinski hanging around through the afternoon before the assault. My guess is that it's a waste of time. Spanish police are doing the same for any possible sightings of him in San Roque. Forensics are rushing through the DNA results – some extra money has been chucked at them apparently – and I have every confidence they will prove that Jasinski is not only a loony, but a murdering son of a bitch as well.'

'I'm sure you're right, guv ...'

'But?' Broderick interrupted. 'There's a "but" coming, isn't there?'

'*But* ... I think I believe him.'

'You believe he didn't kill those three men?'

'I believe *he* believes he didn't kill those men. Whether he can't remember or he just didn't do it, I'm not sure. But when you cautioned him, I think he was truly shocked to learn we had him there on suspicion of murder. He was completely knocked sideways by that, and he wasn't acting. He really wasn't. Jasinski believes he's an innocent man.'

Broderick looked at his detective sergeant for a moment. Her passion was undeniable, even if her reasoning was out of kilter.

'Well, that's neither here nor there, Sullivan,' Broderick said in what he hoped was a calm, reasonable tone. 'We just need to find out who murdered those men – whatever Jasinski thinks or believes is irrelevant. Whether he ends up in solitary confinement or bouncing around in a padded cell, it's all the same to me. So while we wait for the evidence to prove that he's a killer, I suggest we find out the reasons why he became one.'

'The "lies", Sullivan murmured.

'Yes,' Broderick replied, standing to go, 'the "lies".'

CHAPTER 58

THE GLASS-LIKE surface of the villa's infinity pool merged seamlessly into the blue Mediterranean horizon beyond. The mid-morning sun had been gaining in heat as it moved towards its zenith, its rays creating diamond-like sparkles on the pool's edge. Wendall Phillips walked briskly past its diving board, wishing he could plunge into the water's cool depths. It would be a welcome escape from the heat outside the villa and the emotional volcano within it. He had not slept that night. His vigil over Julia Novacs had been unrelenting. The decision not to wake the heavily sedated actress during the night had been the right one; she had not needed to know that Jasinski had gained access to the villa in which she now slumbered. Julia had suffered enough from the assault at the governor's reception and needed to recover, Wendall had reasoned. That situation was about to change. Just after nine o'clock, the phone call had come from Chief Superintendent Massetti informing him of the kidnapping of Isolde and the murder of Josh Cornwallis. From that moment, everything had been thrown into a nightmarish spin.

Anticipating Novacs' reaction, Wendall had planned ahead. A

private jet was put on standby at Málaga airport. A suite at the George V hotel just off the Champs-Elysées in Paris was booked for two nights. A discreet call to Novacs' friend Carla Bruni meant that a sympathetic shoulder to cry on would be available on the star's arrival on French soil. All other conversations, with agents and family, would have to wait.

Novacs had risen at 9.30 and taken breakfast at 10. Wendall had gone into her rooms with the breakfast tray and broken the news before the star had taken the first sip of her favourite herbal tea.

The following hour had proved as traumatic as Wendall had suspected it would be. Novacs had completely fallen to pieces. Distress and anguish had swiftly given way to anger and feelings of retribution as Novacs turned on Wendall. Why hadn't he told her sooner? How had the security team left her so vulnerable? Did they take her for an idiot? At last her tirade abated, and she fell into Wendall's arms, sobbing uncontrollably. From that point, he knew that she would do as she was told and go where she was taken.

Wendall once again looked out across the pool. In ten minutes, they would leave for the airport and their flight to Paris. As he turned to head inside the villa, his phone rang. It was Isolde. Wendall had avoided his increasingly frequent calls all morning. But the time had come to speak.

Chapter 59

SIXTY KILOMETRES SOUTH, in Gibraltar, Tracy Gavin stood outside Julia Novacs' seventy-five foot Winnebago at the *Queen of Diamonds* unit base. Inside the palatial vehicle, Gabriel Isolde was supposed to be resting on the super-king-size bed in the star's boudoir. Tracy had been taking calls from cast and crew all morning. She had also had to keep the press at bay and smooth-talk several deeply panicked executive producers of the movie. Half an hour earlier, Isolde had been released from St Bernard's hospital still suffering from shock. It was clear to Tracy that her boss was in no state to deal with anything, but things had to be dealt with nevertheless. To facilitate this, she had stepped outside of the Winnebago to make his calls for him. All in all, she had managed to hold things together, but there was one person she still desperately needed to talk to.

For the twentieth time in an hour, she picked up Isolde's phone and called Wendall Phillips. To her huge relief, she got straight through to him. Minutes later she wished she hadn't. The news he had given her was the worst imaginable. The star of the movie was leaving Spain within the hour and would not be returning to complete her filming commitments. All future communications would now be through Novacs' agent in Los Angeles. There was also a strong possibility that her lawyers would contact Isolde. Wendall did not go into detail, but Tracy could well imagine the demands they would make. It all pointed to one thing: *Queen of Diamonds* was finished. Over. A complete train wreck.

Taking a moment to compose herself, Tracy plucked up the courage to inform her boss. Reaching for the Winnebago's door handle, she was surprised to discover that it was immovable. Trying with more force, she realised that the door had been locked from the inside.

'Gabriel!' she called, attempting to turn the handle once again. 'Gabriel! Can you let me in?'

CHAPTER 60

'CAKE,' HANNAH PORTILLO announced, 'and wine. *Vino blanco.*
The last two substances ingested by Cornwallis. As his tox screen
identified Rohypnol, I sent samples from his digestive tract for
analysis.'

'Rohypnol was found in both the cake and the wine?' Sullivan
asked, reading the report that the elegant, statuesque pathologist
had delivered to the incident room.

'Yes. A higher percentage of the drug was found in the cake,
strangely enough. I'm sure Forensics will have more to offer. The
cake itself was found in the kitchen.'

'We saw it,' Broderick added. 'Coffee and walnut. My favourite.'

'Thought you'd be more of a jam sponge sort of guy,' Sullivan
said mischievously.

'I wouldn't turn a slice of that away either, Detective Sergeant.'

'Sadly, neither could Cornwallis,' continued Portillo. 'Be
interesting to compare with the Spanish examinations when they
arrive.'

'"When" being the operative word.' Broderick sighed, leaning
back in his chair and putting his feet up on a desk.

'Strange that it should be in two foodstuffs, don't you think?' Sullivan asked Portillo. 'Spiking the drink would have been enough surely.'

'I agree. Unless whoever administered the drug was worried that the victim wouldn't drink enough and brought the cake along as backup.'

Calbot suddenly laughed.

'What's so funny?' Broderick asked the young officer disapprovingly.

'Well, I know he's supposed to be funny in the head, but I can't quite see Jasinski turning up with cakes for his victims, can you?'

'Just what I was thinking,' Sullivan said.

'Could have been a gift. Something like that. A way of making himself welcome in order to gain entry,' Broderick pondered.

'Must have been shop-bought. And locally. We need to check food stores in the vicinity. Morrisons. The Eroski supermarket near the border,' Sullivan said. 'If we find he's bought cake, then I guess we've caught him.'

'I'll get on it,' Calbot said, heading across to his desk.

'So Jasinski's modus operandi was to drug his victims and then finish them off by suffocating them, knowing they could offer no resistance,' Broderick conjectured. 'And the only reason he resorted to smashing Maugham's skull in was because the man didn't eat or drink a sufficient amount to knock him out properly.'

'Still doesn't make sense, guv,' Sullivan replied. 'Why go to the trouble of rendering them physically incapable before asphyxiating them? He's a powerful man and a trained killer. He could have snapped any of them like a twig.'

Before Broderick could formulate an answer, Massetti hobbled into view across the crowded room and nodded for the two detectives to join her.

'What is it, guv?' Broderick asked as he and Sullivan arrived at her side.

'Gabriel Isolde has just been rushed to hospital. A drug overdose by the sounds of it.'

'Jesus,' Sullivan said.

'Get someone over to St Bernard's as quick as you can,' Massetti ordered. 'Meanwhile, the two of you get some results out of Jasinski. Understood?'

'Perfectly, ma'am,' Broderick replied, already heading for the interview room.

'And what's the matter with you?' Massetti asked, turning to Sullivan. 'Not feeling up to the job?'

'I'm just fine, thank you, ma'am,' Sullivan said, choosing to keep her thoughts to herself. 'I'm on my way.'

CHAPTER 61

'MY CLIENT DENIES any involvement in the deaths of Cornwallis, Martínez or Maugham.' The young woman's confident tone did not go unnoticed by Sullivan and Broderick. Having been quickly briefed, Flora O'Harrigan, Jasinski's new sharp-minded and immaculately presented solicitor, was now ready for business. 'The assault on Ms Novacs at the Convent and the subsequent abduction of Mr Isolde were actions driven by the despair caused by not being heard,' she continued. 'My client wishes to tell his story and clear himself of your suspicions. He can then reveal the truth about what brought him to Gibraltar in the first place.'

'So he wants to blame his actions on his medical condition, while getting a platform to explain his motives for committing them,' Broderick replied evenly. 'Sounds a bit "cake and eat it" to me, Ms O'Harrigan.'

'Mr Jasinski just wishes to place his actions in the context of his family history, Chief Inspector. How those actions were influenced by my client's schizophrenia is for others to determine.'

Broderick looked at Sullivan and raised an eyebrow. Jasinski had found a good advocate in O'Harrigan.

'If your client has a story, we'd like to hear it. The more information he gives us, the more we can deduce just how much of a *story* Mr Jasinski is telling,' Broderick replied.

'Or just how much of the *truth*,' O'Harrigan countered. 'Mr Jasinski, please make your statement. If you need to rest, please tell us.'

Jasinski nodded to his lawyer and then looked anxiously towards his interrogators. Taking a deep breath and relaxing his broad shoulders, he began:

'In November of 1942, my grandfather, Czesław Jasinski, disappeared while serving as intelligence officer with Polish Free Army here in Gibraltar. He managed to escape from Nazi-occupied Poland two years before and joined his countrymen in their fight. The price he had to pay for this was that his beloved wife – my grandmother – and their four children were forced to remain in my mother country. They lived in house in isolated woodland between Puszczykowo and the Warta river, to south of Luboń. My family once had money, but all had gone by the time Germans brought war to Polska and the world. My grandfather sent messages to them, but it was difficult, you understand? Germans controlled that part of Poznań with iron grip. The family lived in fear of SS. All lived in fear of them.'

The Pole paused, took another a deep breath and continued:

'My father died three months ago now. All his life he struggle to come to terms with my grandfather's fate here on the Rock and reasons why his family suffered so.'

Jasinski stopped once more. Sullivan and Broderick could see he was distressed. The Pole cleared his throat and said: 'I will tell you this as my father told it to me. You understand?'

Sullivan nodded for him to go on.

'My father was just boy of eight years in 1942. "Child of woods", he call himself, for woods surrounded the family house for many, many miles. One morning he left his mother and three sisters – Alicja, Jolanta and Nadzieja – and went to play with two friends by river. His mother had been making bread with the girls when he left and she had made him promise, she did this always, to play safely and be back by dark. It was a promise my father kept every time. When he walked into woods to meet his friends, he turned to see his mother and sisters waving to him from front steps of their home. My father waved back and went on his way.

'Later that day, light fading, he and his friends returned. His friends were older and could stay out later. They knew that, if they went home with my father, they would be given food and milk. Coming near to house, one of his friends placed a hand on my father's shoulder to stop him. He had seen what my father had not. You understand? Beside house was big truck and big car. They had not seen such a car before, but they knew that it was bad thing. As they came nearer from woods, door of house opened and my father saw his mother and sisters. Soldiers with guns forced them into truck. Two officers left house also and got into car. My father began to cry out, but his friend covered his mouth and dragged him to ground. He saved my father's life. My father looked on as his mother and sisters were driven away. He never saw them again.

'My father and his friends went to house. It was empty. They found only one thing the Germans had left: a photograph on kitchen table. My father's eyes he would not believe. It showed his father – my grandfather, you understand? – in the arms of a woman, a stranger. My father was young, but he knew this was terrible thing. He wanted to burn the photograph, but something stopped him. That same picture is in my rucksack. The one that yesterday I lost. It is reason I am here and reason I have done what I have done.'

'We have the photograph,' Broderick confirmed. 'Please continue.'

'My father was taken in by his uncle and family. Much later they learn that my grandmother and the girls were taken to Fort VII. The first concentration camp of the Nazis in Poland. Twenty thousand Poles die there. Torture and death, by gas or starvation or disease.

'Only after war, my father received news of his beloved mother and sisters. Officially death from typhus. All of them. Unofficially, no imagination can show the horror of their true suffering. Their deaths haunted my father for seventy years.'

Once more, Jasinski stopped to gather himself. Sullivan glanced at her boss. To her mind, Jasinski was telling the truth. The expression on Broderick's face gave no indication if he felt the same.

Jasinski continued:

'And my grandfather? His disappearance was recorded "Missing in action". No confirmation of where he died or what he had been doing. Sometime in the Fifties, a secretary who worked in Polish defence department tells my father, not on record, that a black mark was on my grandfather's file. When my father demanded to see, he was told the file did not exist and warned to question no further – it was "not in the interests of him or his family to do so". You understand? From this, my father's theory comes. My grandfather's disappearance and the deaths of my grandmother and his sisters are connected. "Two tragedies linked by one cause", he would describe it. It is something he believed to be true and something I now know to be so.'

'A belief that led you to take lives in return?' Broderick questioned.

'My client has already answered that question for you, Chief Inspector,' O'Harrigan interjected.

'Not to my satisfaction he hasn't,' Broderick responded.

Jasinski shifted restlessly in his chair. 'I will continue. Yes?'

'Yes,' Broderick answered. 'Continue.'

'My father try hard to find answers. He worked as postman for thirty years and retire on little. No time and no power to follow the matter. There is a saying I have heard which says: "One door closes and the rest, they slam in your face." So it was with him.'

Sullivan nodded. She knew the feeling well.

'But there was a time when my father discover something of what really happened,' Jasinski said, his eyes widening as he continued his story with growing intensity. 'From now on I will call him by his name, Gustaw. Yes?'

Both detectives nodded their assent.

'In 1964, Gustaw had saved enough money to travel here to Gibraltar. An old friend managed to secure a visa for him do so. Not easy in communist times, you understand? My father had good English – taught as boy from his father – and so he wished to journey and investigate for himself. To find the truth he could not get in Polska. Every time he try to go down official routes, in his homeland and here in Gibraltar, all he gets is silence. His one hope was that someone on the Rock would know the young woman in the old photograph he still possessed. After he arrived in Gibraltar, Gustaw visited every building of importance, to show the image to one and all. Government, police, army, church. He drew blank at all of them. Then, on day before he is to return home, luck strikes. A librarian of the old Garrison Library recognises the photograph. She informs him that, several years before, a police inspector named Lorenz had brought the same picture to the library and made similar enquiry. But the woman could not help the inspector then and she could not help Gustaw now.'

THE POISONED ROCK

Sullivan and Broderick glanced at each other. This story was far from what they had expected.

Jasinski continued: 'At the police station in the centre of Gibraltar Town – in "Irish Town" it is called, yes?'

Broderick nodded.

'At that police station, Gustaw is told that Inspector Lorenz had retired and now lives in an apartment right across the street. Within an hour, my father is sitting with Lorenz and showing him the photograph he had brought from Polska and his past ...'

IRISH TOWN, 1964

'... I'M HOPING, Inspector Lorenz, you may help me understand this photograph a little better,' Gustaw Jasinski said, taking an old black and white photograph from his bag. Both men sat in the small, fastidiously tidy apartment that the policeman had been renting for over ten years. The shutters were closed against the bright morning sun, but several laser-like rays forced entry through broken slats to partially illuminate the dim, shadowy interior. The clatter from the cobble-stoned street below and the hubbub from the cafe on the opposite corner seemed to violate the room. Gustaw had been welcomed warmly by the small, balding elderly detective, who swiftly offered his guest his best armchair and supplied him with a cup of hot, delicious coffee.

Recognition and relief filled the old man's face as Gustaw handed the photograph to him. Its edges may have frayed and its image may be fading, but Lorenz knew exactly what it showed.

'Yes,' Lorenz said, moving to a large box on a side table by the kitchen door. For a few moments, Gustaw looked on as the old man rifled through its contents. At last, the policeman removed an old photo album from the box and sat in the chair opposite his guest. Opening the album, he removed an identical copy of Gustaw's photograph.

'Snap!' he exclaimed, handing both pictures to the surprised Pole.

'How is this possible?' Gustaw asked. 'Do you know who that woman is?'

'I'm afraid I don't. But I know what became of her,' Lorenz replied, barely able to hide his excitement.

'And the man? Do you know what happened to him?' Gustaw asked, his heart beating like a drum through his chest.

'I do,' Lorenz replied. 'As soon as you introduced yourself, I knew why you were here. Jasinski – it's a name that's hard to forget.'

'You knew my father?' Gustaw asked.

'No. But I was told of him.'

Lorenz placed the album on a side table and sat forward in his chair. 'The girl in that picture was discovered one night with her throat cut. She had been left in a deserted house up in the Old Town. I'm talking of November 1942, you understand? The civilian population had been mostly evacuated. The whole of Gibraltar was full to breaking point with Allied troops preparing to invade north Africa. The Rock was full of spies, saboteurs and double dealing. It was a dangerous time. That girl,' Lorenz continued, pointing to the photographs in Gustaw's hands, 'that girl was most likely a prostitute working in Gib and La Línea.'

'Oh, dear God,' Gustaw sighed, his worst fears realised.

'When I arrived at the scene, I found that she had not been robbed of her money. I reasoned therefore that her murder was most likely committed by a customer.'

'My father?' Gustaw exclaimed in panic.

'Certainly not.' Lorenz stated firmly. 'Apart from her purse and money, we also recovered at the scene a small photograph of the girl holding a baby. On the back was written "Mama and Rosia".'

'And my father?'

Lorenz raised his hand to silence Gustaw.

'The next day I set about investigating the murder. Within an hour of doing so, I received visitors at police headquarters. Two officers from British intelligence, both stationed on the Rock. The men informed me that they would be taking over the case as it was connected to enemy operations in Gibraltar. My commanding officer made it clear that I would be expected to forget all about it. I had to let the case go.'

'So how did you get hold of that photograph?' Gustaw asked.

'Six months later, a Spanish dockworker was arrested after a brutal fight in a dockside bar. In his bag was discovered a camera and a set of photographs showing scenes similar to that of your father and the murdered girl. All depicted Allied officers in compromising situations with prostitutes. Each photograph had several copies attached. Included in the stash was one of the photographs you now hold before you.'

'I don't understand,' Gustaw replied, frustration growing within him.

'All will become clear, my friend,' the old man said. 'Please be patient. I questioned the Spaniard and he refused to say anything. I brought up the girl's murder and still he would not talk. Then once again I received a visit from the British intelligence officers. As before, they announced that they would carry out the investigation. They then left with the Spaniard and the photographs. All the photographs save one, that is.'

Lorenz nodded towards the less-worn photograph in Gustaw's hands.

'The one of your father I kept. I don't know why. I suppose I was angry at once again being relieved of my duties. Months later the Spaniard killed himself while awaiting trial on charges of spying for the Germans. Word was that the photographs had been used to blackmail serving Allied officers. Forcing them to carry out acts of treachery and sabotage.'

'You are saying that my father became a traitor?' Gustaw interrupted, his confusion turning to anger.

Doggedly the old man continued his account: 'I didn't know. There was nothing I could do. The war continued and my work went on, but always I wondered about that girl. So brutally and callously slaughtered. Who was she? Where were her family? What of the baby Rosia growing up without her mama? These thoughts stayed with me long after the war had ended. Finally, three years ago I retired, and at last I was free to find out who she was. For weeks I visited everywhere, both here and over in La Línea. All fruitless. No one remembered the girl, or if they did, they were not prepared to share that information with a retired Gibraltarian police officer. Eventually I gave up.'

'And that was that?' Gustaw replied, disappointed by the old man's account.

'No, no. As chance would have it, I found myself in Seville two years ago. I was staying with an old colleague who lived there. He had known for years about my interest in the blackmail case and how frustrated I had felt to be sidelined by the intelligence services. One evening, out of the blue, he told me that he knew an elderly British MI6 officer who had retired to a house on the outskirts of the city. Next day he took me to see him. The man in question was in his eighties and in failing health, but he agreed to tell me what little he knew.'

Lorenz paused to sip from a glass of water on the table beside him. The room was hot and the noise from the street below was increasing as midday approached. Gathering himself once more, Lorenz continued.

'His name was Lorimer, and he'd been a station officer in Lisbon for most of the war. He told me that he had been informed of certain facts regarding the case. I'm sad to tell you he confirmed that the man in the picture was a Polish major called Jasinski. Czesław Jasinski.'

GIBRALTAR DOCKS, 1942

MAJOR CZESŁAW JASINSKI stood alone at the far end of the quay. Fifty metres behind him, the business of preparing for battle continued. Army lorries and supply trucks ferrying men and equipment to where they needed to be. Ahead of the major lay the dark, still water of the harbour and, beyond that, the constant stream of naval ships and troop carriers crossing the Bay of Gibraltar.

But here, he was alone. Taking a deep breath, he pulled his right arm back and then, swinging it forward with as much force as he could muster, he sent his briefcase hurtling out across the water. Less than an hour had passed since it had failed to detonate its deadly explosive contents. For nearly half of that time, the major had sat waiting for death to engulf both him and his fellow officers in the room. Death had not come. The military briefing, deep in the tunnels of the Rock, had concluded, and the target of his thwarted assassination had walked smartly from the conference room. Calling out his customary farewell of 'Good luck!', General Dwight Eisenhower had moved swiftly to the Operation Torch command room to continue his preparations for the Allied invasion of north Africa. The great soldier would live and most probably succeed in all he did, the major thought. After all, one man's failure was another man's triumph. Or at least so he hoped. For him, though, it was too late. How had it come to this? Even now he could not understand why he had been chosen. Why God had deemed it necessary to punish Jasinski and his poor helpless family so harshly.

Reaching into his wallet, he took out the tiny capsule that would end the nightmare. He had been given it a year before, on a secret operation to Cairo. It was common currency in the theatres of war he had become expert in. Cyanide. Safe passage to oblivion.

Placing the poison in his mouth, the major looked up once more at the Rock. How transient human life was compared to that never-changing edifice. Turning back at last, he closed his eyes. The faces of his beloved wife and children filled his thoughts once more. Biting down hard on the capsule, he felt a sharp burning at the back of his throat. In the few moments he had left, Jasinski tried to quell the sudden rage of injustice that rose within him. But it was too late. His head now began to swim and an overpowering pain filled his chest. Swaying momentarily, he finally willed his body to fall forward into the waters of the harbour. Something at last had gone to plan. Czesław Jasinski would disappear from the world forever.

Irish Town, 1964

LORENZ PAUSED FOR a moment, the pain in his visitor's eyes all too visible. Slowly, he continued.

The major's body had been pulled from the harbour days before Operation Torch, he told Gustaw. All he knew was that the officer had killed himself. A briefcase containing explosives had been found floating against the harbour wall and criminal activity was immediately suspected. Sabotage missions had been a constant threat on the Rock. Agents and double-agents working for the Abwehr, the Nazi military intelligence service, were an ever-present threat. At least two other officers – another Pole and a Canadian – had been caught up in blackmail plots and turned. The unofficial word was that they had been set up by a German spy operating on the Rock. It was believed that the spy was a woman and that her Abwehr codename was 'Diamant'. That was the *unofficial* word. The *official* word was soon given by British intelligence. The case was now classified and under investigation. The RGP, not for the first or last time, was left out in the cold.

Lorenz saw that Gustaw had tears running down his cheeks. The news that his father had not died a hero but instead had been the victim of a sordid plot was too much for him.

'The girl's identity may never be known,' Lorenz said softly. 'But I'm sorry you've had to wait so long to hear such awful news.'

Gustaw wiped his face with the back of his hand and straightened his back.

'Please ... I need water ...'

POLICE HQ, GIBRALTAR, TODAY

'PLEASE ... I NEED water.' Lech Jasinski looked directly at Sullivan. 'It is difficult for me to pour.' The Pole raised his hands to remind her of his cuffed wrists. Sullivan reached for the jug, poured water into a paper cup and placed it in Jasinski's hands.

'Thank you, Tamara.' He smiled. 'Thank you.'

Although the detectives had listened patiently to Jasinski's story, they knew that, outside the room, pressure was mounting to get a result. Caught between the need to push hard for answers and a requirement to consider Jasinski's medical condition, they had taken the gentler path. Facts were coming, but not enough answers.

'So what did your father do next?' Broderick asked, determined to move on swiftly.

'He went home, Chief Inspector.'

'He left it at that?' Sullivan questioned.

'Not in his mind,' Jasinski replied. 'All his life, it ate away at him. Not knowing who Diamant was. He *knew* Diamant was responsible for deaths of his mother and sisters also. If it was blackmail and my father fail in his mission, the Germans would want to punish him. That is why photograph was left in house and family was taken away to die.'

Jasinski slowly raised the paper cup to his lips and drank the water.

'He knew that for a fact?' Sullivan asked.

'No. But that is what happened. Some things become clear even without all the facts, Tamara.'

'And did he get results?' Broderick pushed.

'Nothing. He received one letter from Lorenz a few weeks after the visit. It surprised my father. Lorenz told him that past should be forgotten and that to continue to pursue this could lead to danger. He did not explain how or why. Not long after, my father learned that Lorenz died. Poisoned. Police were certain it was murder. They could not prove it, though.'

'We'll check,' Broderick said.

'Lorenz's death was a warning, Chief Inspector. One my father took notice of.'

'You're telling us that Lorenz was murdered to stop him investigating further?' Sullivan asked.

'That is what my father believed.'

'And so he stopped looking?'

'Yes. My mother was ill. I was child. There were more pressing matters to concern him.'

'So what changed?' Sullivan asked.

'For years, nothing. Then, just months before he died, he read in newspaper about film – *Queen of Diamonds*. He could not believe his eyes. World may think Queen of Diamonds is made up, but my father knew she had lived and that her real codename was Diamant. When I visited him in hospital, he would tell me about it over and over. The pain and anger were still within him, you understand? So angry that people would make hero out of one so evil. But he was helpless. As he lay dying, I swore to him, my father, that I would find out truth. That is what brought me here. That is why I would not kill. There has been too much death at Diamant's hands already.'

CHAPTER 62

'WELL?'

Massetti projected her question towards the door, over the heads of the busy detectives working in the incident room. Sullivan and Broderick, who had just entered, had not noticed their boss sitting in the far corner. With her crutches beside her, she was resting her swollen ankle on an upturned waste paper basket. The chief super waved them over.

'Well?' she repeated.

'Jasinski's taking another rest,' Broderick answered. 'Headaches are coming back, he says.'

'I bet they are,' Massetti replied.

'He also says he's innocent of the murders. Just wanted to protest about the film,' Sullivan added, perching on the edge of a desk. 'So if you've been hoping for a quick confession, I'm afraid it's not on the cards, ma'am.'

'What do you think, Broderick?' Massetti asked.

'He seems lucid enough. The reasons he gives for coming to Gib and his feelings about the film seem genuine. But the fact is, he was here on the Rock and over in Spain at the time of the killings. We now know that he has motive in spades and a mental condition that could easily have pushed him to murder. He held Isolde at knife-point and, from where I was standing, looked dangerous enough to deliver on his threats.'

'What's the status on Isolde, ma'am?' Sullivan enquired.

'Not brilliant. Locked himself in Julia Novacs' Winnebago and swallowed a bucketload of painkillers. It's touch and go whether he pulls through.'

'Poor man,' Sullivan sighed.

'Novacs has apparently pulled out of the film and taken off for Paris,' Massetti continued. 'Can't say I blame her.'

'Anything yet from Spanish police?' Broderick asked.

'Just added background on the two men. As we know, Martínez was a wealthy businessman – property mostly. Came from poor origins. Brought up in La Línea, but got out when the money came rolling in. Two children living abroad. A recluse in recent years. The Englishman may have a connection with Cornwallis and his work. But why Jasinski should want to murder two elderly men is still anyone's guess.'

All three pondered this for a moment.

'How's the fracture, ma'am?' Sullivan finally asked.

'Possibly the most painful thing I've ever experienced, Sullivan. And I've given birth to two children,' the chief super replied. 'But thanks for your concern.'

DC Calbot approached the trio from the far side of the room.

'Cakes and an estate agent,' he announced.

'What are you talking about?' Broderick demanded.

'Neither of the supermarkets or smaller shops sell the cake we found in Cornwallis's apartment. The manager at Morrisons and several others think it's homemade and not a retail product at all.'

Broderick gave the detective constable a withering look. 'So are we really considering the possibility that Jasinski baked a cake?'

'Just telling you what's been said, guv,' Calbot said.

'And the estate agent?' Massetti questioned.

'An estate agent, as well as a waitress and the landlord of The Angry Friar, have all stated that they saw Jasinski several times as he waited outside the Convent between the hours of 1.00 and 5.30 yesterday. The waitress at the cafe says she was aware of Jasinski hanging around all afternoon.'

'And Portillo's certain of the time of Cornwallis's death?' Massetti asked.

'As much as she can be, ma'am,' Sullivan confirmed. 'She puts it between 3 pm and 6 pm.'

'He might have slipped away,' Broderick suggested.

'To make it across town, murder Cornwallis and then get back again would have taken Jasinski away from the Convent for well over an hour. Most probably more,' Sullivan said.

'Oh, for God's sake!' Massetti cried, slapping the desk in anger. 'I don't need to hear this. We have one suspect and he better be our murderer. I've just seen the three of us on a CNN bulletin, for crying out loud. We're playing on news channels worldwide. So believe me when I tell you, I'm not going to be the one to inform them that we've got the wrong guy. Understood?'

'And if we have?' Sullivan ventured.

'We haven't!' Broderick snapped. 'We need the Wombles to come back with the forensics, that's all. I predict Jasinski's DNA will be all over the shop. So right now, I suggest we don't panic and that we continue with good old-fashioned police work.'

'In what direction, exactly?' Massetti asked.

'For a start, we need to find out why Jasinski needed to kill Martínez and Maugham,' Broderick replied, turning to Sullivan. 'Also check out the Inspector Lorenz story in the RGP archives.

For all we know, Jasinski's entire story could be part of some schizophrenic delusion. Ma'am, if you'd be so good as to keep the pressure up on our Spanish compadres, I'll do the same with Jasinski. Something will give, and soon.'

'It better had,' Massetti said. 'In the meantime, will one of you help me out of this bloody chair?'

CHAPTER 63

JASINSKI SAT IN his empty cell. Through the small hatch in the heavy metal door, a police constable kept constant watch over him. His head ached and his entire body felt wired; he had to clench and unclench his hands to rid himself of the strain.

The worst of it was that he was beginning to believe that he might have killed others. People were saying he had. They were accusing him of crimes that, in his heart, he knew he would not commit. But what if he had? What if he had murdered the men as they said? What if he *had* finally become insane enough to lose control of his mind and actions? Again and again, he had gone over the past few days. He was convinced that he could remember and account for all his actions. The chronology of events since he arrived in Spain was crystal clear to him. Murder had never been a part of his plan. It had never even entered his mind. But if his mind had been lost, how could he really know?

Lech Jasinski lay down on the hard bed and curled into a ball. Only sleep could save him now. Darkness, unconsciousness. He prayed it would come swiftly.

CHAPTER 64

SULLIVAN PASSED THROUGH the iron gates at the front of New Mole House and stepped out onto the pavement. Taking a deep breath and sipping the coffee she had brought from the police canteen, it felt good to clear her head. Only two TV crews remained stationed outside police HQ, awaiting breaking news. The reporters looked at Sullivan and rightly deduced nothing new would come from her direction.

Crossing the road, Sullivan came to a halt by the wall overlooking the dry docks fifteen metres below. Gazing down, she could see the whole site was a hive of activity. Two of the three dry docks were occupied by ships undergoing repair. Engineers and workers scurried about like ants to the sounds of drill and hammer. Out across the busy bay, ships of many sizes lay at anchor or continued on their way to other destinations and ports of call. The afternoon sun on her face was baking, but the gentle breeze made it bearable. The strong scent of the sea and the invisible, life-enhancing force of ozone made Sullivan feel immediately revitalised. A rush of caffeine from her skinny latte had also begun to play its part.

'Wotcha.'

The voice behind her was Calbot's, and for a moment Sullivan's heart sank.

'You can stroll across the road with a nice cup of coffee, but you can't hide, Sarge.' Calbot was pulling what Sullivan recognised as his "handsome" face.

'Clearly not,' she replied, watching him light up a cigarette.

'If you can't stand the heat, get out of the police station,' Calbot continued with a second stab at humour.

'Massetti's under pressure. Shit comes down,' Sullivan said.

'Look, don't think this is out of order, but I'm having a sort of dinner party next week,' Calbot said, leaning against the wall and running his hand through his thick brown hair. 'At my place, just me and two or three others from work. Not sure who. Nobody aggravating, though. Wondered if you might be up for it?'

Taken aback, Sullivan did not quite know how to respond.

Calbot continued: 'I'm a pretty good cook. Italian stuff mainly. Liguine al frutti di mare is my speciality. Not a veggie, are you?'

'No, I'm not,' Sullivan replied with a smile. 'It'll be a Come Dine with Calbot sort of thing, will it?'

'If you like, but without a stupid theme. You don't have to come dressed up as a pop star or a nurse or anything. Unless you want to, that is.'

Try as she might, Sullivan could not help but be charmed by her colleague. He flirted with all the subtlety of a teenager holidaying in Magaluf. But the sheer transparency and obviousness of his guile somehow made up for that.

'I'll think about it,' Sullivan replied.

'To tell the truth, it's a celebration, really.'

'Of what?' she asked.

'It's not official, but DS Marquez is retiring, and everyone knows I'm the next one up for promotion,' Calbot told her, with a confidence that took her breath away. 'Word's out it'll be confirmed beginning of next week.'

'You know that for a fact, do you?' Sullivan asked.

'Nothing's been said, but that's how it works. There's no one else ready for the job, so it has to be mine.'

Unless the position's already been offered to someone else, Sullivan thought. She was not going to burst Calbot's balloon, especially as she had not made up her own mind about the job. However, if she accepted the offer of a permanent job with the RGP, the dinner invitation from Calbot would most likely be rescinded. *Every cloud's got a silver lining,* she mused as she finished her coffee.

'Back to work, I think, Calbot.'

'On my way, Sarge,' Calbot replied, throwing his cigarette to the ground and eyeballing Sullivan's shapely figure as she strode away from him. 'Most definitely on my way.'

CHAPTER 65

SULLIVAN DID NOT have long to wait for the Lorenz files to be delivered to her desk. Historic police records were stored in a section of the government's archive, and a quick phone call from Massetti had elicited an immediate response.

Three files arrived, the first of which contained two pages that confirmed that Inspector Lorenz had been the investigating officer of the young prostitute's murder in November 1942. The second file also confirmed him as the investigating officer in the arrest of the Spanish dockworker who had been found with the compromising photograph of the prostitute and the Polish major. Both reports stated that the cases had been taken over by the Security Intelligence Department of the Rock's Defence Security Office. From that point on, they were classified 'Top secret' and the RGP's involvement terminated. Just as Jasinski had told them.

On the front of the third file was a covering note from a clerk in the archives. She informed Sullivan that the file had been deposited with them after the death of Inspector Lorenz in 1964, and because it appeared to be connected to what the detective was looking for, she had sent it across with the others. Within moments of opening it, Sullivan was grateful that the clerk had done so. The file, was considerably thicker than the other two, included information about the police investigation into Inspector Lorenz's death.

Twenty minutes later, Sullivan was at Broderick's desk, briefing him and Calbot on the file's contents.

'Lorenz was found dead in his apartment on 28 October 1964. The post-mortem concluded that death was caused by arsenic poisoning. There was no suicide note and so foul play was immediately suspected. Police duly took statements from the last people to see him alive. One name on that list might interest you, guv.'

Sullivan handed the document over to the chief inspector to see for himself.

'Dear God!' Broderick exclaimed, after seeing the first name on the list. '"Señor Eduardo Martínez", he read. '"Resident of San Roque, Spain".'

'I've read his statement. Martínez had a cousin named Marisella who disappeared in Gibraltar during the war. She lived in La Línea with her parents and eight-month-old baby – its father had walked out before the child was even born, according to Martínez. One day Marisella went to work at the fruit and vegetable depot here in Gib, but never returned home.'

'And the RGP investigated?' Broderick asked.

'Of course, but apparently came up with nothing. Marisella's family took her disappearance badly. They were a close-knit lot. They had also depended on her income to survive. The repercussions were horrific. Months later, the mother died, apparently from grief, and Martínez says that the baby was placed in an orphanage.'

'And Marisella's father?' Calbot asked.

'Shot himself. Borrowed a revolver from a friend and blew his head off in a field near Jimena de la Frontera.'

Calbot whistled slowly through his teeth. 'Jeez.'

'So Martínez kept the search going?' Broderick questioned, rolling his neck to relieve the tension.

'As best he could, but the years passed and he gave up,' Sullivan continued. 'Then in 1964 he heard that a photograph of a girl resembling his cousin was circulating on the Rock. He made enquiries, which led him to Lorenz's apartment in Irish Town –'

'– where the inspector showed him a picture of a certain young woman in bed with a Polish officer and told him that she was later found murdered,' Calbot interrupted.

'Exactly. That's where Jasinski's story links with the Martínez statement. The Spaniard was devastated by the news. First, by the manner of his cousin's death, and then by the realisation that she'd been working as a prostitute. He then, naturally, wanted to know why her death hadn't been investigated.'

'And Lorenz told him what he'd told Jasinski's father. Tales of Diamant, blackmail, suicide, murder and British intelligence,' Broderick concluded.

'Exactly,' Sullivan confirmed. 'Jasinski's father had only left the Rock a few days prior to the Martínez meeting. It's interesting that Martínez doesn't mention the Pole's name. Maybe Lorenz kept that from him. One thing is clear, though: the case was finally coming together for Lorenz. He told Martínez that he had new information that might identify the Queen of Diamonds. He also mentioned that he was being watched, and that his life might be in danger. The inspector finally warned Martínez to keep a low profile until he got more information. Three days later Lorenz was found poisoned.'

'So what did Martínez do?' Calbot asked, sitting forward in his chair.

'At the time of the statement, he said he was making enquiries with government and the intelligence services in both Gib and the UK,' Sullivan said. 'One can only assume that that was how he came into contact with Graeme Maugham.'

'What about the police investigation into Lorenz's death?' Broderick asked.

'Put on the shelf, sir.'

'But they had a written statement that claimed that Lorenz thought his life was in danger. They must have done something about it,' Broderick replied.

'The investigation could find no evidence to back that up. They even tried to interview Martínez again, but they never got him back over the border.'

Broderick stood and made for the door.

'Let's get this to Massetti.'

CHAPTER 66

POLICE CONSTABLE ARGOS had called the nurse over to the cell door. Through its hatch, they could see Jasinski pacing up and down in a highly agitated state. The Pole had tried to sleep, but his mind was full of dark and bloody images from his past. Women and children lying dead in bombed-out houses in Iraqi villages. Limbless and torn-apart torsos spread across Arabic market places. Victims of teenage suicide bombers. The faces of colleagues flashed in front of him, all friends taken violently by death and haunting him still, their voices rising in volume within his head until finally reaching screaming pitch. He could take no more.

Turning to the wall, Jasinski rushed towards it, smashing his head into its brick-hard centre. The crack of his skull and the snap of nose cartilage sent pain searing through his body. It was not enough. As the blood streamed down his face, and as PC Argos fumbled with the key to the cell door, Jasinski hammered his head once more against the wall. And again. And again. He would not stop until oblivion took him.

Chapter 67

MASSETTI WAS ON the phone as Sullivan and Broderick entered her office.

'Yes, sir. I fully understand.' She waved at the detectives to take a seat. 'We'll have forensic results by midday tomorrow. In the meantime, we're pursuing every line of enquiry. As I said, I fully appreciate your concerns. Thank you for your support, sir.'

The call over, Massetti focused on her officers.

'That was the deputy chief minister. Very understanding, but naturally concerned that we get results ASAP. Says the whole thing is sending out the wrong signals to the world. Threat to the image of Gibraltar – 'a safe haven for people and a safe haven for investment', et cetera, et cetera. So you'd better be here to cheer me up. What have you got, Broderick?'

'A corroborative statement of Jasinski's back story by none other than Eduardo Martínez, ma'am.'

Massettti raised her eyebrows in surprise.

'It seems he met with Inspector Lorenz back in 1964. Just before the policeman died and just after Jasinski's father's visit to the Rock.'

'A statement?' Massetti queried.

'Yes, ma'am,' Sullivan said. 'Martínez was one of the last people to see Lorenz alive. They met just three days before the inspector died of arsenic poisoning. The RGP interviewed him as part of a possible murder investigation. Martínez had visited him because he'd heard that the inspector had a photograph of a woman who looked like a missing relative of his.'

Broderick continued the story. 'It was a copy of the same photograph Gustaw Jasinski had brought with him to the Rock, ma'am. The army officer in the picture was Jasinski's grandfather, Major Czesław Jasinski, and the woman in bed with him was Eduardo Martínez's cousin, Marisella.'

'All very interesting ...' Massetti said thoughtfully. 'But how does that help us with the deaths of our three victims?'

'Both Jasinski and Martínez had lost close relatives, and after meeting Lorenz, they blamed the deaths on an espionage operation allegedly run by a Nazi agent codenamed Diamant, aka the Queen of Diamonds.'

'How much of this has been confirmed by official sources?' Massetti demanded. 'By British intelligence services, for one.'

'None of it, ma'am. Although we've confirmed that the intelligence services took over the case from Lorenz in '42, which suggests that there's some truth in all this. Frustratingly, their investigations remain classified.' Sullivan moved forward in her seat. 'Ma'am, can we run with this for a moment?'

Massetti shrugged. 'Okay.'

'Jasinski, Cornwallis, Martínez and Maugham are joined by one common denominator – the so-called Queen of Diamonds. We have only hearsay as proof that she existed at all, but our three murder victims and Jasinski all seem to have been convinced that she did. Cornwallis wrote a film about her, Martínez and Jasinski believed she was responsible for the deaths of their loved ones, and Maugham was an expert on espionage and spying during the period that Diamant was allegedly active on the Rock. Can we agree on that?'

Massetti and Broderick nodded.

Sullivan continued: 'Three of the men have been murdered in very similar circumstances, and naturally our suspicions have fallen on the fourth member of the group, Jasinski. We know he had a grievance against Cornwallis for attempting to present Diamant as a heroine. But what was his grievance with Martínez and Maugham? Martínez's cousin Marisella was as much a victim as Jasinski's father. Maugham would have had his own story to tell, but at the very least he must have had access to information so far denied to us.'

'So you don't think Jasinski did it?' Massetti questioned.

'I'm not saying that. What I *am* saying is that it doesn't quite add up. I also truly believe that, even if he did kill those men, Jasinski has no recollection of doing so –'

'Blackouts?' Broderick interrupted, slight irritation in his voice.

'Maybe. I just don't buy it.'

'So what *do* you buy, Detective Sergeant?' Massetti asked, glancing at Broderick.

'There's someone else we haven't considered yet, ma'am.'

'Who, for God's sake?' Broderick asked.

A sharp tap on Massetti's door was quickly followed by Sergeant Aldarino's hurried entrance into the room.

'Sorry to interrupt, ma'am. Jasinski's had a fit in the cells. I think you need to come immediately.'

CHAPTER 68

FOR THE SECOND time in as many days, an ambulance pulled away from the front of police HQ. The television crews, which had been waiting patiently outside, had leapt into action and were now following the ambulance at speed. Somehow, as they followed in a police squad car, Sullivan and Broderick found themselves beaten into fourth place.

Broderick looked at the TV vans ahead of them with growing frustration. 'Let's get those bastards for speeding if nothing else,' he told Sullivan, making a note of the vehicles' registration numbers and company logos.

The sight that had greeted the detectives on arrival at Jasinski's cell had been alarming. Three police constables had been called in to restrain the Pole and were now holding him down while the nurse attempted to sedate him. Jasinski's face was almost unrecognisable. His nose had clearly been broken, his lips split and bruised and his hair and face were smeared with blood.

'He went berserk,' Aldarino informed them. 'Just smashed his head against the wall. Nurse says to transfer him to St Bernard's for examination and head X-rays. She thinks his medication may not have been balanced.'

Following the ambulance along Rosia Road through the busy late afternoon traffic, Broderick and Sullivan continued their conversation.

'What were you trying to tell Massetti and me?' Broderick asked.

'I was suggesting that we need to look outside the box, guv,' she replied, shielding her eyes from the bright sun in the west.

'So where do you suggest we start?'

'Let's take Jasinski out of the equation for a moment.'

'What?'

'Just imagine that he only did what he's admitted to doing.'

'Oh, I see. Just the breaking and entering, assault and kidnapping, you mean?'

'Yes,' Sullivan continued, ignoring her boss's tone. 'All that, but none of the murders.'

'Go on.'

'On the night before he died, Cornwallis met with Martínez in San Roque. What if Martínez arranged to see him because he wanted to tell Cornwallis about his own family's experiences at the hands of the Queen of Diamonds? Cornwallis was depicting her as a brave double-agent working for the Allies, yes? What if Martínez's revelations had upset the screenwriter? Upset him enough to change things in his script? Or worse, make him worry that the film might be discredited?'

'A big "what if", Sullivan,' Broderick replied.

'We're outside the box, guv, remember?'

The chief inspector nodded, struggling to remain patient.

'What I'm saying is: what if Martínez had threatened to tell his story?' Sullivan said. 'How would Cornwallis react? His film, his reputation, his future would all be on the line. And not just his. Who would Cornwallis have turned to for help?'

Broderick stared at Sullivan, the penny dropping. 'Are you suggesting ...?'

'Gabriel Isolde.'

'But ...'

'Gabriel Isolde. The only person who would have more to lose from the film's demise than Cornwallis. Years of work, millions of pounds in investment, his professional reputation, all lost because his film's heroine was in reality a double-crossing murderess. How desperate would that have made him to stop the truth from coming to light?'

'Where was Isolde when the killings took place?' Broderick asked, already knowing the answer.

'He's shown on CCTV arriving at the Atlantic Marina Plaza just after 3.00 in the afternoon and leaving at 5.30 to go to the reception.'

'But what about San Roque that evening?'

'He was definitely in Spain. Took the helicopter to Marbella with Novacs and then drove back to Gib. He said he stopped on the way to recce a location at La Alcaidesa. That's barely ten minutes from San Roque,' Sullivan replied with growing excitement.

'And his phone was out of charge for nearly two hours as I recall,' Broderick added. 'Convenient, that.'

'We can place him at or near to both murder scenes. If he had the motive to kill and silence the three men ... he could be our murderer.'

The buzz of Broderick's mobile interrupted their enthusiasm for Sullivan's new theory. The name on the screen was Massetti. Broderick took the call.

'Ma'am?' he answered. 'Not quite at St Bernard's yet. I see.

That's very interesting, ma'am. Right, thank you. Yes, that could be helpful.'

Broderick ended the call and turned to his detective sergeant. 'Cake again,' he announced. 'The Spanish have followed up on our pathology findings. They say Martínez and Maugham had also eaten cake before they died, and like the wine, it had high levels of Rohypnol in it.'

'Cake?' Sullivan queried.

'Slices of *bizcocho* were on the Martínez coffee table with the wine and coffee, remember?' Broderick said. 'It's Spanish sponge cake. Not a patch on a coffee and walnut cake, I grant you, but okay-ish.'

'Unless it's packed full of Rohypnol.'

'Obviously,' Broderick said, regretting his sweet-toothed enthusiasm.

'And I bet it was home-made, just like the Cornwallis one,' Sullivan added. 'Tell me, guv, does Isolde strike you as the kind of man who could bake a cake?'

'Easily, Sullivan,' Broderick replied with a rare smile. 'Very easily.'

CHAPTER 69

PASSING THE SCULPTED family on the Gibraltar Evacuation Monument on Waterport Road, the convoy of vehicles approached St Bernard's hospital. The impressive state-of-the-art medical facility had been created within a large converted office building constructed on land reclaimed from the Bay of Gibraltar. Its Accident & Emergency Department had been alerted and staff were now waiting for the incoming casualty from police HQ.

TV cameras and reporters were up and running at the A&E entrance as Sullivan and Broderick raced from their car and followed Jasinski and the paramedics into the hospital.

'Can you tell us what's happened?' one reporter yelled into Broderick's face.

'Is that Lech Jasinski being admitted to the hospital?' cried another.

'Has he tried to take his own life or has he been the victim of police brutality?'

Sensing that her boss was about to deal with the last question in a less than diplomatic manner, Sullivan placed her hand on the small of his back and firmly pushed him forward and through the doors of the hospital.

'Bastards!' Broderick exclaimed under his breath.

'Yes, guv. But best left to themselves,' Sullivan answered, heading for the reception desk.

Within a minute, a young female doctor was briefing them.

'He seems to have wreaked havoc on himself,' Dr Felice informed the detectives. 'He's in and out of consciousness, and we suspect he may have badly fractured his skull.'

'He went berserk,' Sullivan told her. 'One minute he seemed fine and the next ...'

'Judging from his condition, he might have been avoiding medication,' Felice replied.

'The nurse has been giving him his meds since his arrest,' Broderick informed her.

'You'd be surprised what patients can get away with if they really want to. Be worth checking, though. Either way, it'll be an hour or so before we have a better picture.'

'How's Gabriel Isolde?' Broderick asked, changing tack. 'We'd like talk to him if possible.'

'Mr Isolde is still unconscious, but showing some improvement. I'm afraid he won't be of any assistance to you quite yet, Chief Inspector.'

'I see,' Broderick replied, handing the doctor his card. 'We'll leave two constables with Jasinski and I've asked for another officer to be stationed outside Isolde's door. As soon as you learn anything about either of our patients, please contact me on that number.'

The doctor smiled thinly and headed back into the department.

Broderick sighed. 'Well, that's just great. Two suspects and we can't get near either of them.'

'Massetti's going to have a fit.'

'I don't care about that. What I care about is presenting Massetti with your new theory, backed up with actual evidence.'

'We'll need help from the Cuerpo, guv. Check out Isolde's Spanish alibi. The more we find out about why Martínez met Cornwallis and what the old man had to tell him, the better.'

'The Cuerpo and Guardia will help us,' Broderick observed. 'Leave that to me. I'll call in some favours and I might even ask an old mate of mine to help out. In an unofficial capacity.'

'Sounds intriguing,' Sullivan replied, knowing better than to ask for more details.

'You and Calbot check out Isolde's history more fully and I'll get Massetti to go "upstairs" for some leverage on finding links to British intelligence.'

'Okay, guv.'

'Oh ... and this is awkward ...' Broderick turned to Sullivan tentatively.

'Guv?'

'My sister Cath is taking the girls to Roy's in Casemates Square at 6.00 for a fish and chip supper. She asked me to ask you if you fancied joining them. I'm sure you haven't time, but at least I've asked.'

'Are *you* going, sir?' Sullivan enquired, enjoying Broderick's discomfort at asking.

'I shouldn't, but I promised, and besides, I'm bloody well starving.'

Sullivan checked her watch. It was 5.45 pm already. 'Massetti will have a fit if she ...'

'Aldarino will cover. The slightest development and I'll be back here before you can say "Cod and mushy peas", Broderick countered.

'Well, in that case … I'll make a call and then join you,' Sullivan replied. 'All work and no play can make coppers rather dull in my experience. Wouldn't you agree, guv?'

Broderick didn't know what to say. Settling for a shrug of his shoulders and a muffled grunt, the chief inspector turned to the main door and caught sight of the waiting camera crews. Without hesitation, he turned on his heel and headed in the opposite direction.

'Let's take the back door, Sullivan.'

Chapter 70

RIC DANAHER STEADIED himself and slowly stood upright. Balancing carefully at the apex of the *finca*'s roof, he looked out across the almost uninterrupted landscape spreading westwards as far as the eye could see. The Rock of Gibraltar, forty kilometres southwest of where he stood, was seemingly the only obstacle between him, the sea and the Atlas Mountains of Morocco beyond.

Looking out from his lonely vantage point on the outskirts of the hillside town of Gaucín, Ric felt a sense of calm and belonging. It had been eight years since he had first set eyes on the isolated farmhouse. It had taken him three to finally leave London's Metropolitan Police Service and give himself over to a quieter life in Spain. With a reasonable pension, supplemented by occasional work as a private detective on the Costa del Sol, life was sweet. A feeling enhanced by the closeness he now enjoyed with his daughter Consuela, both geographically and emotionally. The acrimonious divorce from her Spanish mother twenty-three years earlier had made their relationship difficult at first. When his wife had left the UK for Spain with the three-year-old Consuela, Danaher had become determined that his daughter would not disappear from his life. It had not been easy over the years, but buying the farmhouse and making Spain his permanent residence had finally made it possible.

Shielding his eyes against the sun, Danaher looked out on his hillside retreat. Several hundred olive trees spread down the slope towards the river below. Harshly dried vegetation sprouted between outcrops of dark grey rock and slopes of parched thin soil. For two hours, as he had worked unceasingly to repair and replace the red clay tiles on the main part of the old Spanish farmhouse, the scent of myrtle carried on the warm breeze had given his senses the pleasure it had always done.

In the kitchen below, Consuela was busy preparing an early supper for the two of them. She had arrived from her home in Estepona just after lunch and immediately set about imposing order on the *finca*'s interior. By the time Danaher climbed down from the roof and entered his home, he knew it would be clean and tidy. He also knew that it would take him only a few hours to return it to the topsy-turvy domestic landscape he enjoyed and needed. Mixing with the myrtle now came the full, flavoursome smell of one of his daughter's delicious *tagines*. They would eat soon and talk. Then Danaher would walk Consuela to her car and watch her drive off down the dusty narrow track to work. She was on nights this week, and as a detective with the Spanish police in Málaga, the twenty-six-year-old was working long, punishing hours.

Reaching down to manoeuvre yet another tile into place, the stillness of the late afternoon was interrupted by the sound of a mobile ringing. Moments later Consuela appeared on the terrace below, holding Danaher's phone.

'Dad ... it's Gus Broderick calling.'

Now that's interesting, Danaher thought as he gazed down at his beautiful daughter.

'Answer it will you, love? I'm coming right down.'

Chapter 71

AS PREDICTED, MASSETTI had reacted badly to the medical embargo on interviews with Jasinski. Broderick called her from the street as he and Sullivan walked towards Casemates Square. Sullivan could tell that he was relieved not to be talking to her face to face. Both detectives had decided not to inform Massetti of their suspicions about Isolde. Better to build a stronger case for the producer's guilt than risk the chief super chucking it out 'early doors' for lack of detail. Sullivan had called Calbot and told him to concentrate his enquiries on Isolde for the rest of the day, but to keep it under his hat. Broderick, meanwhile, had made a call to Spain.

'We need more background on the Martínez family,' he told Sullivan. 'I've asked a friend of mine to have a sniff around, see what he can find out.'

'And I've told Calbot we'll be back in an hour,' Sullivan replied.

'Good. Fish and chips it is then,' Broderick proclaimed

Chapter 72

CATH AND THE two girls were already sitting at an outside table at Roy's Fish Restaurant on Grand Casemates Square. The area was busy with holiday-makers and locals passing to and from Main Street or stopping at one of the many cafes for an early evening drink or meal.

As Broderick and Sullivan arrived at the family table, Cath rose to greet them.

'Hello, Tamara,' she said, kissing Sullivan on both cheeks. 'I'm so glad you could make it. You know Daisy, of course, but I not sure if you and Penny have met.'

'No, we haven't,' Sullivan confirmed. 'Good to meet you, Penny.'

'And you,' Penny replied with a smile. 'It looks like we'll be seeing a lot of each other from now on, though.'

'Oh, yes?' Broderick questioned. 'How do you figure that one?'

'I got that job in your police canteen. Start next Monday.'

'My sister's very clever,' Daisy announced triumphantly.

'Sounds like it to me,' Sullivan replied. 'Well done, Penny. Looking forward to your finest skinny latte.'

'You got it!' Penny smiled, taking to Sullivan straight away.

'You proud of her, Gus?' Cath asked her silent brother.

'Of course, I am. Nice little gap-filler till she decides which universities she's going to apply for, eh?'

'Thanks, Dad,' Penny responded, pulling a face. 'Cold teas and soggy sandwiches for you next week.'

'Story of my life,' Broderick replied, winking at his eldest daughter.

'Fish and riding whips!' Daisy demanded. 'Roy's are the best in town.'

'They certainly are, sweet pea,' Broderick agreed. 'Cod, chips, mushy peas all round and a pickled gherkin for the guv'nor!'

Within ten minutes, five heaped platefuls of cod and chips had been brought to the table. Daisy cheered at the sight of the feast and everyone set about covering the delicious food with salt, vinegar and large dollops of ketchup. It was, Sullivan happily informed everyone, the best meal she had eaten in years.

As the plates emptied and the girls chatted away to their father, Sullivan enjoyed seeing Broderick as a family man. The change in him was pronounced. The gruff and irritable professional persona had given way to a softer, smiling and more relaxed personality. She had been increasingly aware that his girls were the centre of his life, and now it was easy to understand why.

In a slight lull in the conversation, Sullivan asked about the flooding in the charity shop she had witnessed earlier in the day.

'The man stopped the water,' Daisy announced. 'But everything is wet and smells big time.'

'Bit of a disaster, really,' Cath confirmed. 'But it didn't affect the front of the shop, so we'll carry on from there until it's all sorted. Luckily the main work of the charity is done in the offices just around the corner. The shops here and over in the UK are really about keeping a raised public profile more than fundraising.

Though every little bit helps, of course.'

'Quite a big operation,' Sullivan replied.

'Big enough for me and Sister Clara,' Cath continued. 'The Rock of Ages Foundation is a nipper compared to the big boys – Oxfam, Save the Children and the like – but we still raise nearly £6 million a year. Our new orphanage in Kampala alone looks after nearly three hundred children. Our other projects in Bangladesh, Costa Rica, Haiti and Brazil care for thousands more.'

'And it's just you and Sister Clara running it all?' Sullivan asked in surprise.

'Oh, no,' Cath replied, laughing at the suggestion. 'We have a board of directors and an admin team here on the Rock. Plus teams at our centres abroad. Sister Clara is the boss, but I have quite a lot of responsibility for the day-to-day running of things.'

'Increasingly so,' Broderick chipped in.

'I've been trying to persuade Gus to retire and come work for us instead,' Cath added. 'He'd be good at it, I think. It would be a little less demanding than policing the Rock.'

'I've got a good few years in me yet, thank you very much,' Broderick countered.

'What are you wearing to the ball tomorrow night, Tamara?' Penny asked changing the subject completely. 'I'm going as Katniss Everdeen.'

The question took Sullivan by surprise. 'Ball? What ball?'

'Aunty Cath and Sister Clara's ball,' Daisy explained. 'Fancy dress. Me and Sister Clara are going as *The Sound of Music*.'

'*The Sound of Music?*'

'Yes, Daddy. I'm going as Maria and Sister Clara is going as the Mummy Abbess.'

Sullivan was now thoroughly confused.

'It's one of our fundraisers,' Cath explained. 'At the Rock Hotel tomorrow night. The theme is Hollywood films. It would be lovely if you could come along, Tamara.'

'Well, I'd love to ... if work allows,' Sullivan replied, looking to Broderick.

'Hard to say at the moment,' Broderick told them. 'Poncing about in fancy dress isn't really my cup of tea, but then again I don't really have a say in the matter.'

'No, you don't,' Penny told her father firmly. 'And please dress up as something that isn't embarrassing.'

'Last fancy dress we had, my brother came as a plain-clothes detective,' Cath added, giving Broderick a stern look. 'A little unimaginative.'

'Worked for me,' Broderick said.

'Daddy was rubbish with that one,' Daisy admonished.

'Looks like you're going to have to pull something special out of the bag, guv,' Sullivan said, enjoying seeing her boss squirm.

'And now so will you,' Broderick replied tartly.

Cath reached over and patted Sullivan's hand. 'Don't you worry about that. You're busy. I'll sort you out something wonderful to wear.'

Broderick's mobile buzzed. One look at it was enough to make Gus Broderick grimace.

'Massetti,' he announced. 'I'm afraid our little party's over.'

CHAPTER 73

BACK AT NEW Mole House, Harriet Massetti had been feeling the pressure. She and the Spanish police had issued a joint statement during afternoon confirming that there was a suspected link between the murders of Cornwallis in Gibraltar and the two men in San Roque. Certain members of the press had already drawn this conclusion after the manhunt for Jasinski was launched in Spain the previous evening. Massetti had also spent the best part of the afternoon in exhaustive talks with politicians. The chief minister and the governor of Gibraltar had shared an hour-long conference call, and the minister of justice had visited police HQ for a personal briefing. There were also her hourly updates to the commissioner, who was still desperately trying to get back from New York. Political sensitivities were running high as the story continued to be reported internationally. Sitting in her office with her throbbing ankle propped up on a chair, Massetti felt as though the eyes of the world were on Gibraltar. The demands on the chief super and her team to deliver results were intensifying by the hour.

With this burden in mind, she had decided once again to kick arse. The bollocking she had given Broderick on the phone a few minutes earlier had off-loaded a little stress. That Jasinski had harmed himself while in custody was unacceptable, she had told her chief inspector. Accusations of police brutality were already being made in radio and television news reports. It was an unfortunate and very inconvenient added pressure on a force already under the magnifying glass.

Massetti had always found comfort in the principle of 'Occam's razor' – that the simplest explanation is most likely to be the correct one. Lech Jasinski – a sufferer of severe schizophrenia – shared his father's obsession with the Queen of Diamonds. On his father's recent death, that obsession had become overpowering. Jasinski saw the movie as an obscene rewriting of history, and he would stop at nothing to prevent it happening. The resulting assaults and murders were collectively a campaign of indignation and revenge executed by a powerful man in an unbalanced state of mind. All Broderick and Sullivan had had to do was keep on at Jasinski until he was forced to admit the truth. Instead, of course, their suspect would now be in hospital for days, maybe weeks, and a confession would be unobtainable during that time. It meant that even more attention would now be paid on getting positive crime scene DNA results, which were not due from the lab till the following day.

Massetti closed her eyes. The strong painkillers she had been prescribed were making her feel faint. The mix of this and several sleepless nights finally took their toll. As her head lolled forward, Harriet Massetti drifted into light, anxious slumber. Minutes later, an embarrassed chief superintendent was awoken by a gentle tap on her shoulder from Sergeant Aldarino.

'Sorry to disturb you, ma'am, but we've just got news from the hospital.'

Chapter 74

SULLIVAN AND BRODERICK had already rushed back to St Bernard's and were being briefed by the consultant neurosurgeon, Mr Alex Mbadinuju.

'Mr Jasinski has seriously injured himself, Chief Inspector,' the Nigerian surgeon informed Broderick calmly. 'We have discovered two blood clots on his brain and considerable tissue swelling. Both conditions are the result of the patient fracturing his own skull. Usually such a presentation is the result of an accident. That Mr Jasinski inflicted this injury on himself is most alarming, and suggests considerable mental instability. I have decided that placing him in an induced coma offers the best possible chance of recovery. I am sure you appreciate just how serious this is.'

Both detectives did fully appreciate the situation and its subsequent implications for their investigation. Thanking the consultant, they left the building and headed back to New Mole House.

The first thing they learned on their arrival at HQ was how Jasinski had avoided taking his medications. Several pills had been discovered in his pockets, while others were found floating in a urinal. He had most probably secreted the tablets under his tongue and then attempted to hide them – a wilful attempt to send himself into a psychotic meltdown with inevitable violent and self-harming results.

Back in the incident room, Broderick called the team together and attempted to take stock of the new developments.

'Obviously further questioning of Jasinski is on hold until further notice. It's a mess, but one we've got to put to one side. As it happens, I was about to direct enquiries into a new area of investigation. More on that later after I've spoken with the chief super. But while we await the DNA reports, I suggest we go over the ground covered so far. Cast a forensic eye on everything we have on Jasinski, but also check for anything we may have missed. Anything that strikes you as strange. So far we've fitted the story around Jasinski's probable guilt. Don't be chained to that scenario. Think outside the box. Even if it means leaving Jasinski out of the picture. Agreed, Sullivan?'

'Absolutely, guv.'

'Start at the beginning and work through everything. Let's see what a different perspective throws up,' Broderick ordered. 'Surprise me.'

The briefing at an end, the team returned to their desks and phones. Sullivan turned to her boss. 'Well, that's set the cat among the pigeons.'

'Good,' Broderick replied, looking over the room. 'Now we'll test your new theory to the full.'

'And let Massetti in on it?'

'That as well,' Broderick replied ruefully, 'that as well.'

Calbot approached them from across the room. 'Excuse me, guv. Someone at the front desk asking to see you.'

'Oh aye? Who?'

'Woman called Aina Lascano, guv. Eduardo Martínez's housekeeper.'

Chapter 75

'SEÑORA LASCANO APOLOGISES for her lack of English,' Sergeant Aldarino translated for Sullivan and Broderick. The three police officers sat with the Spanish woman in the small interview room just off the custody suite of New Mole House. Lines on the sixty-year-old woman's face were etched deep into her weathered skin. Her eyes flicked from one detective to the other, apprehension verging on fear evident in her hesitant speech and the constant wringing of her hands. Both Sullivan and Broderick had immediately recognised her from the night before in San Roque.

'She says she's come to us because she's scared,' Sergeant Aldarino continued, as the *señora* spoke almost simultaneously in a deep, husky Andalusian dialect. 'Says she couldn't tell the Spanish police of this. She knows the local officers well – some since they were children – and thinks they'd believe she was stirring things. Making things up. You understand?'

Sullivan and Broderick nodded.

'She says that she was aware of the great sadness that Don Martínez carried in his heart for so many years. She had worked for him for nearly forty of those years and knew him well.'

Tears had sprung into Lascano's eyes. Sullivan instinctively reached across and held the woman's hand for a moment.

'Tell her we understand.'

The sergeant nodded. *'Nosotros entendemos, señora.'*

Lascano smiled and continued as Aldarino translated once again. 'She says Don Martínez and his cousin Marisella were very close growing up. Marisella had been like an elder sister to him. In later years, after the death of his beloved wife, Don Martínez would confide in her – Señora Lascano, that is – although it was often under the influence of too much wine. During these times he had told her terrifying things. Don Martínez believed that a Gibraltarian police inspector called Lorenz had been murdered because of his interest in discovering the identity of Diamant – the Queen of Diamonds. He often told the *señora* that he believed the same fate would befall him if he attempted to track her down. For this reason, he stopped looking.'

Broderick and Sullivan glanced at each other. The *señora's* story confirmed Jasinski's.

Lascano continued, warming to her task. 'One night, several years ago, Martínez went to visit a dying man who lived on the outskirts of San Roque. The man was old and had lived a dreadful life. After the war, he had been accused of informing on his Spanish friends. He and several local men had been recruited during the war by the Germans to spy in Gibraltar. It was believed that the man had then been persuaded to work for the British and had given up his colleagues to the authorities. Two of them had been hanged on the Rock as saboteurs. He had always denied these accusations and they had never been proven, but *"el barro pegado"* – the mud stuck. Despite this, Don Martínez had taken pity on him and, over the years, tried to help him when he could.'

The old woman paused for a moment and took a sip of water from the glass beside her. Clearing her throat, she (and Aldarino) continued the story. 'On the night of his final visit, Don Martínez had found the man delirious. Mistaking the *señor* for a priest, the man had finally confessed to betraying his friends to the British. He also told the *señor* about the terrible things that Diamant had done. He was terrified of her. Said she was evil. Told him she had committed murder many times, including Marisella.'

'Did he give Don Martínez the Queen of Diamonds' real name?' Broderick asked.

Aldarino translated the question and Lascano shook her head. 'No. The only information he gave was an address. A house in Gibraltar.' Lascano stopped to drink once more.

'Did Don Martínez visit that house?' Sullivan enquired.

Lascano took in the question and, through Aldarino, replied: 'No. He didn't have to. He already knew who lived there.'

'Are you saying that the Queen of Diamonds – Diamant, as you call her – was still alive?' Sullivan asked incredulously.

Once more Aldarino translated. Lascano shrugged. 'I do not know. But the knowledge of the address and what the dying man had told him seemed to possess Don Martínez. It robbed him of sleep, turned him into a ghost of his former self. He aged quickly. I couldn't bear to see it.'

'Did he tell you any else?' Broderick asked.

She shook her head again. 'He'd tell me nothing more, fearing that my life would also be in danger.'

Señora Lascano leaned forward towards the detectives, her expression intense. 'The reason I've come to you today is because I believe his fears have come true. When I heard of the death of the English writer, I knew it was connected. He used to tell me, "A little knowledge is a dangerous thing, but much knowledge can kill you." Don Martínez knew Diamant's identity, and because of that, he was murdered. His friend Señor Maugham also. That's what I believe. You must find out the truth. Promise me you will?'

Without waiting for a reply, the *señora* turned to Aldarino and nodded. All she had needed to say had been said.

CHAPTER 76

'THE QUEEN OF DIAMONDS!'

Broderick stood in front of the evidence board in the incident room. Turning to the pictures of the three murdered men pinned to it, he jabbed his finger at each image: 'Cornwallis. Martínez. Maugham.'

He continued: 'These men weren't killed by a ghost from the past. They were murdered by someone who is very much alive and motivated to kill. Señora Lascano told us a story we had heard, in part, before. She believes these murders were the result of these men attempting to discover the identity of a supposed double-agent working on the Rock during World War II. Josh Cornwallis wrote a screenplay about her. Martínez believed his cousin had been murdered by her and that Inspector Lorenz had met a similar fate decades later. Graeme Maugham was a specialist on World War II espionage, so we can presume that he, too, had knowledge of her. Also, Jasinski claims that it was because the Queen of Diamonds was responsible for the death of his grandfather that he came to the Rock – to discredit both her and the film. The common denominator here? All these men shared a deep-seated belief in a person who has officially never existed.'

Broderick turned to Calbot, standing behind the other detectives and sipping from a mug of coffee.

'Do ghosts exist, Calbot? Please tell me we have more to go on than hearsay and ancient paranoia.'

'Not much more, guv,' Calbot responded, moving across to stand next to Broderick. 'Apart from an entry in Wikipedia and a few news articles attempting to puff up the legend of the Queen of Diamonds for entertainment value, we've got nothing. I've been onto MI6, the Foreign Office, the Ministry of Defence, even put in a call to the Imperial War Museum. All about as useful as a kick in the bollocks. It seems the Queen of Diamonds shares many of the qualities we associate with the Loch Ness monster – lots of people believe in her, but nobody can prove it.'

Broderick let out a sigh of frustration.

'Okay,' he conceded, turning to address the group once more. 'Let's hope Massetti can access more information on the subject. In the meantime, Sullivan here has another theory that we need to run past the chief super. The brighter among you will have already gathered that it concerns Gabriel Isolde. Anyone turned up anything of interest on our local movie mogul?'

'As a matter of fact, I was going to flag something up, guv,' Calbot answered. 'I've been talking to Isolde's production co-ordinator, Tracy Gavin. She told me that he hasn't really been himself since he'd heard about Cornwallis and Novacs getting together. She says Isolde worshipped Cornwallis and was very possessive of him.'

'Is she suggesting a relationship between the two men?' Sullivan asked.

'Not a physical or romantic one between the two of them. She says Isolde had given up on that ever happening. However, he was very jealous of the new romance with Novacs and thought it threatened his special relationship with Cornwallis.'

'Doesn't do it for me,' Broderick responded. 'Might work for the Cornwallis murder, but why kill the other two? Besides which, all three murders were premeditated, not the result of a spontaneous fit of jealousy.'

'Gavin also mentioned that Isolde had just sacked his line producer,' Calbot continued. 'The word is that the line producer had been unhappy about some of Isolde's work practices – in particular, taking investment money from certain questionable sources.'

'Such as?' Sullivan asked.

'Gavin didn't know for sure, but she mentioned that Isolde had been in contact with several Eastern European businessmen on the Costa del Sol. Says he was always taking calls from them. Although Isolde never told her outright, she thinks they aren't entirely legit.'

'Good work,' Broderick said, patting Calbot on the shoulder. 'Follow that up. We need to know who they are and how much power they have over Isolde. If nothing else, being in hock to dubious backers would have considerably increased the pressure on him to deliver the film.'

'Maybe our three victims had somehow collectively or individually threatened the making of the film. In that case, certain other parties might have silenced them,' Sullivan said.

'Let's get all this to Massetti. Inform her we're opening a second line of enquiry centred on Isolde.'

'What about Jasinski?' Calbot enquired.

'We're still waiting for the DNA results. If they're negative, he could well be in the clear for the murders,' Broderick replied.

'And that's why we need everything we can get on our new suspect,' Sullivan added.

'Starting with an update on Isolde's condition,' Broderick ordered. 'We need to interview him as soon as possible.'

Chapter 77

IT HAD TAKEN Sullivan and Broderick less than five minutes to convince the chief super of Isolde's new status as a prime suspect.

'If we've been biased towards believing in Jasinski's possible guilt, investigating Isolde could well balance things out,' Sullivan had argued. 'With both motive and access to all of the victims, plus new information about some of his more shady business associates, Isolde is looking like a very plausible suspect, ma'am.'

'Okay,' Massetti had agreed. 'Leave no stone unturned. By the time he's ready for interview, I want you to give him nowhere to go but a full confession.'

'If he's guilty, ma'am,' Broderick added quietly.

'I'm not an idiot, Broderick!' Massetti snapped back. 'I take that for granted. But don't forget that Jasinski is still our best bet. I don't want any of you putting yourself into an induced coma about that fact. Understood?'

Acknowledging this, both detectives headed for the door.

'Oh, just one other thing, ma'am,' Broderick said, turning back. 'We need as much information as we can get on the real Queen of

Diamonds. We think it's pivotal to investigating both Jasinski and Isolde.'

'I'm doing my best, Broderick,' Massetti replied. 'The chief minister has put in an official government request for information to the British intelligence services. The governor has also promised to do what he can.'

'Good, ma'am. Hopefully they'll be a little more influential than Calbot has proved thus far.'

'I would think so!' Massetti replied, trying to hide an involuntary smile. 'If not, we may find ourselves well and truly stuffed.'

'Couldn't have put it better myself, ma'am.'

Chapter 78

THE TRAFFIC CROSSING Vauxhall Bridge early on Thursday evening was as busy as ever. Eleven hundred miles northwest of the Rock and one hour behind Gibraltar time, London was hot and uncomfortably humid.

Looking out from her office window on the eighth floor of the MI6 headquarters building on the Albert Embankment, deputy director of operations, Rachel Shapley, took in the spectacular view across the river Thames and the distant heights of north London beyond. It was a sight that always calmed her and helped her unscramble her thoughts.

The balm offered by this riverside vista was proving particularly welcome now. As both her immediate superiors were engaged in important talks abroad – one in Washington and the other in Israel – an above-average amount of responsibility had been temporarily given to her for the projected forty-eight hours of their absence. It was all proving monstrously challenging. With a morning packed with high-level intelligence meetings in Whitehall and an afternoon spent briefing and being briefed on several new and alarming developments in the Middle East and

Russia, Shapley had paid little attention to an urgent request from the chief minister of Gibraltar. On the face of it, it looked like a minor leak of classified information and, as such, well down the list of pressing international security issues and emergencies.

That had been Shapley's simple view of the matter two hours before – a perspective that had now shifted dramatically. Unable to divest herself of responsibility for it either upwards or downwards, she once more faced the realisation that, for the next twenty-four hours, the buck would stop with her. A short conversation with a senior civil servant at the Foreign Office had provided some unsettling insight into the facts behind the Gibraltar problem. It had become obvious that the situation required her personal intervention. In short, an immediate visit to the Rock. Unfortunately, Shapley could not leave her post until the return of the deputy director from Washington the following evening.

Her head now clear, Shapley realised that she had to do three things. First, inform Gibraltar that the investigation into Graeme Maugham's murder could proceed only with the upmost secrecy. Second, arrange a flight from RAF Northolt to Gibraltar at approximately 1900 hours the following evening. Third and most irritating, tell her sister that she wouldn't be able to attend her nephew's wedding on Saturday morning in Chipping Norton. That piece of news would no doubt deliver a major blow to Shapley family relations for years to come. Not for the first time she ruminated on the negative personal aspects of her job.

Moving away from her office window and back to her desk, Rachel Shapley remembered what her husband had said after viewing the fantastical goings-on in the Bond movie *Skyfall*. Seeing the MI6 headquarters being blown up by the villain Raoul

Silva, he had remarked, 'If you'd been in the office next door to yours, that bastard would have got you.' *On days like this*, Shapley thought, *the Bond baddie would have been welcome.*

CHAPTER 79

THE TRAFALGAR SPORTS Bar was uncharacteristically quiet for a Thursday night. No football match filled the super-sized TV screens that hung on the walls, drawing the eye and focusing attention away from normal conversation. Tonight's customers had only a golf tournament in Australia to entertain them, and this was proving a let-down to those addicted to a pint of Stella and adrenalin-fuelled sports entertainment.

Sullivan had allowed herself to be persuaded by Calbot and the rest of the team to unwind with a quick drink at the end of another punishing day. It had meant walking past her apartment building and the soft inviting bed within, and trekking up to the end of Rosia Road. That was where the Traf was situated, close to the cable car base station and the Alameda Botanic Gardens. On the only other occasion that she had visited the bar, it had been heaving with customers riotously enjoying a Manchester United versus Atlético Madrid cup tie from Old Trafford. She had not stayed long.

Tonight, however, nursing a chilled glass of Pinot Grigio, she was enjoying listening to her colleagues' usual joke-driven banter.

She had expected to work well beyond midnight, but after running a 'hot debrief' with the team on the events of the previous twenty-four hours, Broderick had chucked the day team out of the incident room at 10.30 pm.

'Go home, the lot of you,' he had told them. 'We're all knackered, and tomorrow is lining up to be even more demanding than the last two days have been. Go home and get your heads down.'

His advice had been taken, but not completely acted on. The visit to the Traf had been Calbot's idea, and despite initial reservations, Sullivan now considered it a good one. Not that she had totally relaxed; part of her mind was still processing the day's work.

Earlier in the evening, the team had been told by the Spanish police that certain items belonging to Martínez and Maugham appeared to have been stolen on the night of their murders. Señora Lascano had confirmed that both men's laptops had been taken, as well as a small briefcase belonging to the Englishman and a desk diary and address book used by Martínez.

They had also informed Massetti that two RGP officers had been seen in San Roque on the night, reportedly asking locals to identify a photograph of Josh Cornwallis. The Spanish police were most displeased by this and had demanded an explanation. Massetti had expressed her surprise at the news and promised to investigate further. It was a promise she had little intention of keeping.

News from the hospital was that Isolde had continued to improve slowly and that Jasinski was still in a coma. Frustratingly, there would be no contact with either of the suspects any time soon.

Calbot had set about identifying the film's financial backers. Tracy Gavin had emailed the official list across and added the names of three other people she suspected of being 'unofficial' contributors to Isolde's coffers. As she had suggested, the gentlemen in question were Russian and Romanian in origin and, according to police checks in Málaga, had dubious business interests as well as connections with gambling, sex clubs and property development along the length and breadth of the Costa del Sol.

'Not exactly the sort of people Isolde would be happy inviting to the Oscars,' Calbot had concluded.

Broderick had agreed. 'Not exactly the sort of people you want breathing down your neck, either.'

As expected, Broderick had not taken his own advice to go home, choosing instead to check through the event log and make a start on restructuring the incident room evidence board. It was going to be another long night for the chief inspector.

Back in the Traf, detective constables Vallejo, Cassar and Digby were debating, yet again, UEFA's insistence that the Gibraltar national football team play their games at the Estádio Algarve in Portugal. According to the governing body of European football, the local Victoria Stadium did not meet its rigorous standards, which upset many supporters on the Rock.

'The sooner we get the new stadium built at Europa Point, the better,' Vallejo argued. 'It's bloody daft playing our matches over in Portugal.'

'And expensive to go see them,' Digby added.

'Didn't know you'd been over there.'

'I haven't. But if I did want to go, I couldn't afford it!'

Giving up on his friends' conversation, Calbot turned to Sullivan, who was still lost in her own thoughts. 'Penny for them?'

Sullivan smiled. 'Nothing worth shelling out for, I'm afraid.'

'Busy days. Not that I'm complaining. Beats shoplifting and cigarette smuggling any day.'

'People have been murdered, Calbot. There's never anything good about that.'

Calbot looked suitably shamefaced. 'I didn't mean that. I just meant ...'

'I know what you meant, Calbot,' Sullivan replied. 'No need to explain.'

'About dinner next week,' he said, changing the subject a little too obviously. 'If you think this bunch of muttons are coming, you're wrong.' He nodded towards his fellow officers. 'I've actually invited the chief inspector.'

'Will he come?' Sullivan asked, unable to explain why she felt so alarmed at the prospect.

'No way,' Calbot replied with confidence. 'Never goes anywhere.'

'He's going to a fancy dress ball.'

Calbot shook his head. 'He'll get out of it somehow.'

'So who *will* be coming to yours, then?'

'I'm still thinking about it. If you've got any ideas, let me know.'

'And if you've got any ideas, you'll get more than just my thoughts, Detective Sergeant,' Sullivan replied, softening the reprimand with a twinkle in her eye.

Behind the bar, the barman, bored with the slow-moving events unfolding at the fourteenth hole of the Royal Melbourne Golf Club, changed the channel to watch the news. Immediately the screens were full of scenes filmed earlier at Charles de Gaulle Airport. Sullivan and the rest of the table turned to see the arrival in Paris of Julia Novacs and her entourage. The American star was being greeted with open arms by her friends Carla Bruni and Juliette Binoche. Cameras flashed and reporters jostled to capture the highly stage-managed event. Moments later the screen showed a montage of images: the Rock of Gibraltar, the recently dismantled Queen of Diamonds movie set in Grand Casemates

Square and, finally, a photograph of Josh Cornwallis.

Calbot whistled through his teeth. 'Bloody hell. This is huge.'

Sullivan nodded as she continued to watch the news bulletin play out. 'You bet it is.'

CHAPTER 80

'WE HAVE BEEN informed by the medical team at St Bernard's that Lech Jasinski will be operated on this morning,' Massetti told the throng of reporters gathered once again in the inner courtyard of police HQ. She had begun her press conference at 8 am and now, ten minutes later, was attempting to bring it to a close.

'As you know, we had been questioning Mr Jasinski in connection with the three murders this week, one here in Gibraltar and two in San Roque. We'll continue to pursue our lines of enquiry while Mr Jasinski's in hospital, and widen them to take on board new information and leads pertaining to the case.'

This last statement released a wave of questions from the attending journalists. Unperturbed, Massetti doggedly continued to the end of her prepared brief. 'The RGP is working closely with our Andalusian counterparts, and we'll bring you up to date with our progress as and when appropriate. Thank you.'

She turned and nodded to the two police constables at her side, who immediately moved to support her and her bad ankle. All three headed for the custody suite door on the right-hand side of the courtyard. Massetti was in pain and, with the press looking on, was determined to milk every ounce of sympathy she could out of the situation. Sadly, little appeared to be on offer. Ignoring the barrage of questions and barely disguised accusations of police brutality yelled at her from the press corps, the chief superintendent entered the building and headed straight for the incident room, where she joined Broderick.

The team had been hard at work since before 7 am. Sullivan had already come up with something new on the film producer: 'Isolde's house in Upper Town, ma'am.'

'Didn't know he had one,' said Massetti.

'Left to him by his parents ten years ago,' Sullivan continued. 'Uses it several times a year on his visits from London.'

'Why hasn't he been using it during the filming,' Massetti asked, 'instead of staying at the Plaza?'

'Probably trying to show off his movie mogul bollocks,' Broderick interrupted. 'Posh penthouse fits the part a little better than your average townhouse, don't you think, ma'am?'

'The thing is,' Sullivan continued, 'he may have been using it as *well* as the penthouse. Tracy Gavin had suggested putting up some of the crew at the house, but Isolde vetoed it. She says he seemed annoyed at the idea.'

'So you're suggesting we have a look-see?' Massetti asked.

'I'm suggesting we should have a look-see at both the house and penthouse, ma'am. But we'll need warrants.'

'You'll get them, Sullivan, don't you worry about that,' Massetti stated firmly.

'Excuse me, ma'am?'

All three turned to see Sergeant Aldarino walking across the room with a printed-out email in his hand. 'This has just come through for you from the chief minister's office. Looks important.'

Massetti took the email and read it.

'Well, well, well,' she murmured. 'He's been as good as his word. MI6 is flying someone out here later today. Seems Maugham may have misappropriated some rather important documents. The chief minister also suggests that there should be no mention of this to anyone outside the investigation unless cleared from above.'

'Do we notify the Spanish police, ma'am?' Sullivan asked.

'I'll check that out,' Massetti replied. 'Hopefully we can bat that one over to the government.'

'Still won't be easy, ma'am,' said Broderick.

'Not our immediate problem. Anyway, the Spanish haven't flagged up anything significant about Maugham, so it may well stay that way.'

'Yes, ma'am,' Broderick replied.

'All this supports our thinking about what was going on between Martínez and Cornwallis,' Sullivan said enthusiastically. 'Maugham comes to Spain and gives Martínez some important information. Martínez then gives it to Cornwallis.'

'And within twenty-four hours, all three were dead,' Broderick added.

'Their laptops are missing. Briefcase and diary and maybe more stuff we don't know about, all gone,' Sullivan continued. 'Whoever killed them did so to stop that information getting out. It's as clear as day.'

'No, it's not, Sullivan,' Massetti countered. 'Not until we find out what that information is and who exactly would have suffered by having it revealed.'

'Yes, ma'am,' Sullivan agreed reluctantly.

'Keep on it, but we need hard facts. Until then, the mad and comatose Jasinski is still our most likely culprit. Understood?'

'Understood, ma'am,' Broderick and Sullivan replied, almost in unison.

CHAPTER 81

RIC DANAHER HAD risen early. The journey to Algeciras from his hillside *finca* was not particularly long or arduous, but the challenges it presented to the ex-policeman's sixteen-year-old Mitsubishi Shogun were considerable. The off-roader's regular attendance at the local garage in Gaucín and the many hundreds of euros spent on repairs and servicing should have eased Danaher's concerns about its general roadworthiness. But they had not. On too many journeys recently, the old tin can had let him down badly. But despite this, Danaher could not bring himself to part with it. Consuela had urged her father time and again to dump the old heap and get something better. In her view, an old donkey would have proved a more reliable form of conveyance. And yet the rusty Japanese giant continued to stand at the top of the dusty track that led down the hill to the main road and Jimena beyond.

It had taken Ric just four phone calls to track down a contact regarding Marisella Martínez's orphaned baby, Rosia. As a great believer in the 'six degrees of separation' theory, four phone calls had been a pleasing result. Two of them had been to local government officials in Algeciras and the third to a judge. The fourth had led to him speaking to Juan González, a fellow private investigator. Also known as 'La Rata' – the rat – González was the go-to man for background on both establishment and criminal figures in southern Andalusia.

Danaher had built up his personal contact base slowly and surely during his five years on the Costa and it was now paying dividends. He had actually begun the exercise long before he had left the UK to live in Spain. His policeman's instinct to gather and hoard information meant that he cultivated a network of friends and acquaintances on the Costa del Sol and in Gibraltar, connections that guided and oiled the wheels of his investigations. The Martínez case was proving no exception.

By mid-morning, he had driven to Algeciras and pulled into a car park near the central Plaza Alta. The beautiful square, with its central fountain and magnificent palms, was one of Danaher's favourite spots in the busy city-port. The sun was heading towards its midday high and the temperature in the town – so different from that of the sea and countryside surrounding it – was quite suffocating. A cocktail of heat and thirst made him seek a seat in a small pavement cafe. Ordering a large brandy-infused *carajillo* coffee and a small bottle of *aqua sin gas*, he relaxed at a shaded outside table and collected his thoughts.

His contacts in local government had informed him that, in 1943, the most likely orphanage where the baby Rosia Martínez would have been placed was a small – by municipal standards – children's home known as Casa de los Santos Inocentes – House of the Holy Innocents. Most orphans from La Línea had been taken there during that period. The home was no longer in operation, having been demolished in 1967 to make way for a large connecting road serving the giant CEPSA oil refinery in the Campo de Gibraltar. Danaher had discovered that the records from the orphanage had not been sent to the public records department, but instead had been placed with an Algeciras law firm. Judge Romanez, whom Danaher had contacted next, had been a junior partner with that firm. He was also a regular client of Danaher's. After making his own enquiries, the judge informed the private detective that the records had subsequently been moved to a small firm run by a middle-range lawyer called Miquel Columbus. The mention of Judge Romanez's name had quickly secured a meeting for Danaher at 11.15 am. Finishing his *carajillo*, he paid his bill and headed along the palm-shaded street for his appointment.

Climbing the narrow staircase to the third floor of a half-empty office building three streets west of the Plaza Alta, Danaher knocked and entered the offices of Columbus & Arnez. A middle-aged receptionist with greying hair and the look of the terminally bored took his name and waved him through to Miquel Columbus' office.

'He's expecting you,' she growled, in a resonant Andalusian accent.

If Columbus had been expecting him, he showed little sign of it as Danaher appeared at his door.

'Yes?' the lawyer asked awkwardly, closing the newspaper he had been reading and attempting a look of superiority.

'Ric Danaher.'

'Ah, yes,' Columbus replied. 'Come in. Sit down.'

Danaher crossed the room and took the seat in front of the lawyer's desk. Meanwhile, Columbus reached for a large file that lay across the top of an empty in-tray on the left-hand side of his desk.

'Judge Romanez has asked me to be of assistance to you. You have powerful friends in this city, have you not?'

'If you say so,' Danaher acknowledged, refusing to offer any more information than necessary.

'I have been looking into your request, Señor Danaher,' Columbus continued. 'We do indeed hold the adoption records from the Casa del los Santos Inocentes. They are, as I'm sure you'll understand, strictly confidential, so I fear I may not be able to furnish you with as much information as you desire.'

Danaher took in the somewhat dishevelled appearance of the man before him. Columbus's suit and tie were past their best, a look not helped by the lawyer's ample stomach, which hung over his trousers and acted as a permanent obstacle to the buttoning of his jacket. The inflamed nose and ruddy, veiny cheeks suggested that alcohol played a prominent part in Columbus's life. The sweat on his brow and the heaviness of his breathing also led Danaher to conclude that a good work-out was probably only a distant memory for the fifty-something *abogado*.

'I'd be grateful for whatever information you feel able to give me,' Danaher answered amicably. 'As I told you on the phone, Rosia Martínez was admitted to an orphanage in the spring of 1943. Anything you can do to help me find her would be most appreciated, Señor Columbus.'

Columbus smiled. The respectful tone of the Englishman was pleasing to his ear.

'Well, I have good news for you. According to the file I have before me, a Rosia Isabella Martínez was taken in by the sisters in April of that year. Her actual name, it was noted, was Delgado. Her father's, I believe, but in his absence, the girl's grandparents reverted to their own name, Martínez.'

'Rosia Martínez is who I'm looking for, *señor*. As I say, anything you can do to help me trace her – should she still be alive – would be very useful.'

'Now that is, unfortunately, where I will have to cease to be of use to you, Señor Danaher. Even after so long a time, there are strict rules of confidentiality regarding child adoption. I can confirm that Rosia was adopted at a later date from the orphanage, but her adoptive parents' identity is protected. Notes regarding this case are attached to the file. It seems the couple in question requested complete anonymity. It is the law regarding such matters, Señor Danaher, and as such, it is my legal duty to obey their wishes in this matter.'

'I understand completely, *señor*,' Danaher replied, his smile widening. 'However, I should tell you that, if there was any way to – how can I put it? – *circumnavigate* that necessity, it could prove greatly beneficial to you.'

'I trust you are not suggesting that I would consider a bribe, Señor Danaher.'

'A bribe is very far from what I'm suggesting, *señor*.'

The lawyer could not entirely hide the look of disappointment he felt on hearing this news.

'Then what, exactly?' Columbus demanded, his tone hardening.

'We're both very busy men, *señor*, so I'll get to the point. The benefits I'm suggesting would be those attached to my not revealing to certain interested parties – your wife being perhaps a particularly good example of one – that you have for some years now been seeing, on a weekly basis, a "lady friend" in Cádiz. That this "lady friend" is also the wife of a notable judge of the province may allow you to deduce a second interested party. Needless to say, such information could prove damaging to you both personally and professionally.'

Columbus struggled to his feet, his face turning purple and his paunch miraculously shifting to his chest area. 'This is an outrage! How dare you!' he roared.

Danaher remained seated and placed his forefinger over his lips. 'I think it best not to alert your secretary to the situation, *señor.*'

Columbus stopped in his tracks, his large bulk swaying back and forth behind his desk. After a moment or two, he breathed deeply and addressed the man before him with as much dignity as he could muster. 'Your actions are despicable. I am an honourable man, Señor Danaher.'

'Which is why I chose not to bring up your gambling debts and your many brothel visits in Marbella, Señor Columbus.'

Columbus's head was now spinning and he had to steady himself against the desk. After what seemed an eternity, the Spaniard spoke: 'The file is here before you. I will now leave the room for approximately ten minutes. What you do during that time is none of my concern.'

Columbus moved from behind his desk and walked with an unsteady gait towards the door. Once there, he turned around imperiously to look at Danaher. Sadly for Columbus, the private detective had completely ignored the lawyer's dramatic leave-taking and was already reading from the file. For what little it was worth, the deflated lawyer gritted his teeth and spat at the Englishman.

'*Bastardo!*'

CHAPTER 82

THE BOUGAINVILLEA ADORNING the entrance to the townhouse was at its most colourful and resplendent, drooping heavily over the windows and covering the cracked, patched plasterwork of the walls. Built high up in the Old Town and hidden from street view up a steeply rising passageway, Gabriel Isolde's Gibraltar home had taken Sullivan and Broderick a few minutes to find.

The detectives had not come alone. They were accompanied by a police constable from the Dog Unit whose black labrador Panza had been specially trained to sniff out drugs.

A similar operation was also underway across town at the Atlantic Marina Plaza building, where officers, including Calbot, were searching Isolde's penthouse apartment. Everyone involved knew that it would take very little time for word to get out that Isolde was being investigated by the RGP. The hope was that, by the time it did, there would be some fresh developments, either from the new investigations or from the forensics on Jasinski. With the world's media breathing down their necks, Massetti and the team had to be seen to be doing something.

Broderick had summed things up neatly: 'We may not be clutching at straws, but it feels as if we are.'

The morning had already proved exasperating. Forensics had called to say there would be a delay on the DNA test results, and in spite of Massetti's assurances, the search warrants on the Isolde locations had taken hours to organise. It was now nearing one o'clock and it already felt as though the day was slipping away from them.

Broderick now turned the key – which had been found in Isolde's possessions at the hospital – in the lock of the front door of Isolde's townhouse. Entering the hallway, the first thing that struck the officers was an unmistakable mustiness, a smell redolent with mould and long-closed rooms. The house had obviously not been lived in or even visited for quite some time. Moving through to the sitting-room and then on into the dining-room and kitchen beyond, Sullivan and Broderick were also surprised at the state of the décor. 'Seventies retro' described the style of the fixtures, fittings and furnishings in each room. Multi-coloured carpet or lino covered the floors. A three-piece suite that would have been the height of fashion in the late 1960s filled the sitting-room. An ancient Grundig colour television sat in one corner, and on the main wall the tiled fireplace boasted a log-effect electric heater of dubious taste and doubtful efficiency. The kitchen was even more fixed in time. Formica-topped pale-coloured units lined the room alongside a small electric cooker and a basic refrigerator of Eastern European origin.

Sullivan looked at her boss. 'It's like a museum, guv.'

'Yeah,' Broderick replied. 'One that's lost its funding by the look of things.'

The upstairs and the rest of the house were exactly the same. The room that had been Isolde's bedroom as a teenager had been kept in a perfect state of preservation. It was as if the schoolboy was expected home at any moment. Boxes of Monopoly, Cluedo and Mastermind games were stacked neatly on shelves. Movie posters covered the walls, Hitchcock's *Psycho* and Carpenter's *Halloween* taking pride of place. Sullivan also noted the poster for the original French version of *La Cage aux Folles* covering the door of the wardrobe in the corner. Nothing had changed in the house since the death of Isolde's parents ten years earlier. It was also clear that his parents had altered their living environment little, if at all, during the forty-five years they had occupied the house.

'No wonder Isolde wasn't keen on putting some of the film crew up here,' Sullivan observed.

A careful look around the house revealed nothing of use to the detectives. No laptops. No papers. No Rohypnol. Panza the police dog remained even less impressed with the place, and soon left the building with nothing more than a chew treat in his mouth.

The news from Isolde's penthouse was no better. All hopes of finding anything to confirm suspicions of the Gibraltarian's guilt had come to nothing. Both teams of officers returned to New Mole House and braced themselves for the wrath of Massetti.

Chapter 83

'HAVE YOU NOTICED,' Calbot moaned, 'that that bunch downstairs sprinkle a lot less chocolate on the cappuccinos than they used to?'

The detective constable was sitting at his desk in the incident room staring glumly at his canteen-purchased frothy coffee. Across from him, Sullivan and Broderick were lost in their own thoughts. Massetti had not been there to greet the returning search teams. She was seeing a specialist at St Bernard's for her ankle and would not be back for at least another hour. Everyone was taking advantage of the calm.

On her return to the station, Sullivan had been handed a large carrier bag by Sergeant Aldarino. It had been delivered by Cath an hour before, and the note attached explained its contents:

Sorry to miss you. On the off-chance you'll be able to make it to the fancy dress fundraiser tonight, I've taken the liberty of providing you with a costume. Might be a little big, but with a few pins I'm sure you'll knock it into shape and look just lovely. Don't work too hard, and please tell my brother the same.

Best wishes, Cath

Opening the bag, Sullivan was ashamed to feel her heart sinking. The costume was a Star Wars Princess Leia dress and wig. Her feelings were compounded by the sudden presence of Calbot looking over her shoulder.

'Not bad, Sarge, but I reckon a nurse's outfit would suit you better.'

It did not really matter. The way things were going, the chances of herself or Broderick getting away to the ball that evening were minimal. Neither had mentioned it to the other, which was how, Sullivan presumed, it would continue.

Back in the incident room, Broderick was taking a call from Ric Danaher. Sullivan and Calbot looked on as the chief inspector busily wrote notes on a pad in front of him. After several minutes, he thanked Danaher and ended the call.

'We've got a lead on Marisella Martínez's baby,' he began. 'My friend across the border has been very industrious. The baby Rosia was taken to an orphanage just outside of Algeciras in April 1943. A year later, a Mr and Mrs Ackerman arrived at the home enquiring about adopting a child. Mr Ackerman was South African, his wife was British. They were childless and had both been working in non-military capacities over here in Gib during the first years of the war. They stated that they were moving to Johannesburg and wanted to adopt a Spanish orphan. As non-Spanish citizens, they were at first met with some opposition, but a large donation from the Ackermans to the orphanage oiled the wheels for the adoption to take place. The child that they chose was nineteen-month-old Rosia Martínez. They were told nothing of her family history and were ignorant of the fact that Rosia was the daughter of the missing Marisella Martínez. The couple took their adopted daughter with them, giving a future contact address in Johannesburg.'

Sullivan shook her head in amazement. 'And it took your man just one morning to find that out? Eduardo Martínez spent most of his life chasing that information and failed to find a single lead.'

Broderick nodded sombrely and turned to Calbot. 'Get onto the South African authorities,' he commanded the young detective. 'We need to know what happened to Rosia from then on. Find out as much as you can about the Ackermans, too.'

'Will do, guv.'

'Meanwhile, the two of us are going to visit the Wombles,' Broderick announced to Sullivan as he rose and headed for the door. 'We need to see what's holding up the forensics.'

'Right you are, guv,' Sullivan replied, picking up her mobile and straightening her top.

'Oh, by the way,' Calbot interrupted, looking up from his computer screen with a broad smile, 'may the Force be with you, Sarge.'

'Thank you, Calbot,' Sullivan replied serenely. 'And fuck you, too.'

CHAPTER 84

IT WAS WELL known that Broderick thought the Forensics team on the Rock were a smug, self-satisfied lot. He usually referred to them as 'Wombles' – a name taken from the rubbish-collecting creatures of children's book and television legend. In spite of this, he was always the first to praise their excellent results, often derived from the ever-advancing techniques in the field of forensics. Murderers faced a formidable foe in science. It was a battle they rarely, if ever, won.

On arrival at the oddly named Forensic Scheme Laboratory, Broderick and Sullivan were met by the tall, courteous and scholarly Professor Richard Kemp. His greeting was uncharacteristically effusive: 'Hello, Chief Inspector, DS Sullivan. I trust you're both having a good day!'

Broderick nodded. 'Kemp. What's the score?'

'It's good news. The Jasinski DNA results have just been completed.'

Broderick almost smiled with relief. 'And?'

'Bad news there, I'm afraid,' Kemp replied. 'Unless, that is, you happen to be Jasinski. No trace of his DNA at the Cornwallis murder scene.'

'Are you absolutely sure?' Broderick asked, unable to fully hide his disappointment.

'We tend to be very thorough here in Forensics, Chief Inspector. If we conclude there is none, it absolutely guarantees that there is none.'

'Thank you,' Sullivan said. 'That eliminates Jasinski as a suspect.'

'Almost certainly,' Kemp replied. 'Unless he went to great lengths to protect the crime scene from personal contamination. Reading the report on the timescale, the circumstances and the mental health of the man, I would consider such a possibility to be most unlikely.'

'But not impossible?' Broderick queried.

'I never rule anything out entirely, Chief Inspector. But if you ask me ... Jasinski was never in the room.'

'And how long before you can give us results on Isolde?' Broderick asked.

'He's not on the DNA database, but as a possible suspect we've taken a swab. You'll have to wait a little longer for that one, I'm afraid.'

'Right, thanks.' Broderick said.

'We have, of course, found other samples of DNA. We're checking those against the database now. We'll get the results to you ASAP.'

'Thank you, Professor Kemp,' Sullivan replied with a smile, as both she and Broderick turned to go.

'Oh, by the way,' Kemp added. 'I hear you continue to refer to those of us in this department as "Wombles", Chief Inspector.'

'Oh, shit,' Broderick murmured under his breath.

Kemp continued: 'I only mention it because I'm quite delighted with that one. It is, in many ways, a fine description of us. According to Wikipedia, Wombles are kind and cuddly creatures. Not unlike my assistant William, especially as he now sports a large bushy beard. Wombles also collect things that others discard and then put them to good use. Sums up forensic work rather nicely, I think.'

Sullivan watched as Broderick struggled to remain calm.

With growing amusement, Kemp concluded: 'I'll Womble off, shall I? Good day to you both.' And promptly left the room.

Broderick waited for the professor to close the door. 'Whichever way you look at it, Sullivan, you have to admit that the man is a bit of a prick.'

'I thought he was quite charming, actually, sir.'

Without so much as a glance at his detective sergeant, Broderick turned and headed for the exit. It was clear he did not agree.

CHAPTER 85

BRODERICK PARKED AT the front of the police HQ. Once out of the car, Sullivan took a moment to warm her face in the late afternoon sun. On a normal working day, she would have finished her shift by now and would be sunning herself or swimming from one of the Rock's many sandy beaches. Roused from these thoughts by the approach of reporters demanding fresh information about the case, she turned and followed Broderick through the high metal gates and into the police station's inner courtyard.

Once inside the building, both detectives spent the next forty minutes briefing Massetti and the newly returned commissioner of police. The latter was jetlagged and in no mood to hear anything other than good news. He was soon disappointed. The negative forensic results on Jasinski were not received well, and both senior officers demanded to know where the investigation now stood. Broderick updated them.

'Our main suspect is now Gabriel Isolde. We're awaiting DNA results on him from the scene of the Cornwallis murder and putting pressure on our Spanish colleagues to deliver the same from the San Roque murder investigation. We're also pursuing all lines of enquiry regarding Isolde's possible motive or motives for the crimes – In particular, determining the precise nature of Cornwallis's relationship with Martínez and the information from Maugham given to the screenwriter. We hope our visitor from MI6 will shed some light in that area. We're not relying totally on that, however. We're also following our own enquiries regarding all possible links between the victims and the film *Queen of Diamonds*. These include possible connections between Isolde and criminal elements on the Costa del Sol.'

'Sounds impressive,' Massetti responded. 'But the fact is, with Jasinski out of the picture, we're pretty much back to square one.'

'With respect, ma'am, I'd suggest we're at square *two* and moving as swiftly as possible towards square *three*.'

'Since when did you become the optimist?' Massetti demanded.

Broderick took a deep breath. He had taken enough ear-bashing for one afternoon. Levelling his gaze at his commanding officers, he replied with icy precision: 'We'll get whoever did this, ma'am. I promise you that. It just might not be in time for you to catch the next news bulletin.'

Broderick's words did not go down well with either Massetti or the commissioner, and the meeting was quickly brought to a close. As Sullivan and her boss walked back to the incident room, she was tempted to say 'Oops!', but the look on Broderick's face had convinced her to let the sentiment remain unexpressed.

As they entered the room, Calbot jumped up from his desk and almost pounced on the two of them.

'Got something on the Ackermans, guv!'

'Good,' Broderick grunted, sitting at his desk. 'Any movement would be welcome.'

Sullivan made herself comfortable on a nearby chair. It was

clear from Calbot's theatrical demeanour that he was not going to be rushed.

'I thought this was going to take some time, but then I remembered the contacts I made at the South African embassy in London two years ago on the Vreugdenburg fraud investigation. Luckily I had favours to call in.'

Sergeant Aldarino and two other detectives crossed the room to listen to Calbot, who was pleased with his growing audience.

'The first thing I did was to check records over here. The orphanage stated that the Ackermans had been working in Gib. First piece of evidence that came up was a marriage certificate for the couple. Thirty-one-year-old Max Ackerman married twenty-four-year-old Diana Candoza here on the Rock on 26 February 1944. With that, I got back to my guys in London. They tell me that Ackerman, a South African, had been an intelligence officer for the Brits, based here before the north Africa Invasion in 1942. He was later wounded during the Allied push through Italy in '43, after which he returned to Gib and became engaged to Candoza.'

'What's her background?' Sullivan asked.

'Born in England to an English mother, father a Spanish banker based in London. Found herself in Gib in 1940 and held several clerical posts of varying degrees of military and civil importance until her marriage and move to Johannesburg in 1944. The couple left Gibraltar with their adopted daughter Rosia in late April of that year.'

'Just a few weeks after the first of the Gibraltar evacuees arrived back home from the UK.' Aldarino interjected.

Calbot glared at the sergeant. 'What's that got to do with anything?'

Unruffled, the sergeant said: 'Just an observation. Could be one of the reasons they left. She'd have probably lost her job. By '44, the Rock wasn't a forward operating base any more. Things would have been a lot quieter around here.'

'Be that as it may,' Calbot continued 'the fact is they married and adopted Rosia and then buggered off to South Africa all within a few months. Maybe it was just a whirlwind romance. Brave wounded warrior returns to the Rock, sweeps his girlfriend off her feet and then whisks her south to play happy families in Africa.'

Broderick interrupted. 'Calbot, I am very much hoping that your research is going to get a bit more helpful and a lot less Mills & Boon.'

Calbot checked his notes quickly and went on: 'Max Ackerman's family were wealthy mine owners. Gold, mostly. His father was also a politician, holding ministerial rank in the South African government. The Ackermans moved to a Johannesburg suburb, and Max, like his father, entered politics. For the next five years, all went well it seems, but then, in the spring of 1948, Diana came home one day to find her husband dead.'

Calbot handed Broderick and Sullivan printouts of two newspaper articles that he had downloaded from the Johannesburg Star website. One showed a front page from May 1948. Its headline was bold and clear: '**GARDENER GUILTY OF ACKERMAN MURDER.**' The story below it told of the trial of the Ackermans' gardener, Sehloho Mankana, charged and found guilty of poisoning Max Ackerman with arsenic.

Broderick nodded. 'Interesting. What happened to the wife and daughter?'

Calbot produced another newspaper clipping with the headline '**MURDER WIDOW BECOMES MISSIONARY**'.

'This was published about five months later. It seems Diana Ackerman took Rosia to Kenya and started work at a Christian missionary centre. That's as far as I've traced them. I should be getting an email from Nairobi any moment now, which will hopefully help us discover what happened to them next.'

Broderick stood and stretched his arms. 'All very interesting, Calbot, but sadly nothing to help us with Isolde.'

'Finding out what happened to Rosia may prove helpful further down the line, guv,' Sullivan observed.

'Maybe, maybe not,' Broderick replied. 'We need stuff that's relevant to the last few days. Any word on Isolde's criminal associates up the coast?'

'Still working on it,' Aldarino replied.

Broderick's mobile buzzed. It was Forensics.

'Kemp?' Broderick answered. 'What's new?'

The rest of the team looked on as Broderick listened to the professor. At last, he rang off.

'The DNA results from the Cornwallis apartment. Kemp's found a match on their database. Someone who'd been in the apartment recently and strangely never bothered to mention it to us.'

'Who, guv?' Sullivan asked impatiently.

'Tracy Gavin,' Broderick answered. 'She was charged six years ago in the UK for dangerous driving so her DNA's on record. Let's pay her a visit. I think we're due an explanation, don't you?'

CHAPTER 86

O'REILLY'S IRISH PUB, in the Ocean Village marina complex, was the scene of a wake. Many of the crew and production staff of *Queen of Diamonds* had gathered outside for an early evening drink and some last goodbyes before flights home the next day. Overlooking the yachts moored in the marina and just a few metres along from the Casino – an establishment several of the crew had earmarked to spend time in later – O'Reilly's had become a favourite watering hole for many of the team during their short time filming on the Rock.

Fifty metres away, Sullivan and Broderick walked along the wooden boardwalk, past the restaurants and bars that lined the quay. Broderick wiped his brow with a handkerchief. The early evening air still had considerable heat in it and the chief inspector was feeling its effect.

When Sullivan had contacted Tracy Gavin and told her that she had some further queries to make, Gavin had told her she was at an impromptu end-of-shoot party at the marina and asked if the detective could join her there. But now, as O'Reilly's came into sight, both Sullivan and Broderick were taken aback by the large number of people drinking outside the watering hole.

'Bloody hell!' Broderick exclaimed on seeing the heaving throng. 'How many people does it take to make a movie?'

'Many more than you'd think,' Sullivan replied. 'Keep your eyes out for Gavin, guv.'

Arriving at the pub, the detectives looked around for the production co-ordinator. Not seeing her in the vicinity, Sullivan turned to a couple sitting at the nearest table. The man was in his fifties but dressed much younger. The woman by his side, several years his junior, had her arm around him but was clearly not enjoying herself.

'Excuse me, we're looking for Tracy Gavin. Have you seen her?' Sullivan asked.

'Haven't a fucking clue, sweetie,' the man replied in a strong Glaswegian accent. With a drunken sway of his head, he looked Sullivan up and down, then gestured to the bottle of champagne he had on ice beside him. 'D'ya wanna a drink? You look like you're gasping.'

The woman next to him gave Sullivan a look of disdain and took her arm from around the man's shoulder.

'No,' Sullivan replied. 'Thanks anyway.'

'I'm Jerry,' the man continued, running his fingers through his near shoulder-length grey hair. 'Jerry Callum-Forbes. I was director of the movie we're bidding farewell to. Could have been one of the big ones, you know, if it'd gone the fucking distance. Now the whole thing's just a bloody mess.'

'Sorry about that,' Sullivan said.

Jerry nodded towards the woman at his side. 'Oh, and this is Natasha, my missus.'

Sullivan smiled and nodded to Broderick standing at her side. 'And *this* is Chief Inspector Broderick.'

The colour left the director's face. Broderick leaned forward a little. 'Enjoy your evening, Mr and Mrs Callum-Forbes,' he told them icily. 'Meanwhile, some of us will continue to clear up this bloody mess for you.'

Both detectives turned and headed towards the entrance to the pub. 'Pillock,' Broderick muttered under his breath as he pushed his way through the crowd.

The interior of the pub was no less busy, but after a minute, Sullivan and Broderick found Tracy Gavin standing at the end of the bar. She was laughing and flirting with a couple of good-looking men, both of whom had an air of wealth and privilege.

'Sorry to interrupt, Ms Gavin,' Broderick said, drawing her attention away from her handsome companions. 'May we have a word? Somewhere a little quieter, if possible.'

'Outside I think, Chief Inspector,' Tracy suggested, excusing herself from the men and leading the way out.

Much to Broderick's annoyance, their passage out of the pub and through the multitude of film people took a good ten minutes as Gavin was stopped every few metres by friends and colleagues keen to chat and gossip about the film's demise. At last the three of them cleared the front of the building and moved along the boardwalk to a quieter spot at the end of the quay.

'Sorry about that,' Gavin apologised. 'All very sad. Particularly as Gabriel isn't here.'

'We've just heard that he's out of intensive care, Ms Gavin,' Broderick informed her. 'We're hoping to interview him a little later.'

'Makes me feel guilty really. Being down here having a party. But it's what Gabriel would want. The show goes on and all that.'

'Even when the show clearly isn't?' Broderick queried.

'It's tradition, Chief Inspector. Movie people work hard and party hard. Even in the face of adversity.'

'Fair enough,' Broderick conceded. 'We're not all made the same, are we?'

'So what can I do for you both?' Gavin asked.

'At any time during this week, were you in Josh Cornwallis's apartment?' Sullivan asked.

The look of shock on Gavin's face confirmed that the question had taken her by complete surprise. 'I'm sorry? I beg your pardon?'

'It's a straightforward question, Ms Gavin,' Broderick said. 'Were you in his apartment and, if so, when and why?'

The repetition of the question appeared to rob Gavin of oxygen. Her shoulders collapsed and her head bowed low as if she were about to faint.

Sullivan reached to support her. 'Steady now,' she said. 'Take your time.'

After taking several deep breaths, Gavin attempted to respond. 'How did you find out?'

'You don't need to know that for now,' Broderick answered. 'When were you in the apartment?'

'Oh, my God. You think it was me? Me who killed him?'

'Just answer the question, please, Tracy,' Sullivan said a little more delicately.

Gavin's cheeks flushed and her eyes began to dart left and right, her mind racing. She was desperately trying to focus on what to say and do.

'The truth, please, Ms Gavin,' Broderick insisted.

The pressure was at last too much. 'Tuesday afternoon,' she blurted out. 'We had our first night-shoot that evening, which went through to the following morning.'

'Your first and last night-shoot,' Broderick observed.

'Why exactly were you at the apartment?' Sullivan pressed her. 'Were you there on business with Mr Cornwallis?'

'No. Josh wasn't there.'

'Wasn't there?' Broderick asked incredulously. 'What do you mean?'

'He was in Marbella with Julia. He was flying back with her late in the afternoon.'

'Why were you there then? Do you make a habit of visiting other people's apartments when they're not there?' Broderick questioned.

'It was all a mistake. I'm so sorry.'

'Sorry for what, Tracy?' Sullivan asked patiently.

'It was just stupid. I knew Josh wouldn't be there, wouldn't be back till later ... The fact is, Josh had left his keys at the production office the day before and then had gone off to Marbella with Julia. I promised him I'd pop them back to the reception desk at the Plaza in time for his return.'

'So why go *into* his apartment? What were you thinking?' Broderick asked.

'It wasn't *my* idea!' Gavin replied with alarm.

'You mean there was someone else with you?' Sullivan asked, keeping a steadying hand on Gavin's arm.

'Yes. He said we wouldn't get caught. Said Josh would never know ...' Gavin continued desperately.

'Who said that, Tracy? We need to know,' Sullivan asked.

'... We'd said we wouldn't. Not again. There was no future in it. I knew that. But I couldn't help myself. He's very persuasive.'

'Who is, Tracy? Who are you talking about?' Broderick demanded.

'Jerry. Jerry Callum-bloody-Forbes.'

'Oh, Jesus!' Sullivan let go of Gavin's arm and stepped back. Half in amazement, half in disgust.

Gavin continued with her story. 'We worked together last year on the film *Ivanhoe*. I knew it was stupid. I just fell for his charm.

He said he was going to leave his wife. That we'd move in together. Never happened, of course. I thought it was over. I thought we could just be, you know, professional. But from the first day I knew I wasn't over him.'

Broderick looked at her in amazement. 'But he's over there with his wife,' he said, gesturing towards the pub.

'I know. That's why we went to Josh's apartment. Jerry's apartment was on the next floor up. He said it was too good an opportunity to miss and I listened to him. I thought we'd get away with it. I'm sorry. That's all it was.'

'You should have told us,' Sullivan reprimanded.

'I thought about it. I even asked Jerry, but he told me to keep quiet. Said we'd be found out and the repercussions would be huge. Personally and professionally. I was scared. Terrified. You have to believe me, though, we had nothing to do with Josh's death. Nothing.'

'It's hard to know what to believe at the moment,' Broderick said. 'But you're going to have to come with us and make a statement.'

'What, now?'

'All we have is your word for it, Ms Gavin. We'll have to question both you and Mr Callum-Forbes in greater detail at police HQ to eliminate you from our enquiries.'

Tracy Gavin swayed once more as Broderick's words sank in. 'Jerry? You're going to bring Jerry in as well?'

'Yes. We are,' Sullivan told the near-hysterical woman, keeping her words simple.

'We'll get a car to take him in separately,' Broderick continued. 'Don't want you two getting your stories straight along the way, do we?'

'But everyone will know. Please don't do this here. Not at the party,' Gavin pleaded.

Sullivan took pity on her. 'We'll get the patrol car to park out of sight and the officers to remain with it. It'll be as discreet as possible, Tracy. I promise.'

'But you don't know Jerry. He won't come without a fight,' Gavin told them with real fear in her voice.

'Well, if that proves to be the case,' Broderick replied, 'it'll be a pleasure to see Mr Callum-Forbes biting off more than he can chew.'

Broderick didn't have to wait long for the pleasure to begin.

The director's *third* mistake was to throw a wild punch at Broderick's head. That it failed to make contact compounded Jerry Callum-Forbes' misery. His *second* mistake had been to tell the chief inspector to fuck off. This, on top of his *first* miscalculation – to laugh derisively in Broderick's face – had led to Callum-Forbes being pinned face down on the deck outside the pub and handcuffed like a common criminal.

Gavin had left with Sullivan a few minutes before and been placed in a patrol car with two uniformed officers. On returning to O'Reilly's, Sullivan tried to control the crowd of outraged film personnel, none of whom understood the reason for their director's sudden and dramatic arrest. On top of this, the event had been infiltrated by several news reporters. They were quick to film the arrest with their phone cameras and even quicker to fire off a tirade of questions, none of which Sullivan or Broderick were prepared to answer. An explanation would have to wait until the images had been played across the news networks for all the world to see. For now, the two detectives led the still-protesting Callum-Forbes away from the throng.

CHAPTER 87

WITH GAVIN AND Callum-Forbes awaiting interview in separate rooms, Sullivan and Broderick returned to the incident room. Calbot was on them as soon as they walked through the door, insisting they sit down and listen to what he had to say.

'You're not going to believe this!' he informed them excitedly.

'Try me,' Broderick replied, wearily leaning back in his chair.

'Diana Ackerman moved to Nairobi with her daughter in 1948 and worked as a helper at the All Saints Christian Missionary in the city for nearly three years. I spoke to someone there who agreed to check their records. It seems they both left Kenya in 1951, giving the mission a rather large financial donation as a parting gift. In fact, it still has an Ackerman Wing.'

'Fascinating, Calbot,' Broderick replied flatly. 'Did they have any idea where they went?'

'The woman at the mission did. It seems Diana and Rosia Ackerman left Nairobi and moved back to Gibraltar.'

'Holy shit,' Broderick responded, nearly falling off his chair.

'It gets better,' Calbot continued, barely able to contain his excitement. 'I checked with the main records office. Matilda

Ramón actually stayed on there for an extra hour to help me –'

'Get on with it, Calbot,' Broderick interjected roughly.

'Matilda dug up a marriage certificate. In 1953, Diana Ackerman married a Gibraltarian called Paul Ruiz.'

'Paul Ruiz?' Broderick interrupted. 'As in Sir Paul Ruiz, the shipping millionaire?'

'He wasn't a "sir" then, guv, but that's the guy, yeah,' Calbot confirmed triumphantly.

'Dear God!' Broderick exclaimed.

Sullivan looked on in bewilderment. 'Someone famous, I take it?'

'Just a bit by the sounds of it,' Calbot told her.

'More than just a bit, Calbot,' Broderick said. 'But Rosia Martínez ... Ackerman ... did she ...?'

Calbot jumped in. 'Rosia Ackerman took the name Ruiz, and she and her mother moved into the Ruiz residence here on the Rock. But here's the thing. Five years later, at the age of sixteen, Rosia joined an order of Carmelite nuns in London. The name she took there was Clara.'

'Are you telling me ...?' Broderick was now standing, a look of utter disbelief on his face. 'Are you telling me that Sister Clara ... my friend ... is Rosia Martínez?'

Calbot paused for a moment as he realised just how shocking his news was for Broderick. 'Yes, guv. It seems that way.'

Broderick turned away from his fellow detectives and stared out of the window.

Sullivan stepped in with a question of her own. 'How the hell have you found out about all this so quickly, Calbot?' she asked.

'I struck lucky with Matilda Ramón. It seems her mother had been at school with Rosia here on the Rock, in the years before she left for London. She's known the Ruiz family all her life. She told me how Paul and Diana set up the Rock of Ages Foundation and how Rosia – Sister Clara, that is – left the Carmelites and joined her mother in running the charity in the late Sixties.'

Broderick turned back to his colleagues. '"Ruiz" is new to me. I've only ever known her as Sister Clara. That's what everyone calls her.'

'Yes, guv,' Sullivan agreed. 'But we now know that she was also Rosia Ackerman, and before that Rosia Martínez. Eduardo's niece.'

Sullivan had another question: 'Does Sister Clara know that she was adopted, guv?'

Broderick shrugged. 'No idea. I've never heard of anything being mentioned about her past.'

'Well, I think we'd better find out more about it pretty smartly,' Sullivan replied.

The ringing of her mobile interrupted any further thoughts. 'It's your sister, guv,' she informed Broderick. 'She's FaceTiming me.'

Before Broderick could ask what exactly FaceTiming was, Sullivan had pushed the 'Accept call' button on her mobile and Cath's face appeared on the screen.

Sullivan had to admit that Cath's smile was the only thing she recognised from the image in front of her. Broderick's sister was sporting a short-cropped grey wig and a pair of dark sunglasses. She also wore a raincoat with its collar up and held a revolver in her hand.

'Hello there, Tamara,' Cath began. 'As the two of you seem unlikely to get up here for the jollities, we thought we'd give you a preview of our Hollywood alter egos.'

'Wow,' Sullivan replied, rather lamely. 'You look … extraordinary.'

'I'm Judi Dench as M,' Cathy informed her with a laugh. 'Not a brilliantly accurate replica of the spy mistress from the Bond movies, but the best I could manage. Some cheeky bugger just told me I look more like Danger Mouse.'

THE POISONED ROCK

'You look great,' Sullivan lied. 'Let me show your brother.' Sullivan turned and handed the iPhone to Broderick.

'Erm,' he murmured. 'Yeah. How are the girls?'

'Penny is here. Have a look, Gus.' Immediately Broderick's eldest daughter appeared on the screen dressed as Katniss Everdeen.

'What do you think, Dad?'

'You look great. Who the hell are you?'

'Duh. No point telling you, Dad. You've no idea who she is any way. Wait till you see Daisy and Sister Clara.'

Once again the screen image whipped around, this time revealing Daisy in her *Sound of Music* costume.

'Hi, Dad!' Daisy yelled. 'I'm Julie Andrews.'

Much to Broderick's discomfort, both Sullivan and Calbot had stepped behind him for a better view.

'So you are, sweet-pea,' he told his youngest.

'I can sing as well, Daddy,' Daisy announced and promptly launched into a rendition of 'Do-Re-Mi'.

'Very good, sweet-pea,' Broderick said, 'but I think I'm going to have to go now. Have fun.'

'You haven't seen Sister Clara yet,' Daisy pointed out. 'She's been promoted. She's Mother Superior now.'

Once more the image on the screen whirled around to reveal Sister Clara. She stood smiling at the camera wearing a full nun's habit.

'Hello, Gus,' she said. 'Sorry you and Tamara aren't here. Don't the girls look good? All three of them!'

'Yes, they do,' Broderick replied. 'Look, we may come up shortly anyway, Sister Clara. I don't want to spoil the fun, but we need to have a talk with you.'

'Gosh, how intriguing. What about?'

'Oh, just some things you may be able to help us with.'

Cath's face suddenly replaced Sister Clara's on the screen.

'Well, that's just charming, Gus. We're supposed to be having fun up here,' she admonished.

'Sorry Cath. Can't be helped.'

'Well, you can tell Tamara that she's not getting in if she's not wearing her Princess Leia costume. And if you think you're going to get away with turning up as a plain-clothes detective for the second year in a row, think again, brother of mine.'

With that, the screen went blank.

Broderick looked up to see Calbot smiling down at him. 'That told you, guv,' the young man said.

'And now I'm telling *you*, Detective Constable,' Broderick replied, his eyes narrowing. 'Two statements from Gavin and Callum-Forbes and as quick as you like. I think they're just opportunists guilty of nothing more than a spot of sexual squatting, but if there are any discrepancies between their stories, let me know straight away.'

With a resigned nod, Calbot headed off towards the interview rooms. Meanwhile, Broderick glanced around to see where Sullivan had got to. He found her at a desk on the far side of the incident room directing her full attention to the computer screen in front of her. Broderick called across to her.

'Let's get up to the Rock Hotel, Sullivan.'

'Do you mind if I don't come with you, guv?' Sullivan replied, her eyes not moving from the screen.

'Why not? What are you up to?'

'I don't really know, sir,' Sullivan replied, sitting back in her chair and shaking her head. 'I've just got this niggling feeling that I've missed something. I can't explain why, but I think I need to go over everything again. Do you mind?'

'Sure this isn't just you getting out of wearing your *Star Wars* costume?'

Sullivan smiled. 'That's a bonus, I guess. Are you really going to tell Sister Clara who she really is, guv?'

'Not sure,' Broderick replied. 'It's not really an appropriate occasion to pass on such news. I think I'll just find out how much she knows. If she's ignorant of it all, I'll probably wait till the morning. Her knowing or not knowing doesn't really help us proceed with the investigation, does it?'

'Not really, guv.'

Sergeant Aldarino popped his head around the door.

'The chief super is rather keen to see you, sir. She's a bit concerned with the news stories coming in about us arresting a Hollywood film director.'

'Tell her you just missed me, will you, Sergeant? I've got other things to get on with.'

Aldarino nodded and left. Broderick followed a few moments later, leaving his detective sergeant to focus on her computer screen.

Once again, Sullivan had been drawn back to the CCTV recording of the Atlantic Marina Plaza reception on the afternoon of Josh Cornwallis's murder. The black and white images played out in front of her, showing the busy reception area packed with minimally costumed porn artistes, visiting buyers and other attendees at the Blue Job X launch party. Once more, she saw Isolde's arrival and his journey across the foyer to the lifts to the apartments, hidden out of sight behind the porn channel's large 'Welcome' stand, full of public relations staff.

Sullivan had viewed these images many times before: Isolde weaving his way through the throng of artistes dressed as Flash Gordons, Barbarellas, gladiators, US Navy Seals, bishops, nurses and a host of other glamorous and kitsch porn fantasy characters. After the first three or four viewings, Sullivan had tended to fast forward to Isolde's departure from the building later in the afternoon. Now she decided to view the recording all the way through again.

Within minutes, she was glad she had. On the screen before her was something she had noted previously but had considered unimportant. A few fleeting images on the periphery of the screen that now made Sullivan's mouth turn dry and her heart pound. Again and again, she checked the screen, isolating and magnifying the image as best she could. The picture was not as clear as she would have liked, but in her gut, she knew exactly what she was seeing.

With her mind racing, she now reached for her mobile and leapt to her feet. If her suspicions were accurate, she had identified the murderer. If they were wrong, she would be derided as a fool and an incompetent. Her niggling feeling had quickly developed into the strongest lead they had. Sullivan knew she had no choice but to run with it.

CHAPTER 88

HIGHER UP THE Rock, on Europa Road, Broderick arrived at the Rock Hotel. The large white art deco building, with over a hundred rooms and suites, stood majestically above him. Getting out of his car, he quickly crossed the road to the hotel's large outside swimming pool and bar. Next to these luxury amenities stood a huge banqueting marquee called the Khaima. This giant tent, decorated in a rich Moroccan style, was the venue for the evening's charity fundraiser.

Guests, dressed in an array of costumes, were arriving in large numbers by taxi and mini-bus. From what he could see, Marilyn Monroe and Darth Vader were particularly well represented, as were Superman, Laurel and Hardy, and Miss Piggy. Looking down at his well-worn light grey suit, Broderick felt a tinge of guilt for letting down his sister yet again. That he was there at all was entirely down to his profession. Although everyone around him seemed to be pleasure bent, Broderick was here on business.

The people checking tickets at the entrance to the Khaima were from the charity, knew Broderick and let him pass freely into the marquee. The inside was laid out with immaculately set white-clothed tables, and ornate Arabic lanterns dangled from the ceiling, creating flickering light and adding warmth to the atmosphere. In the far corner, a small quartet was playing movie theme tunes, while a buffet table, heaving with food, took up the best part of an entire side of the marquee. Broderick estimated that there were already over a hundred people in the room and more were arriving all the time. It was a good turn out; Cath would be pleased.

Moving through the happy party-goers, he searched the Khaima for Cath and Sister Clara. A tap on his shoulder made him spin around. Behind him stood the darkly bewigged and stylishly suited Oskar Izzo.

'Hello, Gus. What do you think?'

'About what?'

Izzo stepped back a pace, allowing Broderick a better view of his celebrity transformation. 'George Clooney. *Ocean's Eleven*,' Izzo boasted. 'An uncanny resemblance, don't you think?'

Looking down at the five-foot-six, eighty-one year-old, Broderick did not know what to think.

'If you say so, Mr Izzo. Have you seen my sister?'

'I have. I upset her, I fear. I told her she looked like Mrs Doubtfire.'

'Ah, yes. Well.'

'How is it all going with this Novacs business? Murders, too, I hear. You have your man, I hope. The Pole?'

'I can't talk about that, Mr Izzo. Excuse me, please,' Broderick replied, stepping abruptly to one side and moving off through the throng.

Seconds later, his sister came into view. Cath was talking to a security guard at the exit that led out to the poolside and bar. As Broderick approached, Cath turned and looked straight at him, as if she instinctively knew her brother was there. Her expression immediately alarmed Broderick. Something was wrong.

'Thank goodness you're here, Gus!' Cath clutched her brother's arm and urgently took him to one side. 'Maybe I'm just being stupid, but something rather strange has happened.'

'What?'

'Sister Clara and I were supposed to have been officially welcoming the guests as they arrived, but she's disappeared. I've checked everywhere, and now that security man tells me that she and Daisy left about twenty minutes ago. The man says they took a taxi from the front entrance.'

'Daisy left with her?' Broderick replied.

'That's what the man said. I can't think why they would leave. Is it some surprise I don't know about? Maybe she's unwell.'

'It'll be nothing,' Gus comforted his sister. 'Perhaps she left something behind at home. You mustn't worry. Just get on with things while I find them both.'

Broderick's mobile sounded in his pocket. Reaching for it, he saw Sullivan's name on the screen. 'What is it, Sullivan?' he asked, aware of how abrupt he sounded.

'It's about Sister Clara, guv,' Sullivan answered.

'What about her?'

'It's not conclusive, but I'm certain I've found her on the CCTV footage from the Plaza on the afternoon of the Cornwallis murder.'

'What the hell are you talking about?' Broderick demanded.

'It was seeing Sister Clara with Daisy on my mobile. Dressed as a nun, I mean. I knew I'd seen someone like that before, and recently. I've been trawling back over the recording. Minutes after Isolde enters the reception area, you can just make out the figure of a nun passing along the outer edge of the picture. It's crowded and full of people dressed up in God knows what, but it's a nun alright. The same figure also leaves by way of the reception an hour and a quarter later.'

'And you can identify the nun as being Sister Clara?' Broderick asked as calmly as he could.

'The face is hidden, guv. It's almost as though she knows where the camera is. But the outfit seems identical to Sister Clara's.'

'For God's sake, Sullivan!' Broderick exploded. 'All nuns look the bloody same! It could be anyone.'

'Yes it could, guv, but it isn't. I know it's Clara, because I realised it's not the first time I've seen her dressed that way.'

'This had better be good, Detective Sergeant.'

'Later that day, both of us were in San Roque looking for Jasinski. As we were walking up through the town towards the Plaza de la Iglesia, can you remember what we saw?'

'I haven't got time for a quiz, Sullivan. Get on with it,' Broderick ordered.

'An open lorry with fruit boxes drove down the street. It was closely followed by a nun. She was riding a small motorcycle. Remember? I thought it was sweet. You did, too. I saw you smile.'

'Yes, I remember.'

'The thing is, I caught a fleeting glimpse of her face as she passed. When I saw Sister Clara wearing the nun's habit on FaceTime, she looked different but at the same time familiar. I couldn't figure it out. I mean, I knew I'd never seen her dressed that way before, but then it hit me. The fact is, guv, I had. They were the same person. It was Sister Clara I saw in San Roque on the night of the Martínez and Maugham murders. I'm also convinced that it's her on the CCTV recording of the Plaza reception on the afternoon that Josh Cornwallis was murdered.'

In the Khaima, Cath looked on as the blood drained from her brother's face.

'What is it, Gus?' she asked. 'What's going on?'

Broderick pulled himself together and responded to Sullivan on the other end of the phone. 'Sister Clara's disappeared from the ball up here and taken my daughter with her,' he said, a terrifying picture building in his mind. 'We need to find them and quickly, you understand?'

'Of course. I'm on it.'

'She may head to her home. She lives at Sovereign Villa. It's at the top of Sovereign Passage halfway along Prince Edward's Road. I'm on my way. Get backup and meet me there straight away.'

Before Sullivan could reply, Broderick had ended the call. He now turned to his sister. 'I'm going to sort this out, Cath. You're not to worry.'

'But Gus ...?'

'Just trust me,' Broderick told her firmly. 'Everything's going to be fine.'

Leaving the Khaima, the chief inspector ran across the street. A minute later, he was behind the wheel of his Mercedes and speeding downhill towards Prince Edward's Road. His daughter was in danger. He had never felt fear like it. He punched the steering wheel in frustration. He had to protect Daisy. No matter what it took.

Chapter 89

REACHING THE TOP of the passageway steps and crossing the cobbled courtyard at the front of Sovereign Villa, Broderick could hear the siren of an approaching RGP patrol car.

The iron gate set in the high whitewashed walls surrounding the property was open, and Broderick swiftly climbed more steps up to the garden and front door of the three-storey villa. To his surprise, the large oak door leading into the entry hall of the house was also wide open. Moving cautiously, Broderick took in the immaculate grandness of his surroundings. He had visited the house only once in the few years he had known Sister Clara and had been impressed by her home and its position high above the town.

'Daisy!' he called. 'Daisy! Are you here?'

Silence greeted him.

Broderick checked the downstairs rooms before moving on to the floors above. Returning down the stairs to the ground floor, he arrived in the hall just as Sullivan and two uniformed officers entered through the front door.

'They're not here,' Broderick informed them. 'But I think they were. All the doors were open. They can't be far away.'

'All available officers are out looking for them, guv,' Sullivan replied. 'Border Control's been notified, as has the Marine Unit.'

'I don't want anyone putting my daughter's life in danger. Call Aldarino and tell him to put out a call. No one is to approach them. If that woman's as dangerous as you think she might be, I'm going to be the only one to talk to her. Understood?'

'Yes, guv,' said Sullivan, reaching for her mobile. 'Calbot thinks he has an idea of where Sister Clara may go, sir.'

'Where, for God's sake?' Broderick asked, his desperation rising.

'Sister Clara's mother is in a special nursing home out near Little Bay,' Sullivan replied. 'Been there for some years apparently.'

'Her mother?' Broderick questioned incredulously. 'There's never been a mention of her from Sister Clara. Nor from Cath. I'd assumed she was long dead.'

'No, guv. She's pretty ancient, but she's still with us. Clara must know that she can't get off the Rock. Where else is she likely to go?'

Without hesitation, Broderick moved for the door. 'Let's get there,' he commanded.

Chapter 90

LEAVING THE UNIFORMED officers to keep watch on Sovereign Villa, Broderick and Sullivan took the Mercedes and raced southwards along Europa Road towards Little Bay. The sun was low in the west now, but its warmth and deep red glow permeated the evening sky. In half an hour it would drop over the horizon and darkness would engulf the Rock.

As Broderick drove, Sullivan took a call from Calbot back at HQ. The detective constable had called the nursing home.

'Sister Clara and Daisy Broderick arrived there a few minutes ago,' he told her. 'They've already gone through to her mother's room.'

Sullivan promptly requested backup, insisting a distance be kept until Chief Inspector Broderick ordered otherwise. The last thing they wanted was to spook Sister Clara.

'Understood,' Calbot confirmed.

Next to call Sullivan was a near-hysterical Chief Superintendent Massetti. Sullivan put her on speaker.

'I don't know what the two of you think you're playing at, but it had better be on the money. First, it's Jasinski. Then it's Isolde.

Next thing I know you've brought in a famous film director and his squeeze for questioning. Now you're chasing Gibraltar's answer to Mother Teresa and requesting backup at an old people's nursing home. I hope I'm convincing you that I'm somewhat apprehensive about your next move.'

Sullivan looked at Broderick. The chief inspector kept his eyes fixed on the road.

'We are responding to new developments, ma'am. We have reason to suspect Sister Clara of involvement in the deaths of Cornwallis, Martínez and Maugham. I might also remind you that she's in the company of Chief Inspector Broderick's daughter Daisy, who's most likely being held against her will.'

Massetti was silent for a moment.

'Ma'am?' Sullivan enquired.

'Tell Broderick to do what he considers appropriate, but remind him that he is emotionally involved. I'm coming out to Little Bay myself. Backup's on its way. Take the utmost care. Both of you.'

Massetti ended the call. Once again Sullivan looked at Broderick. Once again he would not meet her eyes.

CHAPTER 91

ALTHOUGH BUENA VISTA House was a nursing home, it was not immediately recognisable as such. Less than a decade old, its publicity described it as a 'state-of-the- art nursing facility for 21st-century elders'. From its position high above the sandy beach of Little Bay, near the southernmost tip of Gibraltar, the select facility offered its occupants large balconied suites with beautiful views across the bay and to the coast of Spain beyond. Most of its aged residents enjoyed these from the comfort of their monitored beds. If you added in the round-the-clock nursing care and surroundings that resembled a luxury hotel, the average cost of care per week was rumoured to be €3,500. Locals joked that you needed a Swiss bank account or a Gibraltar-based off-shore one to die there. Either way, the facility had a long waiting list of people wishing to pass away in five-star surroundings.

The nursing home's manager and a staff nurse were already waiting at the main entrance as the Mercedes pulled up in front. Both Broderick and Sullivan jumped out and were quickly escorted into Buena Vista House and led to a lift that took them to the top floor of the building. Here, the plushest and most expensive nursing suites were to be found. Sullivan noted that the beautifully decorated, pine-scented interior of the building was a far cry from the cabbage- and urine-smelling establishments she usually associated with elderly care. Along the top corridor, she noticed that the suites had brass name plates and the one they were about to enter was called the 'Lady Hamilton'.

Broderick tapped gently on the door and waited. A moment later, the door opened and he looked down at his daughter's smiling face.

'Daddy!' Daisy Broderick exclaimed, moving forward to hug her father. 'Sister Clara said you'd come to get us.'

Broderick felt his knees almost buckle with relief as he wrapped his arms around his youngest child. 'Hello, sweet-pea,' he gasped. 'It's okay. Everything's okay.'

'I know it is, Daddy,' Daisy replied, puzzled. 'Can we go back to the ball now?'

'Of course you can, sweet-pea. I just need to talk with Sister Clara first.'

'She's here, Daddy,' Daisy said, dancing away from her father's arms and into the suite's sitting-room. 'She had to see her mummy. Her mummy's not well and she's very, very old.'

Broderick signalled for the manager and the nurse to remain in the corridor. He and Sullivan then followed Daisy to the bedroom through large double doors to the left of the sitting area.

Moving swiftly through, both detectives were met with an unsettling sight. At the far end of the enormous room, Sister Clara sat beside the bed of a small and extremely elderly woman. Surrounding the two of them was an array of medical machinery with various wires and tubes that all led to the skeletal figure of Diana, Lady Ruiz. The old lady seemed unaware of the new visitors to her room. Her trance-like stare passed them by as she looked out towards the balcony windows and the magnificent view beyond. Sister Clara, still clad in her nun's garments, slowly turned to greet the two detectives.

'Hello, Gus, Tamara,' she began, her polite smile at odds with the deep sadness in her eyes. 'I'm so sorry to put you both to such trouble. I'm afraid things have got most awfully out of control.'

Before Broderick could reply, Daisy interrupted: 'Can we go back, Sister Clara? Your mummy's okay and you've got the gun now.'

Broderick's entire body tensed once more. 'Gun? What gun, sweet-pea?'

'It's alright, Daddy,' Daisy answered. 'Sister Clara said she needed the gun in case the Germans came. She said it's what they should have done in *The Sound of Music*. It's cool.'

Broderick swiftly took his daughter's hand and led her from the room.

'Good idea, sweet-pea,' he told her. 'We'll help Sister Clara, while you wait in the car downstairs.'

Still standing in the corridor were the manager and staff nurse.

Daisy protested. 'Why can't I wait with you, Daddy?'

'Because our friends here are going to take you down to my car.' And Broderick gave the manager his daughter's hand.

Outside the building the sound of sirens alerted them to the arrival of police backup.

'You might get a lift back to the ball in a special police car. Would you like that, sweet-pea?'

Daisy nodded excitedly. 'Yes, please!'

Broderick looked to the manager and whispered: 'Please take her down and tell my colleagues that Sister Clara has a gun up here, will you?'

'Of course,' the woman replied gravely.

'Off you go then,' Broderick told them, giving Daisy a comforting smile. 'I'll be down shortly, sweet-pea.'

The two women and Daisy headed back along the corridor towards the lift. Turning on his heel, Broderick re-entered the suite.

'Daisy okay?' Sullivan asked as he walked back into the bedroom. Broderick nodded, his eyes firmly set on Sister Clara.

The older woman now held an old automatic pistol in her hand. 'I've no wish to cause you any more alarm, Gus. You're not in danger. I've no intention of using this to harm anyone other than myself.'

'There'll be no need for that, Sister Clara,' Broderick replied firmly.

'Will you please hand the gun to me, Sister Clara?' Sullivan asked.

'I think not, if you don't mind, Tamara. I have things I need to tell you. Things you both should know. I'd be grateful if you'd allow me a little time to do that.'

Sullivan looked at Broderick. The chief inspector considered for a moment before replying: 'Talk to us, Sister Clara. Tell us what's happened.'

As Sister Clara placed the pistol on the bed, both Broderick and Sullivan weighed up the chances of reaching it before the older woman could grab it. Instinctively they separately concluded such an action would fail.

A look of pain shot across Sister Clara's face. Then, taking a deep breath and steadying herself, she spoke: 'My mother has been here almost eight years now. They've looked after her well. She has, of course, deteriorated steadily over that time. Her strokes have left her totally immobile and without sight or speech, but her hearing and mind remain intact. She won't show it, but she knows exactly what's going on here. She's been expecting it for decades. Even I have had the last eight years to prepare. The events of the last few days took me completely by surprise. My reactions to them weren't planned, Gus. I'm afraid they were a knee-jerk response to the hell I found myself thrown into. I assure you that, with hindsight, I would have done things differently, but I accept the consequences of what I did do.'

'Sister Clara, are you confessing to the murders of Josh Cornwallis, Don Martínez and Graeme Maugham?' Broderick asked.

For a moment, Sister Clara's large green eyes filled with tears. 'Yes, Gus. I am.'

Sullivan took a step forward. 'Perhaps it would be better to do this elsewhere, Sister Clara. Leave your mother in peace.'

'Please come no closer, Tamara,' Sister Clara implored, reaching once more for the gun. 'I really have nothing to lose by turning this weapon on myself. And that would rob you of my full confession.'

Sullivan paused a moment before stepping back.

'Thank you, dear,' Sister Clara said, replacing the gun on the bed.

The sun across the bay hung in the sky like a gigantic orb, filling the room with an intense red and purple glow. The electronic bleeps and pulses from the monitoring machines, together with the old woman's occasional rasping breaths, lent the entire tableau an other-worldly quality.

Sister Clara cleared her throat and carried on: 'The most immediate thing you need to know is how and why those poor men died. The simple explanation is that they were about to destroy everything I've worked for during the last fifty years. I've not taken these actions to protect my reputation, whatever that may be. Nor indeed my parents' legacy. I killed those men because

THE POISONED ROCK

I thought I had no choice. I believed it was the only way I could protect the thousands of men, women and children that the Rock of Ages Foundation helps every year. People without hope or any real means of survival. People who would perish without the charity's help.'

The ringing of Broderick's mobile interrupted her.

Broderick checked the screen. 'It's Chief Superintendent Massetti. May I speak with her, please?' he asked.

'Of course,' Sister Clara conceded.

The detective touched the green button and put the phone to his ear. 'Ma'am?'

'Broderick, I need to know exactly what the situation is,' Massatti asked. 'Can you speak freely?'

'To some extent, ma'am.'

'Does Sister Clara have a gun?'

'Yes, ma'am.'

'Is she threatening you?'

'No, ma'am,' Broderick answered calmly. 'Neither Detective Sergeant Sullivan or myself are being held against our will. We're talking to Sister Clara in the hope of persuading her to hand over the gun and leave here with us peacefully.'

'Okay, Broderick. Armed officers are taking position in the corridor outside the room. Leave the phone line open so I can hear exactly what's going on. The slightest problem and I'll order them in. Don't take any chances, you understand?'

'Perfectly, ma'am. May I ask that you get Daisy away from here? Get her back to my sister at the Rock Hotel.'

'Already happening, Gus,' Massetti replied. 'Good luck.'

A relieved Broderick looked at his mobile's screen and pretended to touch the 'Call finished' button, but instead, the line remained open with Massetti listening intently on the other end.

'You're a good father, Gus,' Sister Clara said. 'Your daughters are a credit to you.'

'Thank you,' Broderick replied. 'Perhaps you'd now like to tell us exactly what's happened.'

'Of course,' she said, reaching into a pocket and pulling out a black velvet purse. Loosening the lace band that held it tightly closed, she emptied its contents onto the bed in front of her.

'I discovered these,' she declared, as a shower of diamonds poured from the purse onto the bed. Neither Sullivan or Broderick had ever seen such a dazzling stream of precious stones. It was impossible to guess how many there were, but Broderick estimated that it had to be a cache of least twenty stones of differing shapes and sizes.

'Impressive, wouldn't you agree?' Sister Clara continued.

'Very,' Broderick returned. 'Are they yours?'

'No, no. My mother's hidden hoard,' Sister Clara replied, unable to hide a hint of distaste. 'Soon after she came here to the Buena Vista, she experienced the first of her strokes. For many weeks, it was touch and go whether she'd survive. Naturally, I prepared for her passing by attempting to get her affairs in order. I started with her home in Spain. She hadn't lived here on the Rock for decades. She and my stepfather spent most of their lives travelling the world, but they passed the rest of their time at their homes in Seville and London. Most of the bigger financial and business matters had been attended to by my mother herself. It was the smaller, personal matters I needed to address. One afternoon, while examining the contents of the safe in her study in Seville, I came across the key to a safe deposit box that she rented from a local bank. As my mother had given me power of attorney, I saw no harm in investigating the box's contents. In it, I discovered these diamonds.'

Taking a handkerchief from her sleeve, she reached across and gently wiped a small dribble of saliva from the old woman's chin.

'Hard to imagine now, but my mother was quite a formidable person in her prime. The Rock of Ages Foundation was her idea. With my stepfather's support, she fought to establish it. I had always taken it for granted that the charity would be her legacy. Something the world would know her for and appreciate long after she was gone. The fact is, if the truth about her life becomes known, she'll be remembered for very different things.'

At that moment, Sullivan thought she saw a flicker in Lady Ruiz's eyes. It passed in an instant but was enough to confirm to Sullivan that the old woman was aware of every word that was being said. Sister Clara folded her handkerchief and placed it on the cabinet beside her.

'Her life has run along two very different parallel lines. One life public and benevolent. The other secretive and shameful.'

Sister Clara stopped for a moment. It appeared as though the full weight of what she had to say might prove too much for her.

'Perhaps we *should* do this elsewhere,' Broderick suggested.

'No, no. It has to be here and now,' Sister Clara replied, regaining her composure. 'I have to tell you things in order. I'm easily confused at the moment. The effects of shock, I'm afraid.'

Once again Sister Clara paused to collect her thoughts. 'My earliest memories are of living with the missionaries in Nairobi, after my father was murdered in Johannesburg. Do you know about that?' Broderick and Sullivan both nodded. 'Well, our journey through Africa to Kenya opened my mother's eyes to what she saw as the "real suffering of the world".'

Sullivan and Broderick glanced at each other, both sharing the same thought: *Is Sister Clara still unaware that she's adopted?*

'My mother had never seen poverty and death on such a scale before. She had never seen the huge disparity between the nations of the world. Those with wealth and those with nothing or next to nothing. By the time we arrived in Kenya, she'd decided to help those without hope. Working at the mission, she soon realised that religion would not affect the situation – only money and aid could make an immediate difference. But little was changing. She became disillusioned over there. Going to South Africa wasn't desirable. She told me that my father's murder there made it too painful for her to contemplate a return. She was going to do something – and she did. It took her nearly twenty years to get the foundation fully established. Quite something, really.'

'I'm sure,' Sullivan acknowledged.

'I don't think she meant to stay here long, but she, as a widow with a young daughter, had had a sympathetic welcome on the Rock. People were very kind. None kinder than Paul Ruiz. Within eighteen months they were married and that was that.'

'And the diamonds?' Broderick asked, impatient to move on.

'The diamonds here hold the key to the whole Pandora's box,' Sister Clara said, picking up one of the larger stones and holding it to the light. Its sparkling transparency was suddenly infused with the ever-deepening crimson glow of the sunset. For a moment, it looked as though the diamond was transforming into a precious ruby.

'It's turned red,' she murmured, almost mesmerised by its beauty.

For a moment, all three looked on as refracted beams of coloured light spread out from the stone and danced on the walls of the room. Sister Clara broke the spell as she returned the diamond to its place among the others and continued in a more matter-of-fact tone.

'My mother made a remarkable recovery from her first stroke, and so I took the opportunity to ask her about what I'd found. To my huge surprise, my discovery didn't surprise her. It seems it had been her intention for me to find the diamonds as I did. Nothing unusual about that – always in control, my mother ...' Sister Clara reached for Lady Ruiz's hand and held it. '... until now, perhaps.'

Once again, Sullivan saw a fleeting glimpse of defiance in the old woman's eyes. An expression that went unnoticed by Sister Clara.

'My mother confessed, as best she could, that she had no regrets about her life other than having to lie to her only child.'

'And the diamonds?' Sullivan asked again.

'She told me they'd been her payment for services rendered. Diamonds were the currency in which my mother was paid for her work on the Rock during World War II.'

'World War II?' Broderick exclaimed. 'What the hell was she doing to get that kind of reward?'

'It's quite simple, Gus. My mother was a spy. A highly valued and well-paid one. An interesting story. The sort of story some people might even turn into a film.'

Sister Clara could see that Broderick was struggling to take everything in. 'I think Tamara might be a little ahead of you on this one, Gus.'

Broderick turned to the detective sergeant, but before he could ask the question, she answered him: 'I think she's telling us that Lady Ruiz here was the Queen of Diamonds, guv.'

'Yes ... I am, Tamara.'

Sister Clara slowly reached into her bag and pulled out the top secret file that Graeme Maugham had brought with him from England.

'And this file confirms it. When I first confronted my mother, here in this very room, she only confessed part of the truth. The part that has become the legend. The sanitised version Josh Cornwallis dramatised in his film script. The Queen of Diamonds depicted as a hero. A lone woman spy working for the Allies to bring about the defeat of Nazi Germany. I wanted desperately to believe her, but as she told me, I remembered something. An incident I'd almost erased from memory. I remembered that I'd once received a letter from a retired inspector, formerly with the Gibraltar police. This was back in the early 1960s. I'm afraid I forget his name now.'

'Inspector Lorenz?' Sullivan interrupted. A sharp look from Broderick made her wish she had kept her mouth shut.

'Yes,' Sister Clara confirmed. 'I believe that was his name. The letter was sent to my convent in England. As I never received letters of any kind, it was deemed important enough to let me read it. As I recall, it stated that Lorenz was making enquiries about my mother's activities in Gibraltar during World War II. He wrote that he had some important questions he'd like to ask me regarding my mother's possible work as a German intelligence operative. A Nazi spy who later became a British double-agent. He said he'd be prepared to travel to the UK to meet me, if I'd be allowed to see him.'

'And were you?' Broderick asked.

'Of course not. I didn't even reply. It didn't stop Lorenz from coming, though. One afternoon, about a month later, the mother superior informed me that I had a visitor. A Mr Lorenz. Not even my mother had visited me at the convent, and I have to say I was far from pleased. I refused to see him.'

'Weren't you interested in what he had to say?' Sullivan asked.

'I wasn't. I wrote to my mother and told her of Lorenz's enquiries. She wrote back and told me that the man was off his head, and that I shouldn't give it a moment's further thought. And I didn't. Until eight years ago, when my mother admitted the truth. Or part of the truth.'

'Which part did she omit?' Sullivan asked.

'The part about once being a German intelligence operative.'

'And when you confronted her with that?' Sullivan continued.

'She neither admitted nor denied it. She told me that life on the Rock had been very difficult during those years, and that she had only done what she believed was right. I didn't press her further.'

'And the whole truth was delivered to you this week by Cornwallis and the Maugham file.'

'Yes. The full story, as poor Mr Maugham discovered, was quite different.'

'Different enough for you to end up murdering three men?' Broderick said, aghast.

'Yes,' Sister Clara confessed, a look of genuine anguish filling her face.

'Why did he and the others have to die, Sister Clara?' Sullivan asked.

'Because I panicked. When the making of the film was announced, I knew things would change. After all, my mother had told me she was the Queen of Diamonds. It was her story. But something else happened. Something I hadn't wanted to face up to. The truth was that I didn't believe her story. Not fully. It was just an instinct, at first easily dismissed, but it had never fully gone away. For eight years it had haunted me. What if there was more? What if my mother had lied and Lorenz had told the truth? The diamonds seemed to be a huge reward for her work. What exactly had they bought? To my horror, I realised that I didn't believe her. And so I read everything I could about the film. I found out all I could about those who were making it. The fact is, when Josh Cornwallis contacted me this week, I knew exactly who he was.'

'Cornwallis contacted you?' Broderick asked.

'He left a note at Sovereign Villa asking me to meet him urgently. He said he knew secrets and had urgent questions he needed to ask.'

'And so you went to see him,' Sullivan added, moving a little nearer to the bed.

'I had no choice,' Sister Clara replied. 'All my fears came tumbling in on me at once. Every scenario led to the same conclusion. Josh Cornwallis had discovered that my mother was the Queen of Diamonds. That was bad enough, but I sensed there was more. I felt sick to my stomach. I almost fainted. What did he know? I had to somehow find out, but I also had to protect myself and my mother for as long as I could.'

It was clear that the sheer effort of confession was taking its toll on Sister Clara. She reached for the glass of water beside her and took a sip. Sullivan and Broderick waited for her to regain her composure and carry on.

'A plan came to me out of the blue. Born out of terror, really. I convinced myself that it was the best I could do. Not knowing how much or how little Josh Cornwallis knew meant that I had to cover all possibilities, to give myself options. It just so happened that I'd unpacked my old nun's habit in preparation for this evening's ball. I hadn't worn it since I had left the order and was pleased that it was still in good condition. I was even more delighted that it still fit me well. Looking at it, I realised that, wearing the habit afforded me some kind of disguise. Putting it on, I saw that the real me, the person many recognise as Sister Clara, simply disappeared. It's often said, and with good reason, that "all nuns look alike". It was this that persuaded me to wear it on my visit to the Marina Plaza. At the very least, I thought it might disarm Cornwallis and render me, in his eyes, harmless.'

'Why would you need that?' Sullivan asked.

'Because if the need arose, I'd decided that I'd have to harm him.'

In the bed, Lady Ruiz's arm twitched and jerked upward. Sister Clara looked unsurprised. 'She does that. Involuntary spasms. Can be quite alarming, but she's alright.'

'Does she need a nurse?' Sullivan asked.

'Oh, no. I don't think so, Tamara. Thank you for your concern.'

'So what happened next?' Broderick asked, anxiously.

'I did what I always do when I need to think clearly.'

'Pray?' Broderick offered.

'No, alas. I simply went to my kitchen and baked a cake.'

'The cake containing the Rohypnol, you mean?' Sullivan asked.

'The same,' Sister Clara confirmed. 'For most of her life, my mother had suffered from chronic insomnia.'

'I'm not surprised,' Broderick interrupted before he could stop himself.

Sister Clara carried on as if the comment had gone unheard. 'She'd take the drug to relax and ease the relentless anxiety and exhaustion of her condition. Over time I used it, too. Indeed, I accrued a surplus of it in my bathroom cabinet. I reasoned that, if I could somehow get Josh Cornwallis to take a dose, it might render him physically helpless. It would also impair his memory, allowing me to obtain what information I could while leaving the young man unable to remember our meeting. With luck, the drug would make him forget he'd seen me at all.'

'But it all went wrong,' Sullivan said flatly.

'At first, no. I baked the cake, mixing in powdered Rohypnol and adding extra flavouring to mask any taste of the drug. I walked to the apartment building, passing several friends and acquaintances, none of whom recognised me. When I reached the Marina Plaza, there was a huge reception party going on. So, checking where the security cameras were positioned, I slowly worked my way around the edge of the room until I reached the lifts. On answering his door, Josh Cornwallis seemed surprised to see me, but when I told him that I was the resident of Sovereign Villa, he welcomed me in and accepted the cake. He didn't take long to get down to business and quickly showed me Maugham's file. He told me about its contents and from whom he'd received it. What he told me about my mother's activities while working for the Germans here in Gibraltar during the war was truly shocking. Her work as a blackmailer and murderer was far worse than anything I could have anticipated. Looking through the file, he showed me document after document that confirmed the stories he was telling. My mother had been a cold-hearted mercenary. Inspector Lorenz had been right. She held no real allegiance to any country or political creed. She worked just for the diamonds and for the thrill of power and danger.

'As he told me all this, Josh became agitated. He said his film would be discredited if the truth got out. He told me the only thing he could do was convince his producer to stop production and begin again with a screenplay that told the real story. I'm afraid I couldn't have cared less about that. My only thought was to stop the truth coming out at all. I noticed that he'd eaten a generous slice of the cake and was becoming incoherent. Then, while he wasn't looking, I took the opportunity to lace his drink with more Rohypnol, to find out who also knew about my mother. He said that, to his knowledge, it was just an old Spaniard in San Roque called Don Eduardo Martínez and whoever had given him the file. Slowly, Josh began to lose control of his body. His speech became slurred and I realised at that moment I could not let him live. I had to stop him and the others from revealing the truth. Which is why

I took a cushion, covered his face and pressed down hard until he breathed no more.'

Sister Clara fell silent. Sullivan and Broderick looked on in shock. At last Broderick was able to speak. 'What happened next?'

'I took his laptop and phone and then walked home. Once there, I went to my kitchen and baked another cake. This time a Spanish *bizcocho*. A gift for Don Martínez.'

'How did you find him?' Sullivan asked.

'That was easy. I knew who he was already. He'd been mayor of San Roque and a very successful businessman. I'd even been to a reception at his house once – many years ago, but I remembered it. I even remembered its rear courtyard leading out onto a series of passageways. His home telephone number wasn't ex-directory and so I called it from a pay phone just off Main Street here in Gibraltar. His housekeeper answered and I pretended to be a representative from a delivery company wishing to drop off a parcel for Don Martínez. My Spanish is good and she didn't question me. I enquired if delivery could be made some time that evening. She informed me that she left at 7 pm, but that Don Martínez would be in and, if not, his house guest might take the parcel on his behalf. I found myself asking if the guest was Spanish. She told me he was an Englishman, but that his Spanish was good so communication wouldn't be a problem. I thanked her and rang off. It didn't take me long to work out who the guest was. It had to be Maugham. A taxi to San Roque was of no use, but in my garage, I had an old motor scooter I used to ride – to my surprise, it started first time.'

Broderick looked at Sullivan. His detective sergeant had been right about that, too.

'And so, early that evening, I set off for San Roque. It is a journey I've done often over the years. I have many friends in San Roque. Many friends.'

Sister Clara, lost to the past, continued to recount the murderous events of that night. As she spoke, the two detectives once again weighed up their chances of crossing the room and overpowering her before she could take up the gun. Despite Sullivan's subtle attempts to move closer, it was clear to both that it wouldn't work. They had no choice but to remain patient and listen.

'I crossed the border with ease and rode to the town. I arrived mid-evening, parked the motor scooter on a side street, and then walked to the rear of the Martínez house. At the back door, Don Martínez was shocked to see me. I told him I needed to speak urgently and so, reluctantly, he let me in. I gave him the cake and assured him I was alone. I also told him I was scared and that I desperately needed to know exactly was going on. This seemed to reassure him. He led me through to meet Maugham and minutes later they confirmed that the files from England were authentic. Then, as they ate the *bizcocho,* Don Martínez told the story of his cousin Marisella's violent death. A murder that he believed my mother had carried out while working for the Germans in 1942. I asked them who else, other than Josh Cornwallis, knew of these facts. Both were convinced that it was now just the three of them. This was all I needed to know. Not long after that, Don Martínez gave way to the Rohypnol's effects. Graeme Maugham, however, did not. I had no choice but to strike him across the head with a heavy ornament I found on a nearby table. The poor man tried to rise again, but I hit him once more and he died. Don Martínez, I fear, met a similar end to that of Josh Cornwallis. It was a terrible scene.'

'We know,' Broderick informed her coldly. 'We saw it for ourselves.'

In the bed, Lady Ruiz's arm began to shake uncontrollably. Almost immediately her entire body was overcome by a series of grotesque convulsions. Her eyes opened wide to reveal white bloodshot eyeballs, and her breathing became a series of rasps of increasing pain. The support machines beside the bed went into meltdown as their alarms pierced the quiet stillness of the room.

The shock of this made Sister Clara stand and step away from the bed. Taking their chance, both Sullivan and Broderick ran towards her, Broderick securing the gun and Sullivan pushing the emergency button above the bedstead. Simultaneously, the door of the bedroom burst open and three armed police officers entered the room. The first moved to Sister Clara and forced her against the wall; the other two trained their guns on the clearly traumatised woman.

Next into the bedroom came Massetti, balancing on her crutches, and Calbot. On seeing her two colleagues, Sullivan yelled an instruction that needed no clarification.

'For God's sake, get a nurse here. Now!'

CHAPTER 92

THE MASSIVE STROKE that took the life of Diana, Lady Ruiz completed its work in seconds, leaving only a withered shell of wrinkled flesh and bone behind. Sister Clara asked if she could close her mother's eyes and say a prayer. This she was allowed to do, before being led away to a police car and the journey to New Mole House.

The first thing Gus Broderick did upon leaving Buena Vista House was rush to the Rock Hotel and check that Daisy had arrived back at the ball safe and well. He saw immediately that his daughter was enjoying herself. She'd come third in the fancy dress competition and was now at the centre of the dance floor enjoying the disco. Cath, standing next to her brother, was desperate to know what had happened to Sister Clara.

'I'm sorry, Sis,' Broderick told her. 'I know how upset you must be, but I can't say anything at the moment. I'll let you know as soon as I can. Promise.'

Although distressed, Cath knew better than to press her brother further.

Ten minutes later, Broderick, Sullivan, Massetti and Calbot arrived back at police HQ expecting something of a hero's welcome.

Instead they were met by a sombre-faced Sergeant Aldarino.

'You have visitors waiting for you in your office, ma'am,' he informed Massetti. 'Commissioner Barrolli would like you to brief him immediately. Chief Inspector Broderick, DS Sullivan and DC Calbot are to wait outside your office so he can talk with them, too. The commissioner has also made it clear that no mention of tonight's events are to be made to any other personnel here at the station until he's given clearance.'

'What the hell's going on, Aldarino?' Massetti asked.

'I couldn't say, ma'am. He's got someone from London with him and he seems a little vexed,' the sergeant replied.

'Do we have to ask his permission for a cup of tea as well, Aldarino?' Broderick asked sarcastically.

'Commissioner Barrolli gave no direct orders regarding that, sir,' Aldarino replied. 'I'm sure I can rustle up a brew and a plate of biscuits while you wait.'

As Massetti entered her office, her three colleagues reluctantly took seats outside. During the hour-and-a-half wait, Aldarino was kept busy bringing tea and biscuits for the waiting trio and taking messages into the chief super's office. Patience was running short by the time the office door finally opened and Police Commissioner Thomas Barrolli asked them to step inside. They found Massetti sitting at her desk, her foot perched on an upturned waste paper basket. At her side stood a tall, elegant-looking woman in her mid-forties.

'Well, well, well,' the commissioner began. 'It's been quite an evening, by the sound of things.'

Broderick nodded. 'Sir.'

'Thank you for waiting. We've had a lot to deal with one way or another. Firstly, I'd like to introduce you to Rachel Shapley,' Barrolli said. 'Ms Shapley is deputy director of operations for SIS, better known to you and me as MI6. She's arrived here from London tonight because of a special interest in the Queen of Diamonds case and, of course, in the events of the past week.'

Rachel Shapley took a half-step forward and smiled at the assembled officers. 'I'm delighted to meet you. It seems you've achieved some extraordinarily fine results in a very short period of time. You're to be congratulated.'

'Thank you,' Broderick replied.

The commissioner continued: 'As you're aware, it's a case that's generated a great deal of interest in the world's media and a great deal of anxiety here on the Rock. It seems you may have caught the perpetrator of these murders, but I have to tell you, things are a lot more complicated than they presently appear.'

'With respect, sir,' Broderick interrupted, 'they seem complicated enough.'

'I'm sure, Chief Inspector,' Barrolli responded curtly. 'Nevertheless, I think it best if I hand you over to Ms Shapley for an initial insight into our thinking on this.'

Sullivan looked across to Massetti. It was clear from the chief super's expression that she was far from happy with the unfolding situation.

'Thank you, Thomas,' Shapley said, taking another step forward. 'What I have to say will most probably surprise you. As you know, the late Graeme Maugham stole a top secret file from the cabinet secretary's special archives. It contained many things of a highly sensitive nature. Things that would continue to place the file beyond declassification for some considerable time. From my understanding of what has occurred tonight, the four of you have been privy to some of the information within those documents by way of Sister Clara's confession. You'll be aware that, as police officers, you've signed the Official Secrets Act, and because of this,

I'd ask that you now keep all the facts you've heard and those I'm about to tell you completely confidential.'

Broderick looked questioningly at Massetti. The chief super shrugged. 'I'm as baffled as you are, Chief Inspector,' she said.

'Then I'll endeavour to make myself clearer,' Shapley said. 'You must all be exhausted, so I'll try to get to the point as quickly as I can. Much of what I have to say now isn't to be found in the Maugham file. It's in another, even larger file held by MI6. Diana Ruiz has been known to the British intelligence services in one guise or another for over seventy years, but we only made the connection to her in the present cases after hearing about Maugham's murder yesterday.'

'And you didn't think to inform us sooner?' Massetti asked angrily.

'I'm afraid we moved as quickly as we could. Besides, we weren't absolutely convinced. Before I get into that, let me tell you more about Ruiz.

'Although she went by several names during her lifetime, she was born Diana Candoza in London in 1920. She had wealthy parents, was well schooled but, in her teens, became something of a rebel. At the age of sixteen, she ran away to Spain, where she joined the International Brigade on the Republican side, fighting Franco's Nationalists in that country's civil war. Within weeks, she was captured, interrogated, most probably tortured and finally turned by Franco's intelligence operatives into a spy. In this guise, she was allowed to escape and rejoin the brigade. For the rest of the war, she successfully worked against the Republicans, passing highly sensitive information to her Nationalist colleagues.

'At the end of the conflict, she stayed in Spain and lived with a Nationalist major named Carlos Ortiz, the man who had interrogated her after her capture. Soon after moving with him to Algeciras in the December of 1939, she fell pregnant. Then Ortiz disappeared and Diana was forced to have the baby alone. In September 1940, the child was taken in by a local orphanage. We know that Diana Candoza then made her way to the Rock and got a job dealing with freight imports out near the military airfield – the present-day airport.

'During her time in Algeciras, she had been recruited by the Nazi Abwehr and persuaded to become a spy for them here on the Rock. Her ambitious missions for the Abwehr over the following years are all documented in Maugham's file. It's clear that she was a ruthless operative who thought nothing of sending people to their deaths. She was even personally responsible for at least two murders herself.'

Shapley could see that her audience was beginning to wonder why they were being given such detailed information.

'I'm sorry if this is a lot to take in, but you'll see its relevance to today's events shortly,' she said, straightening her back. 'Our intelligence officers working on the Rock eventually became suspicious of her, and it soon became obvious that she was a spy. At this point, it was decided to attempt to turn her into a double-agent. One officer in particular took control of this process and achieved almost immediate success.

'Within a short time, the German agent, codenamed Diamant, had become our very own Queen of Diamonds, recruited as an operative just prior to the ill-fated flight of the Polish prime minister-in-exile, General Władysław Sikorski in July 1943. He was killed when his plane crashed seconds after take-off from the runway here in Gibraltar. It's long been the subject of conspiracy theories, many claiming that he was assassinated, but this was always officially denied. In fact, many in the service thought the 'accident' had been arranged by Stalin, who had fallen out with

Sikorski. Certain documents in the file that Maugham smuggled out of the UK point to the fact that such theories are most probably true. I'll return to this shortly.'

'Would you care for some water?' the police commissioner offered.

'I'm just fine, thank you, Thomas,' she smiled wearily and then continued her story: 'For the next year, Diana Candoza seemed to work successfully for British intelligence, but despite this, she was still considered dangerous. Mainly because she was no ordinary spy. She was a mercenary, demanding payment from us in diamonds in exactly the same way she'd demanded them from the Germans. In 1944, with her espionage work diminishing, she married an unsuspecting South African called Ackerman and left Gibraltar for Johannesburg. Prior to this, the couple had adopted a child from an orphanage in Algeciras – the same orphanage where she'd left her own child four years previously. Perhaps she'd gone searching for it and found it gone, the adopted child becoming in some sense a replacement. We'll never know for sure. However, it seems highly likely she knew exactly who her newly adopted child was – Rosia Martinez, the daughter of a woman she had murdered. Was the adoption born out of guilt? A need for redemption? Again, we'll never know.'

A shocked silence greeted this information. Shapley moved quickly on.

'And so the Ackerman family flew south to start a new life. That could well have been the last we ever heard of her. However, sometime in 1962, MI6's attention was drawn to a Lady Ruiz, a resident of the Rock and wife of the hugely influential international businessman Sir Paul Ruiz. Her name had been flagged up by the Soviet defector Anatoly Golitsyn. You may remember that he was one of the Russians that MI6 used to help identify the spy, Kim

Philby. Golitsyn stated in interview that he'd heard that a major KGB agent was the wife of a leading executive with connections to Gibraltar. It didn't take MI6 long to discover that Diana Ruiz had once been the British double-cross spy known to the agency as the Queen of Diamonds.'

'Excuse me,' Sullivan interrupted. 'Did you say KGB spy?'

'Indeed I did,' Shapley replied. 'I said this case was more complicated than you imagined. On Golitsyn's tip-off, MI6 officers went back decades through the files and investigated further. One hugely important piece of information finally identified Ruiz as a KGB operative. The name of the intelligence officer who had turned her from a German spy into a British double-agent in 1943 was the then head of MI6's Iberian section – Kim Philby.'

GIBRALTAR, JULY 1943

THE NEXT FEW minutes would be vital.

Hidden high on the upper reaches of the Rock, the British intelligence officer checked his watch and raised a silver-plated drinking flask to his lips. Two large gulps of fine malt whisky brought a burning sensation to the back of his throat. A delicious discomfort. The time was now precisely 23.05.

The man had a 360-degree view from his position on the Rock. The Bay of Gibraltar to the west, with Spain and Africa to the north and south. Ignoring those panoramas, the tall and darkly handsome head of MI6's Iberian section focused intently on the Mediterranean, its blackened canvas spreading endlessly before him to the east. Conditions were perfect. The air balmy and warm, the stars diamond bright in the night sky above. It was hard to believe that there was a war going on.

Returning the near-empty flask to his jacket pocket, the officer tried to visualise the events taking place on the nearby Gibraltar airfield. The commander-in-chief of the Polish army and prime minister of the Polish government-in-exile, General Władysław Sikorski, would by now have boarded his plane. With him, his daughter and members of his staff. The general would be weary from his two-month tour of the Middle East, inspecting his forces and raising the morale of the Polish troops. With his beloved country divided between German and Soviet occupation, the path he was treading continued to be a dangerous and potentially treacherous one.

The B24 Liberator would be ready for take-off at the side of the short Gibraltar runway. The airfield had been built on land reclaimed from the sea, and was prone to dangerous updrafts of air currents circling the Rock. Take-off and landing were challenges for even the most experienced of pilots.

As soon as clearance was given, the Liberator's Czech pilot, Eduard Prchal, would commence his journey towards the western end of the runway.

Some 240 metres above him on the towering limestone Rock, the officer reached once more for his whisky flask and readied himself for a show.

The next few minutes would be vital.

Many feet below, on the northern edge of Gibraltar Town, someone else was watching.

Standing on the roof of a three storey-building on the town side of the Gibraltar airfield, a woman waited nervously for the final stages of her operation to be over. She had been involved in many acts of espionage since arriving on the Rock two years earlier, but this one was different in both scale and expectations. It was also different in one other respect. Her loyalties had changed. The direction of the war had shifted, and so had her allegiance. It was a brave new world for those who had the guts to exploit it.

THE POISONED ROCK

In peace time, the building below her had been occupied by an insurance company. Requisitioned by the army, it had served many purposes over the war years. Most recently it had been used as a records and processing office for all military and civilian air supply and cargo services. The work was highly classified and the young woman had held an important clerical position within the department. English-born, she had retained civilian status on the Rock and was completely trusted by her superiors.

Often working late into the night, she knew her presence in the empty building was never considered suspicious in any way. The guards who stood sentry at the main doors were used to the young Englishwoman leaving her workplace late in the evening. Tonight would be no exception. At 22.45, she had left her office on the second floor, taking care to keep her desk lamp on, and made her way to the roof. Supposedly out of bounds to all personnel, she had gained possession of the key. Climbing the narrow stairs to the top of the building, she had unlocked the small, metal-reinforced door that led out onto the large expanse of flat roof. Moving swiftly to the airfield side of the building, she was relieved to see that her view of the entire runway was practically unimpaired.

The airfield was full of operational planes of all shapes and sizes. Fighters, bombers and supply aircraft stood almost wing tip to wing tip along the length of the runway on both sides. All awaited refuelling, maintenance or orders for new missions. As the sole Allied airbase on the Continent, its position and security were of unimaginable importance in the fight against Hitler and the Axis powers.

Pulling the collar of her blouse up around her neck and readjusting a wisp of her honey-coloured shoulder-length hair, the woman scanned the airfield for one particular aircraft. The B24 Liberator came immediately into view, pulling away from the side of the runway and moving to the end of it in preparation for take-off. The woman's heartbeat increased alarmingly. Her part in what was about to happen had been pivotal. Blackmail, torture and murder had been her methods. Although still only twenty-three, she was experienced in the dark arts of espionage and took great pride in her abilities and achievements. If all went to plan in the next few minutes, she would be rewarded handsomely, although the thrill of anticipation she felt was almost reward enough.

Minutes later, the Liberator thrust forward, down the terrifyingly short runway and started its ascent into the skies to the east of Gibraltar. The woman looked on as the plane climbed normally, before dipping its nose to gather speed. At this moment, she knew that the Liberator's pilot would be struggling to control the aircraft's elevator controls, all unaccountably and irreversibly jammed. He alone among those on board would know the seriousness of the malfunction at such a vital point in the flight.

Moments later, unable to respond to the pilot's demands, the plane lost speed, shook violently and nose-dived. Within seconds it had crashed into the dark and unforgiving waters of the Mediterranean. From take-off to fatal submergence had taken sixteen-and-a-half seconds. It would take the best part of a minute for the alarm bell to ring out across the airfield and for an emergency truck to move urgently towards the eastern end of the runway. From her secret vantage point, the woman looked on with growing excitement, guessing correctly that all rescue efforts would be in vain. The next day the world would wake to the news that General Władysław Sikorski, his daughter and his entire staff were dead.

The woman let out a deep sigh of satisfaction, smiled and walked purposefully back towards the rooftop door. Operation complete.

Present Day

SHAPLEY ADJUSTED HER collar. The room was hot, the air conditioning seemingly ineffectual. She continued to brief the detectives.

'Logically, we now know that Philby must have turned Ruiz into a triple-agent working for the Soviets. Her job and connections on the Rock would have proved immensely useful in enabling the sabotage of Sikorski's doomed aircraft. Philby gave her the operation to test her loyalty to both himself and the Soviet NKVD intelligence service. Once she'd passed that test, he made much of her to MI6 as his new double-cross spy on the Rock. British intelligence bought it hook, line and sinker. Stalin must have been delighted.'

'Bully for him,' Broderick murmured under his breath.

Ignoring him, Shapley continued: 'When Diana Candoza finally left Gibraltar for South Africa, we believe she left spying behind – although it's thought she most probably had a hand in her husband's murder. On leaving South Africa for Kenya, she was reactivated as an agent by a Soviet consulate official in Nairobi. She subsequently moved to Gibraltar to recommence her spying career. You might say the Russians hid her in plain sight.'

Shapley now reached for the glass of water that the commissioner had offered previously. As she drank thirstily, Sullivan asked the question that was on everyone's mind. 'So if you knew she was a Russian spy in 1962, why didn't you arrest her?'

Shapley smiled, pleased to have got her information across so well. 'The oldest intelligence trick in the book – we let her carry on, but under extremely close observation. She had no idea she'd been outed and so continued to work for another twenty-seven years for what had by then become the KGB. Until the Berlin Wall came down, in fact. For most of that time, MI6 made sure she was fed clever misinformation. Enough useful bits and pieces to please her handlers, but also many other things that led to more revelations about KGB operations and operatives during the Cold War than we could ever have imagined possible. She became of less use to both us and the Russians over time. But even towards the end of her spying years, she was still unwittingly providing us with enough intelligence to keep us more than interested.'

'So over a period of fifty years, Ruiz had been a spy for Franco's Nationalists, the German Abwehr, British intelligence *and* the Soviet KGB?' Massetti asked incredulously.

'Yes, indeed. A truly extraordinary career,' Shapley conceded.

'And Sister Clara has no idea about her mother's work with the KGB?' Massetti continued.

'None whatsoever.'

'Sister Clara also has no idea that Diana Ruiz isn't her real mother,' Sullivan added pointedly. 'She was born Rosia Martínez. In 1942, her real mother, Marisella, was brutally murdered by Ruiz – known then as Diana Candoza, or Diament – after the poor girl became caught up in an espionage plot to kill Eisenhower. Rosia Martínez – a.k.a. Sister Clara – is also unknowingly a cousin of

Eduardo Martínez, who she poisoned and suffocated to death in San Roque earlier this week.'

'I'd prefer not to be the one to tell her that,' Broderick muttered.

'None of you will have to,' Shapley said, 'for the very good reason that we have no intention of telling her.'

The silence that greeted Shapley's remark was born out of genuine shock. Nobody wanted to ask a question lest they appeared foolish for missing the reasoning behind the MI6 officer's announcement. Recognising this, Shapley came to their rescue.

'MI6 and both the British and Gibraltar governments at the highest levels have decided that the truth about Diana Ruiz's long career must remain secret. There are many things about her activities that are still far too sensitive for us to allow the full story to spill into the public domain. As well as any political considerations, our ongoing intelligence work and special relationships might be compromised. A restless and territorially ambitious Russia is changing the political climate. A new Cold War is becoming a daily reality. The events and revelations of your investigations over the last few days could cause great embarrassment and danger to both the UK and the British Overseas Territory of Gibraltar.'

'Excuse me, ma'am,' Sullivan spoke at last. 'We've just arrested Sister Clara for three murders. The story will have to be told on those grounds alone.'

Barrillo gave Shapley a nervous look. He was not prepared to reply to Sullivan's observation. Shapley had no such fears. 'We have a plan. A plan that depends on your co-operation and loyal support.'

'I have no idea where you're going with this,' Broderick replied. 'But I have to say, I'm feeling pretty uncomfortable about things so far.'

Massetti, Sullivan and Calbot all nodded their agreement.

'I understand your feelings, Chief Inspector,' Shapley said. 'They're to be expected. All I'd ask is that you appreciate that some decisions of state, particularly those involving national security and diplomatic processes, have to be obeyed without explanation of their need or, perhaps, morality. I've already probably explained too much.'

'May I ask what this plan involves?' Massetti asked.

For the first time since the meeting had begun, Shapley allowed herself a thin smile. 'Of course. MI6 will take over the case in its entirety. The Maugham file will be returned to the UK and remain classified. As I pointed out, the officers in this room are the only people who were privy to Sister Clara's confession and the information it contained. You'll be bound as officers of the Crown to abide by the Official Secrets Act regarding that information. As for Sister Clara, no charges will be brought against her.'

'But she bloody well killed three men, for God's sake!' Broderick exploded.

'Chief Inspector Broderick, I insist that you listen courteously to what Ms Shapley has to say!' Barrillo admonished the chief inspector, his face red with anger.

'It's not right! That's all I'm saying.'

'I understand your concerns, Chief Inspector,' Shapley said. 'But as I've tried to explain, this is a highly sensitive case which demands extreme measures.'

Broderick bit his tongue.

'I can only say that an *arrangement* will be made with Sister Clara,' Shapley went on. 'One that keeps both her and her adoptive mother's story secret. Such action would also protect her foundation and its international aid projects. We all think that it's important for their work to continue unaffected.'

'And what about her victims?' Sullivan asked. 'They were *murdered*!'

'I know,' Shapley replied, attempting a look of compassion. 'It's a tragic but universal truth that sometimes the few must suffer for the sake of the many. I fear this is considered to be one of those occasions.'

'And where's the justice in all this?' Massetti interrupted.

'I'm afraid I can't answer that,' Shapley replied. 'All of us see only part of the picture. It's unfair and unjust to those murdered here this week. Of that, there's no doubt. I'm truly sorry for them and for the difficulties you all have experienced during your investigations. But that doesn't take away from the seriousness – and, indeed, the rightness – of the decisions being made above us. I have a duty to carry out those decisions, and so do all of you.'

Massetti now turned to Barrolli for support. 'Where do you stand on this, sir?' she asked.

Barrolli shifted his weight from one foot to the other. He had the look of a man who wished he was still several thousand miles away in New York.

'I don't like it any more than you, Massetti,' he answered. 'But in matters pertaining to intelligence and defence, we toe the line. During the last hour or so, Ms Shapley and I have been in communication with both of our governments at the highest levels and we're bound by their decisions in this case. It's our job now to facilitate them to our best abilities.'

'Well, that's crystal clear,' Broderick commented. 'So where does that leave our murder investigation?'

'Outside of these walls, people believe our prime suspect is Jasinski,' Barrolli answered. 'Latest word from the hospital is that that unfortunate individual remains in a deep coma. His prognosis is bleak. There's also concern about permanent brain damage should he awaken. All can see that we're hampered in our investigations in that direction. The press believe Jasinski to be the most likely perpetrator of the crimes, as do our police colleagues across the border. It's therefore our intention to keep the case open until such time as Jasinski recovers and can help us further.'

'A scenario that may never happen,' Sullivan observed.

'So Jasinski's the patsy,' Broderick added. 'Poor fucker.'

'I think that will be all for tonight,' Barrolli said sharply. 'Ms Shapley and I are going to interview Sister Clara now. The outcome of that will be relayed to you as soon as possible. I think you all understand what's needed from you. Once again, we greatly appreciate your work on this case and value your candour and future support for our work with Ms Shapley and MI6.'

With that, both Barrolli and Shapley left the room, leaving behind four stunned detectives. Massetti broke the silence first. 'I'm sorry. I don't know what to say to you.'

'Just when you thought you'd seen it all ...' Broderick said.

'If we don't agree with it, maybe we should make a stand?' Calbot added. 'Say something?'

'And be branded as whistle-blowers? We all know what happens to them,' Massetti said. 'Besides, what if they're right? What if revealing the truth did lead to the damage they suggest?'

'We'll never bloody well know, ma'am. That's the only truth they've left us with,' Broderick replied, looking towards the silent Sullivan. 'You've gone quiet, Sullivan. What are your thoughts?'

Sullivan took a deep breath as she tried to make sense of what had just taken place. 'I just feel sorry. Sorry for Josh Cornwallis, Martínez and Maugham. I feel sorry for Jasinski. I feel sorry for Gabriel Isolde. I feel sorry for Marisella Martínez and all the other victims of that evil woman who died tonight. I even feel sorry for

Sister Clara. She's as much a victim in her own way as the others. But most of all, I just feel helpless.'

'We all do, Sullivan,' Massetti said softly.

'There's just one small consolation, I suppose,' Broderick added after a moment. 'The world may never find out about it, but the fact is we *nailed* the bitch. She died knowing she'd been found out. That she hadn't got away with it after all. It's what finally killed her.'

'And the devil in hell can deal with the rest,' Massetti added.

Broderick moved to the door of the office. 'I need a drink. Anyone coming?'

'But you never go for a drink, guv,' Sullivan said with surprise.

'Well, I am tonight,' Broderick replied. 'I suggest we raise a glass to honour those who have suffered. Not much of a gesture, but right now just about the best we can do. Or the best we're *allowed* to do. After that, it's my firm intention to drink you all under the bloody table.'

Over the following week, the world's press continued to revel in the 'Novacs incident' (as they insisted on calling it). The official line - that Jasinski was the chief suspect in the investigation of the three murdered men – was accepted by virtually everyone and arrangements were now being made to move the coma patient back to his native Poland.

Gabriel Isolde recovered quickly and, in the face of bankruptcy and following threats from a major Russian investor, had discharged himself from hospital and flown to Thailand. The word was that he had gone to convalesce at a spiritual sanctuary. His actual whereabouts in Asia were, in fact, anybody's guess.

An unexpected piece of information arrived from the Marbella police investigation into the murder of Krystle Changtai. Officers following the money that the solicitor had embezzled, had discovered something of interest. Changtai had taken over half a million pounds from one client in particular – Mikhail Volkov, a Russian steel magnate with connections to the Costa del Sol's criminal underworld. Volkov had also invested in the film *Queen of Diamonds*. Inspector Juan Cordobas was now investigating a possible link between the Russian millionaire and the death of Changtai. Sullivan and Broderick thanked their Marbella colleagues for their contribution and filed it accordingly.

Cath Broderick had taken Sister Clara's abrupt departure from the Rock very badly. The story that her dear friend had decided to disappear indefinitely to England had shocked not only her, but everyone else at the Rock of Ages Foundation. When the charity's directors called an emergency meeting to discuss the sudden departure of their president, it was quickly decided that Cath should continue to steer the charity, but now as managing director, and that a new honorary president be appointed as soon as possible. The name proposed for that role by several directors, including Cath, was one of the Rock of Ages' most generous benefactors: Oskar Izzo.

At a Carmelite convent in rural Oxfordshire, just 24 hours after her forced departure from the Rock, Sister Clara began her new life of silent devotion.

EPILOGUE

GIBRALTAR'S NORTH FRONT Cemetery, situated between the southeast side of the airport and the north face of the Rock, contains hundreds of war graves honouring the dead of two world wars. Surrounding the large military section of the cemetery are other areas that include burial sections for members of the Catholic, Presbyterian, Church of England and Jewish faiths. The sight of so many graves is often the first or last thing people see before take-off or on landing just a few metres away on the airport runway.

Entering by the main gate, Tamara Sullivan made her way to the Catholic section of the cemetery. It did not take her long to find what she was looking for. The small gravestone honouring the life of 'ALBERT JOHN LORENZ, 1897–1964', seemed to stand out from the others. The burning midday sun made its mottled marble shine brighter than those surrounding it. Under Lorenz's name was the carved epitaph: 'AN HONOURABLE AND DEDICATED OFFICER OF THE ROYAL GIBRALTAR POLICE'.

Kneeling down beside the grave, Sullivan placed a single white rose at the foot of the gravestone. A tribute to a fellow police officer. It had come as no surprise to discover that Inspector Lorenz had visited England just a week before his death. His attempt to interview Sister Clara there had failed. The young nun had then informed her mother of the policeman's visit and Diana Ruiz had dealt with the matter by poisoning Lorenz on his return – a death from arsenic which, in retrospect, mirrored that of her murdered husband, Max Ackerman. That was the theory and Sullivan believed it. Another death. Another victim.

Standing up now, Sullivan looked across to the main terminal of Gibraltar's International airport. The gleaming glass-and-metal exterior of the impressively designed building was pleasing to her eye. It was also a reminder of how quickly her time on the Rock had passed, and how imminent her return to the UK was.

Once again Sullivan felt the pull of this place. The feeling of being at home on this impressive limestone outcrop, with its Mediterranean climate and warm, generous people. *Should I go or should I stay?* Sullivan thought, feeling the sun on her face and breathing in the hot, sea-salted air. Before she could attempt an answer to that question, a familiar voice interrupted her thoughts.

'You found him then?'

Sullivan turned to see Gus Broderick standing a few paces behind her.

'Nice thought,' he added, looking down at Lorenz's gravestone. 'The flower.'

'What are you doing here?' Sullivan asked.

'Got the day off. I'm driving Cath and the girls up to Gaucín to see Ric Danaher and his daughter. Ric's finally completed the roof on his *finca* and he wants to celebrate. It's taken him seven years to finish it, so I reckon we're in for quite a party.'

'How'd you know I was here?' Sullivan asked.

'I didn't. We were driving by and Daisy spotted you walking

through the gate. They're over in the car. This place gives them the creeps. I hope you don't mind, but I thought I'd find out what you were up to.'

'Paying my respects, I suppose,' Sullivan replied.

'He deserves them. He was a brave man. Must have known he was in danger, but he didn't give up.'

'Unlike us.'

'We haven't given up. We're just having to bide our time,' Broderick replied. 'The fact is, we know the truth, and in my experience, secrets don't remain secrets for ever.'

'Diana Ruiz and Sister Clara got away with murder, and there's nothing we can do about it.'

For the first time, Broderick saw how hurt his colleague really was. 'Sunday afternoons. BBC2,' he said.

'I beg your pardon?' Sullivan replied.

'Me and my dad. Every Sunday when I was a lad, we'd sit down in the front room and watch an old movie. Anything, so long as it was good. Westerns were our favourite. Gary Cooper, John Wayne, Jimmy Stewart, Alan Ladd. If they were playing cowboys, me and my dad would be watching. At the end of every film, he'd say the same thing to me: "The man in the white hat always wins in the end." For years after that, whenever I found myself down or angry or frustrated with the world, I'd call home and my old man would say the exact same thing to me: "Don't you worry about it, son. The man in the white hat always wins in the end."'

'And does he?' Sullivan asked. 'Always win?'

Broderick paused for a moment and looked her straight in the eye. 'Eventually, Sullivan. Eventually.'

For a while, they both looked down at the gravestone and the single flower that lay at its foot.

'I haven't got a flower,' Broderick said gently. 'I don't do flowers. It looks like this will have to do instead.'

Slowly and a little awkwardly, Broderick stood to attention and raised his right arm in a police salute. At his side, after a moment, Sullivan did the same.

The sound of a car horn broke their reverie.

'That'll be Penny, I expect,' Broderick said. 'Patience is a virtue unknown to the teenage mind.'

'Hope you all have fun,' Sullivan said. 'I guess I'll see you on Monday.'

'And, hopefully, many more Mondays after that, Detective Sergeant.'

Sullivan found herself quite taken aback by Broderick's words. 'Well ... y-yes ... s-sir – hopefully,' she stammered.

'Good,' Broderick replied with a smile. 'That's very good.'

Slowly, Chief Inspector Gus Broderick turned round and headed back along the path towards the cemetery gates and his waiting family. Sullivan looked on until his tall, powerful and untidily dressed figure disappeared from view. Allowing herself a smile for the first time in several days, Tamara Sullivan looked up at the gigantic and immovable Rock of Gibraltar that towered above her.

'You're right, guv,' she whispered to herself. 'It *is* good.'

If you've enjoyed this Sullivan and Broderick murder investigation, please sign up to robertdaws.net for news about the next novel, Killing Rock, plus free offers and competitions. Also, a free download of Tunnel Vision – a Sullivan and Broderick ghost story. Thank you.

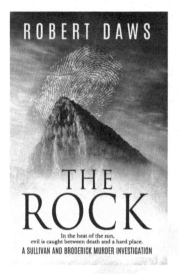

£7.99
ISBN 978-1911331193
URBANE PUBLICATIONS

The Rock. Gibraltar. 1966. In a fading colonial house the dead body of a beautiful woman lays dripping in blood. The Rock. Present day. Detective Sergeant Tamara Sullivan arrives on The Rock on a three-month secondment from the London Metropolitan Police Service. Her reasons for being here are not happy ones, and she braces herself for a tedious twelve weeks in the sun. After all, murders are rare on the small, prosperous and sun-kissed Rock of Gibraltar and catching murderers is what Sullivan does best. It is a talent Sullivan shares with her new boss, Chief Inspector Gus Broderick of the Royal Gibraltar Police Force. He's an old-fashioned cop who regards his new colleague with mild disdain. But when a young police constable is found hanging from the ceiling of his apartment, Sullivan and Broderick begin to unravel a dark and dangerous secret that will test their skills and working relationship to the limit.

Acknowledgments

I have been a yearly visitor to Gibraltar for some twenty-five years. The warmth and spirit of its people, together with the wonder and magnitude of the Rock on which they live, have never ceased to amaze me. Even as I write, I am looking forward to my next visit.

I would like to thank those within London's Metropolitan Police Service and the Royal Gibraltar Police who have given their time to offer help and guidance. It has been invaluable. Thanks also to Stuart Green and Peter Canessa, and to my friends at the marvellous Gibraltar Tourist Service and Gibraltar Literary Festival.

I hope I will be forgiven for having played hard and fast with the internal geography of the Gibraltar police headquarters, as well as Gibraltar's main general hospital, St Bernard's. I have also changed the names of several places and establishments. Other than that, I have tried to be as accurate as possible with situation and location.

Huge thanks to my agents at Independent, Paul Stevens and Will Peterson, for years and years of help, energy and kindness. Good men.

To Laura Mackie and Sally Haynes for having faith and acting on it.

To Matthew Smith, my publisher at Urbane, for his energy, faith and terrific creativity. A man with a vision.

To Samantha and Norbert Oetting – for SEO, marketing and a thousand other things I know next to nothing about.

Thanks also to my editor Nancy Duin – a great professional.

To Mr and Mrs James, for their invaluable support, friendship and encouragement.

To Adam Croft for passing on his huge experience of publishing and fine ales.

To Debbie at The Cover Collection. Invaluable help and a willingness to walk the extra mile.

To Katie, Jo, Mike, Kate, Emma, Jane and Steve for help in tough times.

For Ben, Betsy and May for being lovely and remaining only mildly interested in what I do.

Last, but not least, to my wife Amy, for her wisdom, patience and wonderfully creative mind. A dear writer friend, Christopher Matthew, once wrote, 'Eighty-five percent of a writer's life is spent thinking and thinking very hard. Unfortunately for writers, unless they are seen to be pounding away at a laptop keyboard, nobody really thinks they are working at all.' Amy has always understood this strange process, even when my 'thinking' has drifted into a pleasant little afternoon siesta.

ROBERT DAWS

As an actor, Robert Daws has appeared in leading roles in a number of award-winning and long-running British television series, including Jeeves and Wooster, Casualty, The House of Eliott, Outside Edge, Roger Roger, Sword of Honour, Take A Girl Like You, Doc Martin, New Tricks, Midsomer Murders, Rock and Chips, The Royal, Death in Paradise, Father Brown and Poldark. He has recently completed filming a second visit to Midsomer Murders and will shortly begin work on the film, An Unkind Word.

His recent work for the stage includes the national tours of Michael Frayn's Alarms and Excursions, and David Harrower's Blackbird. In the West End, he has recently appeared as Dr John Watson in The Secret of Sherlock Holmes, Geoffrey Hammond in Public Property, Jim Hacker in Yes, Prime Minister and John Betjeman in Summoned by Betjeman. He is returning to the stage in 2017 in Alan Ayckbourn's classic comedy, How The Other Half Loves.

His many BBC radio performances include Arthur Lowe in Dear Arthur, Love John, Ronnie Barker in Goodnight from Him and Chief Inspector Trueman in Trueman and Riley, the long-running police detective series he co-created with writer Brian B Thompson.

Robert's third Sullivan and Broderick novel – Killing Rock – will be published in 2017, as will his thriller, Progeny. His first novella, The Rock, has been optioned and is being developed for television. He is currently co-adapting the international bestseller, Her Last Tomorrow, by Adam Croft for television, as well as writing a new thriller for the stage with award winning television and stage writer, Richard Harris.